DREAM IN SHACKLES

ROMANCE IN TOSHALI SERIES BOOK 1

S A SPENCER

BLISS PUBLISHING

Bliss Publishing, the Bliss Publishing logo, are the trademarks of Bliss Publishing Pty Ltd.

ISBN: 978 0 6451171 6 5

Editor: Traci Finlay

Cover design by Nisha Dutta

i.nishadutta@gmail.com

CHAPTER 1

I ra remained standing. Desire stirred in her chest. She hadn't felt such strong desire in over a year, since her husband Rahul had died.

Sam stood up and closed the door. "Why don't you sit down? You seem to be quite tired," he said as he took Ira's hand. His touch made her feel so warm inside. She liked his touch and let herself go into the embrace of his muscular hands. She was surprised how quickly she had relaxed and lowered herself onto the sofa. He sat beside her on the sofa, caressing her hands and kissing them. Ira felt a rush spreading through her body. She did not know why, but she enjoyed the feel of his hands on her. She gave him a smile.

She wanted to forget that she was not at her own home at Raghupur, but in Toshali. An apartment her college-going son Varun was sharing with Sam.

Only an hour ago, Ira sat on the balcony, alone. She felt a sudden urge to run into a new life. Her heart fluttered. Her eyes watered. She felt a need to do something which would take her away from the monotony of her life. Hadn't she been stuck in one place since her husband's death? She felt she was not the same person anymore. Impulse to get out of this dark hole ran in her veins. She wanted to feel new emotions, and she wanted to be with someone who loved her.

Then Sam came home and instigated all those feelings for which she had just been yearning.

Sam coming back early from the office surprised her, but it didn't bother her—even though Varun was still in classes, leaving her alone with her son's roommate.

"I am feeling exhausted, and I need to rest," she said as she leaned back.

"You are tired, I guess. Maybe it is because of the journey? You are quite tense. How do you feel now?" Sam asked as he stroked her hair.

"I am okay now," she replied as she looked into his eyes. "It seems my stress level is normal today," she added as she looked away. She'd never been this close to Sam before. It wasn't entirely comfortable, but it didn't feel like an invasion, either. It felt...welcoming.

Sam moved closer to Ira. He put his arm around her shoulder and held her close. "I was thinking about you and missing you. I was pondering about you when I was on my way here," he murmured.

"Thanks for thinking of me," Ira replied as she placed her hand on his. She expected his hand to feel foreign, but it was warm and inviting, like slipping on a glove. She'd never touched Sam's hands like this before.

"I will make sure that you are always safe," Sam replied as he pulled her closer to him. "Let's go to my bedroom. I will make you feel relaxed."

Like a mesmerised person, Ira got up and walked to Sam's room, his arm wrapped around her. He kicked the door shut behind him.

"You are going to make love to me now, aren't you?" Ira's voice cracked as she pushed her head closer to his.

"Yes, I will make love to you now," Sam replied.

He pulled her towards him.

A faint sound tickled Ira's ears, like someone unlocking and entering the apartment.

Heat flushed up Ira's chest, neck, and into her face. Something was wrong. No, everything she was doing or going to do was wrong. Did she really hear someone open the apartment door and enter? The soft footsteps sounded like pounding ones to Ira and a quiver of recognition shot through her. Varun had been sharing this rented apartment of Sam's for the last six months when he left his mother's home in

Raghupur and joined college in Toshali City. The air suddenly became stuffy in Sam's bedroom.

"Stop, Sam." Her whisper was full of panic.

Samuel had wrapped his arms around her waist, holding her in a tight hug, and one of his palms was massaging her breasts. "Don't worry, Ira. Varun won't come home from the college until evening. I know his college timings. It is only three in the afternoon."

"You know nothing about my son." She pushed his hand away from her chest. "You are only his flatmate, not his mother." She suppressed her scream and yanked herself away from Samuel.

She tiptoed to the door and opened it a crack, peeking out.

"You're overthinking, Ira." A ghost of a smile crossed Sam's face. "Didn't I tell you Varun won't be here until evening? And no one else has the key to open the door and come inside. There is no need to spoil the fun. We can have..."

"Have what, Sam?" Ira's voice pitched up. "We can't have fun. Not like this. I came to Toshali to spend a few days with my son and stay in his apartment. Not to romance with his flatmate. Mistake. My mistake. No, blunder." She stomped out of Sam's bedroom.

"But Ira." He followed her to the lounge room.

She threw herself onto the sofa and buried her head into a pillow. A sob started in her stomach and soared out of her mouth. *Am I an irresponsible woman? A dirty one? What was I going to do?*

A warm hand crawled over her back. Sam's masculine perfume massaged her senses. A familiar smell swirled inside her heart. She looked up.

"I'm sorry, Ira."

"Do...don't...don't touch me." She pushed Sam's hand from her back. "You are my son's flatmate. Only about five years older than him. And he is still a student, not even eighteen. And how long have I known you? Since the day before yesterday when I came here from Raghupur? I am sorry. It's my fault."

"No, Ira. My mistake."

Ira got up and cast a desperate glance around, as if ready to run to safety. A place where she could wash out the sin she just attempted. Her whole upper body heaved, as if seeking oxygen. She plunked herself down on the sofa again, lacking courage to look at Samuel. Her eyes panned up and down her skirt to make sure there was no crease from Sam's embrace.

Samuel was still sitting on the adjacent sofa, guilt painted on his face.

"Go to your room, Sam." She wiped her eyes with the hem of the skirt.

"Ira—sorry, Mrs. Ray," he said, his voice warm and low, "you are a gorgeous woman. Neither of us is at fault. You were like a magnet, and it pulled me to you."

Ira glanced up, and for the first time since the incident, she met Sam's gaze. A child's innocence was radiating from his eyes. He was young enough to be her son. How could this man seduce her and take her to his bedroom so effortlessly? Who was a magnet? She or Sam?

"Your panic is unnecessary, Ir... Mrs. Ray. I still adore you and would do anything to put a smile on your face."

Was Sam trying to seduce her again?

Sam got up from the sofa. "I will make tea for both of us."

The same jumpy feeling snaked again into Ira's mind. Varun had said his last class would end at four p.m., and it would take him at least fifteen minutes to get from campus to the apartment.

Did Varun come home and realise his mother was inside a closed room with his flatmate, Sam? Did he run away? What would he be feeling? How could his widow mother have such an affair? *What a shame!*

Ira was curled up into herself on the sofa when Sam came back with two cups of tea and stood near her. After setting the cups on the coffee table, he put his hands in his pocket and his shoulders hunched.

"Can I sit near you Ira, on the sofa?"

Ira felt her strength regenerating. A giggle formed but stopped at her throat. "Can't you sit across from me?"

"Y...yah, of course."

She took a sip of tea from the cup; it was too hot and tasteless, her mouth burnt. She set the mug on the coffee table and glanced outside—dark clouds that had built up in the sky mocked her.

4

But that scent again knocked at her memory. It was not even a year now since Rahul died. Same Hugo for Men, the one she had given him for their first anniversary. It became his favourite, so much so that he never even tried another brand. Why is this Sam using the same cologne? Did Varun tell him what brand his father had used?

"B... But, Ira, I still appreciate you and your beauty."

Ira lifted her face and tried to follow his gaze—it was as if he were staring at her chest.

"You mean, love?"

"Right, Ira." Sam chuckled for the first time. "I lo—"

"Stop, Sam." Heat radiated from her eyes. "Don't assume those three magic words will cast a spell on me."

"I truly, Ira... Trust me."

"What will happen to that love, Sam? Would you marry me? Would we continue like a couple?" She felt her eyes pooling.

"We can, maybe...take time to think."

"Take time? I am not a college girl anymore, Sam, where I could go with one man now and then another, and then decide which one is suitable for me. You know, my older sister's son is your age, and he calls me 'aunt.'" Ira rubbed her forehead. "I had come here to spend a few days with my son in the city, not to romance with his friend."

Samuel didn't reply. An unspoken scream moved through Ira. How would she face Varun when he'd come back?

Her tense mood morphed into a softening of her attitude.

"Do you have a girlfriend, Sam?"

"No, Ira."

"Did you ever have one?"

Samuel buried his gaze in the teacup. "Y...yeah."

"When? Recently?"

"No. A while ago."

"A while...meaning what? One month? One year?"

"Over three years ago, Ira."

Was she interrogating the young man?

"I am sorry. I'm being rude to you."

"No, Ira. That's all right. Your every word sounds sweet to me."

A chuckle stopped at her lips. Was he still hoping to make love with her? She didn't know if she would ever come back to the city of Toshali and stay in this apartment with her son.

"I'm not angry with you, Sam. I am the older one here. A hundred percent responsible for what happened. I would appreciate—"

"Please, Ira. My mouth will be tight-lipped. And trust me, nothing happened. Toshali is a large, multicultural city. Here, no one minds or even cares about such things."

Nothing happened? Didn't he insert his hand inside her top and try to explore?

"But I'm from Raghupur, a small country town where petty matters spread through spicy gossips. No widow in our traditional hometown would have ever dreamt of another love life. Too much social stigma. A middle-aged widow with a man almost her son's age! They won't call it a romance." Ira struggled to control a sob. "*Whore*. They use this term liberally. Abuses would shower from everywhere. A disgraced woman can't even walk on the street. I was born and brought up in Mumbai. Raghupur became my home only after marrying Rahul. This place is a hundred years behind Mumbai, or even Toshali. You can't imagine if you have never lived in such a town. I crossed the line."

Ira inhaled a deep breath. She could do nothing now other than make a truce with herself and Sam.

"Sam," she said, filling her voice with affection, "did you not find another girlfriend, or even try? See, I have nothing to do with this. I'm still trying to become your friend. I am not even going to be your girlfriend. Just a..."

Samuel stared at the floor, as if unaware of her presence.

"I didn't get one, no. Ira, you are lucky you are a woman. I mean, any female in this country is lucky because of the poor sex ratio. Boys are outnumbering girls."

Sam was right. Eighty girls per a hundred boys. Why did she and Rahul decide that the 'one child policy irrespective of the child's gender' was the best? They could've planned for another child, and who knows if that could have been a girl?

Sam was tall and handsome, and he worked in a multinational company. Any such man would have been a dream match for any young woman. How quickly the times changed! Would her son also struggle to find a match when he became an adult?

Which led her thoughts down another path... What if her suspicion that Varun secretly wore her dresses were true? But she couldn't think about that now. One issue at a time.

"I understand, Sam. Every parent in India thought getting a boy was economically right. Though I and my late husband had not planned for our only child to be a male, so many parents got rid of the female embryo, which has now become a nightmare for their own sons, who struggle to find love."

Sam nodded sadly—a personification of this struggle she just described.

Bitterness filled Ira's mind. How could doctors be so greedy to help parents get rid of female embryos even though the government had banned sex determination tests? She remembered when she had been to a clinic for the ultrasound for her own pregnancy. The doctor in charge had demanded bribe money to let them know the sex of her child, because it was illegal.

She had bluntly replied, "No, doctor. Just let us know if the child is healthy. We will love to have a girl or boy; whatever God has planned for us."

How could she ever forget the smile of appreciation on Rahul's face?

"What a shame," She murmured absently.

"Shame?" Sam sounded nervous.

"No, nothing." Ira realised she had gone back in her past. She stood up straight and looked at her watch. "I remembered some urgent work at home in Raghupur, Sam. Two hours if I get a non-stop bus. Please tell Varun I am going back." She got up and breezed into the bedroom, then she trudged out of the flat carrying her suitcase, Sam watching silently.

The bus stand was at a walking distance. Ira took out the phone from her handbag and switched it off.

Sam watched her from the door. She couldn't even say bye to him, couldn't even send a text message to Varun. Wouldn't Varun ask, "*Mum, you came here for the first time after I moved to Toshali to spend time with me for an entire week, so why are you going back suddenly?*" How would she answer him?

How dare she?

CHAPTER 2

The sky was overcast, and it could have started raining at any time. Ira ran to her apartment building and switched on her mobile after entering. She didn't dare to look at her mobile during the two hours from Toshali City to Raghupur, the sleepy country-town which she had called home. Varun must have come back from his classes and looked for her by now.

No missed calls appeared on her phone. No texts or voice mails even. Was her fear valid? Did Varun find out his mother was making love with his flatmate? Did he run away so as not to embarrass her? Or to save himself from the embarrassment?

Thunder growled.

She could imagine Varun's voice now. "Mum, why did you go back? What was the urgent work, Mum?"

Ira unlocked her mobile again. No, Varun didn't call her.

You are a strong woman, Ira. You will overcome it.

She laid her suitcase on the floor and slumped on her sofa.

What did I do?

Since Rahul's death a year ago, Ira's life had been upside down. Her schoolteacher job was her only consolation as far as the financial side. Fighting with Rahul's brothers for his share of ancestral property was an actual nightmare for her. She had told herself several times, *I'm strong enough to handle all this. I will see that Varun never suffers in receiving higher education.*

Varun was devoting less time to his friends and more time to her. The death had brought mother and son closer than before. She knew Varun's way of life sometimes worried Rahul. He never liked the way Varun kept his room decorated with dolls, colourful pictures, and arts.

It was a month before Rahul was diagnosed with blood cancer. Ira and Rahul had gone to the market together. She bought a doll for Varun.

Rahul rolled his eyes when he saw it. "Who would think we have a boy at home who loves dolls?"

"What's wrong with this?" Ira pleaded. "Don't you appreciate the fact that your boy always keeps his room neat? Unlike his cousins."

"That's worrying me, Ira." Rahul frowned when they proceeded to a food court. "I'll admit my friend's sons never keep things uncluttered, but his daughter is not the same. And I was also more like his son than Varun. That's how boys behave. Most often."

A delicious smell tingled Ira's nose. She glanced at the counter on her side. A cook was dipping a round shaped spicy mashed potato in gram-flour paste and dropping it in boiling oil in a large deep fryer. Another man on his side was making burgers for the customers.

"Most boys like..."

"Potato-vada burgers."

Rahul stopped walking and stared at Ira. "Potato-vada burgers? No. I meant, most boys love..."

"How about eating some potato-vada burgers, Rahul? Smells so yummy."

"Smells yummy!" Rahul mocked. "Just watch how much oil is going in there. And see my waistline."

"So, what else would you like to have? Masala Dosa? Less oil than deep fried Vadas. Even Upma."

Rahul glanced around. "Weren't all these people selling food on the street a few months ago? Raghupur got a western style mall with a food court. And what are we getting here? No McDonald's, no KFCs. Just visit any mall in Toshali. You will notice the difference."

"Chicken tikka, prawn tikka, mouth-watering and spicy!" a hawker shouted from the other end of the food court.

"*Pani puri*, tangy and tasty!" The sound came from another stall. Ira's mouth watered thinking of the deep-fried puff-pastry balls filled with spicy potato and tamarind chutney. Another day! She had made up her mind to have a potato-vada burger now.

"Food court! This is a western concept, Ira. This is the same old wine in a brand-new bottle. The same street hawkers are selling food here." Rahul laughed.

Ira grabbed Rahul's hand and giggled. "How many days can you survive eating McDonald's and KFC food? Are they better for your waistline? The foods here are the soul of our country." She turned to the side and asked, "Brother, can you please make two plates of potato-vada burgers for us? And with fried green chilli on the side, please."

"Sauce or tamarind chutney, ma'am?"

"A bit of tamarind and also some coriander-mint chutney. No sauce."

The man took only a minute or two to place two burgers on paper plates. Ira took them. "We are on that table there," she said, "if you can send two cups of masala chai after a while."

"Sure, ma'am," the man replied with a smile and attended to another customer.

Ira and Rahul settled on a table. It was around five p.m. and after-office customers slowly started entering the area. She cast a quick glance around. Almost fifteen small stalls with varieties of Indian foods catered to the food court. And most of the faces were known to her from the street across the mall. The walls were all decorated with the paintings imitating the arts of the twelfth century Konark temple. The tables and chairs in the food court were designed like antique furniture in some king's palace of the past century.

"Do you know why big names like McDonald's are not coming to this food court?" Rahul said, lifting his burger to take the first bite.

"Why?" Ira dipped her burger in the tamarind chutney. "Because of these street vendors? Below their dignity? No, they can't shout like these people to advertise."

"I think so." Rahul stopped eating and said, "If they want to do business in a small town like this, they must learn to share space with the local people here."

Ira noticed a smile of pride in Rahul for his native place. The smile that had attracted her so much that she had left a multicultural Mumbai to make Raghupur her hometown.

The server came with two cups of steaming masala chai and placed them on the table.

"Thanks," Rahul said to the man and gazed at Ira. "We were talking about boys."

Ira laughed at her husband and recollected at which point their heated discussion took a break. "That is the point, Rahul. *Most often.* Which law says boys should always remain disorganised? That they can't take care of their stuff? Shouldn't decorate their rooms? After all, my Varun is a boy, not a monkey that would throw stuff here and there."

"Monkey? You are comparing my childhood with monkeys?" Rahul set down his chai.

Ira let out a giggle. "Yes. Monkeys never take care of their things. They destroy them. And you should be happy that your son keeps his life in order, not frown about it and speak against him."

Rahul wiped his fingers with the tissue and lifted the chai cup. A smile brightened his face.

"Okay, my darling. Who can argue with you? You always win. But..."

"But what?" Ira pinched his hand. "You are like a naughty boy. Naughtier than your son. People complain when their children don't learn discipline. But you are complaining your child is more disciplined than his peers. What is wrong with you? Do you have any other grievances against your boy?"

"Yes, but never mind."

"No, Rahul. Please tell me. I want to know what other shortcomings my child has."

"Nothing that important." Rahul folded his arms across his chest.

"No, Rahul. Please. There's something else you don't like."

"Not that serious. But I don't understand why he frequents the kitchen. I mean, helping the mother sometimes is good, but should he cook like girls?"

"Wow, my hero husband," Ira giggled and set the empty cup on the table. "Cooking is a girl's job? I work fulltime and bring in money. And I also cook all the meals like a housewife. I have never whined, always have given you the benefit as you grew in a patriarchal environment. Not your fault. But times are changing, Rahul. I don't expect my son to continue the male chauvinistic attitudes of his forefathers, at least. He should help his spouse when he grows up. At least in this matter, he shouldn't be like you."

Rahul stared blankly at her. "Ready to go?"

The couple finished their shopping and went home. Varun was home from school and was collecting dried clothes from the terrace.

"Mum, the housemaid is not coming for three days. I will fold the clothes until she comes back."

"She had taken three days off to visit her in-laws. But today she should have come."

"She called Mrs. Mishra, the side-door neighbour," Varun looked up, "and said she is sick."

"Oh, no." Ira's frustration was clouded inside her appreciation for Varun. "So, you thought to help Mum? That's my good boy." She ruffled his hair.

Rahul didn't comment but went out to meet his brother, who lived only a kilometre away. Ira moved to the bedroom to change clothes. When she came back to the drawing room, she watched Varun in silence. He was folding each piece of clothing and piling them, including her undergarments. Varun picked up another piece from the clothes stack—her bra—and neatly folded it and set it aside.

What is so bad about this? she thought. Her sister-in-law (Rahul's older brother's wife) always cautioned boys to never touch women's undergarments, not even mothers' and sisters'. She found that awkward. Wasn't that like a forbidden apple, though? Wouldn't the boys mature better sexually if parents opened up with them?

A silent smile escaped her mouth. At least her only child would be a better husband when he grew up.

Now, Rahul was no longer in her life.

Seated on the sofa, Ira opened her eyes. Rahul's scent was alive in her senses. That Hugo for Men.

She got up and moved to their wedding photo hanging on the wall. She inhaled a deep breath as she kissed him in the photo and gazed at him intently. "I love you, Rahul."

A sad chuckle escaped her mouth. He was not a perfect husband, but still a loving one. Ira wiped her tears. Blood cancer snatched her man from her without giving enough notice. Ira had never blamed him for not helping her enough with the household chores. He was, however, changing and even started helping with domestic tasks a few months before his death. Ira was pleasantly surprised. After all, she had gotten maids. Why would she taunt a man who was loving but ignorant because of the small, traditional town upbringing?

Her thoughts flew to the days when she was pregnant and both Rahul and she had decided against a sex-determination test. Even the patriarchal-cultured Rahul was against eliminating the girl child like many of his friends were opting for. She had even imagined her firstborn being a girl and had bought all girly clothes and dolls.

Those pink toys didn't go to waste. Rather, they were Varun's favourite when he was a toddler. Ira had loved it even when Rahul had sulked.

"Why should we keep boys and girls in separate watertight compartments, Rahul?" she had debated when Rahul had commented about Varun. "Like blue for boys and pink for girls. Dolls for girls and cars for boys? Don't I like to drive and am even a better driver than you?"

"One minor accident didn't make me a terrible driver." Rahul stood in front of Ira, hands behind his back, a smile on his face. "You know what, Ira? If you want to talk about it, I'll listen to you. But I don't want to argue. If we both start arguing, then it's going to be like this for the rest of our lives."

She stared at the photo and felt her eyes pooling. "I miss you so much, Rahul. I don't know why you are coming to my mind again and again today."

Ira left for the bedroom to change clothes, but she couldn't stop her thoughts from digging into the past. She had determined to train her son to be different. Varun would receive the perfection which Rahul didn't. But could a person gain all the positive qualities? All the qualities which she would appreciate?

Yes. Varun was different. But she loved the way he was.

Standing before the dressing-table mirror, she combed her long hair and tied it back, then she pulled on a ball cap.

Long hair!

Ira giggled, remembering that day not long ago when Varun had appeared before her, tying his hair into a bun. As soon as Ira opened the door, Varun wrapped her in a big hug. She struggled to come out of his clasp to see what he had done.

"Your dad, when alive, always warned you when your hair was long enough for a cut. I say nothing, and you get a bun?" She was conscious Varun would be eighteen soon.

Varun chuckled. "Mum, Dad would have said, 'Don't act like a girl.' But I am not offending his soul. Do I have to be a hundred percent like my father? Genes blend, Mum. I am a mixture of you and Dad, not his replica."

He was right. Didn't Ira sometimes feel the absence of a daughter and imagine Varun as a girl when he helped her in the kitchen? When he folded the clothes?

Thankfully, to Ira's surprise, nobody in Raghupur raised an eyelid at Varun's long hair. But Ira suspected that Varun might be trying her dresses on when nobody was home. A few times she had noticed her wardrobe not in the exact condition after returning home. She never wanted to ask Varun about this, though. She never felt the timing was right.

Day by day, her imagination was taking shape in her son's behaviour. But not the exact way she would have loved. Whatever, boys having buns was not something new.

"Mum, would you mind if I also pierce my ears? Even some movie stars are doing this nowadays."

She had forced out a smile of approval. Men piercing their ears had become normal. But in big cities. What about Raghupur? How would her in-laws and even neighbours react? And Varun's friends?

That evening, after Ira relented and took Varun to pierce his ears, Varun had sat near her on the sofa and hugged her. "Love you, Mum. You are the best mum of the world."

"Love you, my boy." She planted a kiss on his cheeks.

"Mum, you are doing so much for me. I don't think I am doing enough for you."

"Says who? Nowadays, you are spending less time with your friends and more with me, since your dad passed away. You help me in the kitchen, fold the clothes, and talk so nicely to me." She ruffled his hair bun.

But now she was afraid to face her own boy.

Ira came back to the drawing room and checked the phone, which she had left on the coffee table. There were still no messages or missed calls from Varun. Did she lose the trust of her son forever? She tapped the phone icon and selected Varun's name. She must talk to him and give a reason why she suddenly left Toshali. But what would be that reason?

CHAPTER 3

The next morning, Ira rolled over on her bed and felt a biting pain across her back. Thunder rumbled across the sky. The air was sultry, and a storm was brewing. She felt a cold sweat run down her spine. Lightning flashed.

She felt frightened. She did not know what was going to happen next. She hoped this storm would pass soon, and the rain would cease.

She looked at the clock. It read 8:15. She wondered if Varun had tried to call her, or even returned her text from last night.

Her smart phone had dozens of WhatsApp messages. But not even one reply from Varun to her text message: *Sorry, but I had to go home.* Shaking off the unease, she stretched and yawned. She had slept very little last night, checking her mobile frequently for anything from Varun. Her brain was whirring with thoughts of yesterday.

She got up and ambled to the kitchen. The morning light was just filtering through the windows. Thankfully, the thunder had stopped, and instead of her usual practice of drinking steaming tea in the morning, she poured herself some milk and sat down.

A knock on the door.

Must be Shanti, her maid. She never pressed the calling bell. Who else could be? She dragged her feet and opened the door.

"Came back early, *madamji*? Mrs. Gupta said you came home last evening. She had seen you entering the lift. How is Varun? Spent a pleasant time with him?"

Ira forced a smile. "Yes, of course."

Shanti breezed past Ira into the living room. "How is his place, ma'am? Toshali is a big city. Much bigger than our Raghupur. Rents are so costly there. He must share a room with friends."

"Oh, yes." Ira was not in a mood to talk. But she was happy Shanti at least enquired about Ira coming back early and that she came to work. Otherwise, Ira would have done all the cleaning.

Shanti had been her maid since Ira came to Raghupur after marrying Rahul. She even continued with her after they moved to this new apartment, and was a big support when Rahul died. She had known Varun since his birth, and he was attached to her. So many times Varun had said, "Mum, Shanti is like another mother to me."

"Yes, Shanti. He is sharing a flat with another man."

"Man? Like an aged man?"

"No, I mean, his flatmate is not a student. He has finished his studies and is working. Five or six years older than Varun."

"So nice, *madamji*. When you go to spend time there, you practically have two sons, instead of one."

Two sons? I'm almost going to lose my only son forever after what I did with his flatmate. He had definitely come home when I was with Sam and must've run away. Such a shame.

"Would you like to have some tea, Shanti? I woke up late, only a few minutes ago." Escaping to the kitchen was the only option for Ira to avoid further embarrassing talks.

"You rest, *madamji*. I will make tea for both of us."

"No, Shanti—" Ira got up from the sofa— "you have so much to do. How much more rest do I need?"

She trudged to the kitchen and poured water into the kettle.

How long would she hide her shame?

The calling bell buzzed just when Ira had dressed after taking a shower. She had given money to Shanti to buy vegetables from the shop across the street. Was she back so early? But she always knocked on the door!

"Hi, Mum." Varun took her into a tight hug the moment Ira opened the door.

"I'm sorry. I'm so sorry for leaving like that." Ira kissed her son's forehead, but then looked away. She felt her voice lacked the emotion she usually had when she welcomed Varun home from Toshali. Her heart jumped in her ribs fearing what she would say if Varun asked her why she came back.

"Mum, I'm hungry."

A cool wave passed through Ira's skin. Thank God Varun didn't enquire further. "I will make something quickly for you." She turned around to go to the kitchen. "And you freshen up."

"Mum, no cooking now." Varun opened his backpack and took out a packet. "I bought some vadas from the Raghupur bus depot. They are still fresh."

A faint aroma of the deep-fried snacks spread across the room when he opened the packet.

Ira served them on two plates, and both settled on the sofa.

"Good, you plan to spend the weekend with me," she said before taking the first bite.

"I will be here all next week, Mum. Not going back tomorrow." Varun had buried his gaze into the plate and was eating quickly.

"All of next week? But I have a job, going to the school."

"Don't worry, Mum. I know how to cook."

What would he do here, missing his college classes? Ira noticed Varun had yet to meet her gaze since he came home. Is this a sign of the coming storm? She decided to not talk to Varun about it now.

At eleven in the morning, Ira was cooking lunch in the kitchen, and Varun was busy chopping vegetables for a salad. Ira stilled for a moment and watched him. How many mothers in Raghupur were lucky enough to get a son like this? All the teen boys spent their free time with friends, assuming it was a birthright for young males to enjoy life this way.

And young girls? They were expected to help their mothers with household chores.

She stepped closer to Varun and ruffled his hair.

He raised his eyes and met her gaze.

"My darling boy, I love that you are the symbol of the new trend. This breaking out of the patriarchal society norm."

Varun blushed and looked down. "But Mum, I really love you, and..."

"And what?"

"And I also want to learn how you cook the Chicken Bharta."

"I know, Varun, it's your favourite dish. So I'm cooking it today, especially for you." Motherly affection bubbled in her heart.

"The aroma from the simmering Chicken Bharta is bringing out saliva from my mouth." He brought out plates and spoons to the dining table.

Ira placed the dishes in the middle of the table and served the food.

"Mmm, love this, Mum," Varun said immediately after one spoonful of Chicken Bharta.

She replied with a smile and began eating.

Varun stopped eating halfway through and stared at her. A storm broke out in her veins.

"What, Varun? Need something?"

"Mum, can I ask you something?"

Ira put her spoon down and looked at him.

"Why did you stop wearing fashionable clothes after Dad died? You looked so beautiful in the trendy jeans and skirts."

Thank God he didn't ask about what happened with Sam. Regardless, she couldn't say anything. A sob gathered in the back of her throat, but she swallowed it.

"Nineteen years ago, when I married your dad," Ira swallowed again, "when I walked out of the home wearing the same western style dresses I was wearing in Mumbai, do you know what neighbours said?"

Varun rested his spoon on the table and gazed at her, eyes wide. "What?"

"They didn't say anything to me, but to your dad. 'Rahul, your wife seems of easy virtue. Beware, she might elope with anyone.' Your dad was studying in Mumbai and had seen the trends there. He came to my defence. He said, 'She is my wife. You don't bother about her. I am her man and I know what she is doing. I have full trust in the woman I love.'"

A smile of pride appeared on his lips. "And our dearest Uncle Rohan?"

"He would joke with me saying I am a Bollywood item girl. Married women in Raghupur were expected to dress differently than unmarried ones."

"Unbelievable, Mum. How come I didn't know this?"

"Because you were not born, my dear." Ira chuckled.

"Oh! I see." Varun chortled too.

"Yes, after so many years there has been change here, but in terms of the culture of larger cities, Raghupur is still fifty years behind. Some other married women got courage and began wearing clothes which were considered too sexy. I mean skirts, tight jeans, sleeveless tops. People got used to it. When more and more women began wearing them, it didn't look racy to anyone."

"Then what is the problem now, Mum?"

Ira's shoulders dropped. "Because I became a widow. These people are brainwashed with the traditions they have followed for ages. A widowed woman should mourn her husband her entire life by discarding anything considered fashionable. No lipstick, no ornaments, and only light-coloured clothing—if not white. I am taking a middle path, though. Not adhering strictly to the norm these people think is right, and not putting on clothes that look sexy. But the situation is different when I am in Toshali."

"Did anybody make any comments to you? Please tell me. I will take care of them." Varun clenched his fists.

"Nobody talks openly, unfortunately. But they'll pass remarks when you least expect it."

"Mum, don't you think people will get used to this the way they did after your marriage?"

Ira stirred her spoon in the raita pot for a while and then looked at Varun. "Maybe. But then your dad was beside me to give me moral support."

"Mum, I can do the same."

"No, my child. There is a difference between a husband defending his wife's clothing and a son doing the same."

Varun didn't reply. He lifted his spoon and resumed eating.

"Mum, yesterday, I had thought of taking you to a restaurant in Toshali. Can we go to one here tonight?"

Ira finished her dinner. She set the spoon on the plate and said, "Of course, my child. Why not?"

"Thanks, Mum. I will choose the best skirt and top from your wardrobe for you."

Ira stilled for a moment, staring at the plate.

"Mum?"

"Okay, dear." She lifted her gaze. "But I will wear them only on occasions. Don't forget we are living in a small, conventional, Indian town. It will take a long time for people to accept that even widows are humans, and they too can love fashion."

"That's nice, Mum." Varun planted a kiss on her cheeks.

CHAPTER 4

The weight of a dozen eyes in the restaurant pushed unease into Ira's chest. Varun was sitting across from her at a corner table, facing the wall. She peered at her own top; it was a bit deep at the neck—perfectly normal in a city like Mumbai or even Toshali. She had moved around in Raghupur wearing sensual clothes when Rahul was alive and loved the stares. Why was she so much more conscious now? She cast a quick glance around again. Women were mostly in traditional salwar kameez or saree, expect a few. Faces appeared familiar, but not their names. And the stares looked demeaning. Or was that in her mind?

The evening itself looked scary.

"Varun, can we exchange seats?"

Varun was holding the menu in front of his face. He placed it on the table and met Ira's gaze. "All right, Mum." He stood up.

Ira quickly adjusted her top and smoothed her skirt. She drank a glass of water after moving to Varun's position, showing her back to all those prying eyes.

"What's wrong, Mum? Are you all right?"

"So many familiar people are here, Varun. This skirt and the top are too much for them, not expected from a widow," Ira almost whispered.

"Don't worry, Mum. Who cares about what people will think? Didn't you wear them when Dad was alive? You are not here with your boyfriend, but your son." Varun began checking the menu again.

"Don't use that word so loudly, Varun." Another wave of discomfort passed through her nerves.

Varun didn't acknowledge her; he just looked at the menu. "Mum, what would you like to have?"

Ira took another look at the menu, but after looking at a few dishes, she tossed it to the side. "Why don't you choose something for us?"

Varun set the menu on the table. "No Mum, you cooked my favourite dish for lunch. I'm not a superb cook like you, but I would love to eat your favourite dish."

Ira lifted her menu and surfed through the dishes again. A pleasant aroma from the table next to them aroused her tastebuds. She cast a sideways glance. "How about mutton biryani, Varun?"

"Good, I was thinking the same."

Varun immediately called the server and placed the order. Ira pulled out her smart phone and checked her WhatsApp and Facebook. But then she saw Varun was focussing his phone camera on her.

"Mum, smile please. One photo of my beautiful mother."

Ira tried her best to bring out a smile, but she wasn't sure she could grin through her shame.

Within five minutes, the server girl came with biryani and raita. Varun left his chair and came to stand on Ira's side, holding his phone for a selfie. "Mum, you have chosen the perfect dish for the evening. Let me take a selfie—you, me, and the biryani."

Once again, the smile didn't slip easily across her face.

"Another photo facing us, please," someone shouted from a table behind her.

Varun swung around and cast an angry glance around the dining hall. Then he moved back to his seat. "Sorry, Mum, I chose a fitting top for you. But you look so sexy in this. I love when you wear that top with this skirt. You look like a fairy."

Ira didn't have the courage to swing back and see who said it. "Enough, Varun," she hissed at him, knowing well it was fruitless even if Varun could find who said it. She didn't want to draw more attention. "Can we eat now?" She reached for her spoon and began eating.

Tasteless, she wanted to say, but Varun commented, "This is yummy. Do you like it?"

"Me? Yes, of course." She drank some water to push the rice through her throat.

She didn't realise when and how she finished her dinner. *Why am I so afraid of what people will think of me? Wasn't I always an extrovert?*

Varun put the spoon on the empty plate.

"All right, Varun. I'm going to pay the bill, and you get a cab." She left her seat and almost sprinted to the counter, avoiding eye contact with anyone in the cafeteria.

Rahul always loved an outing with Ira when she put on fashionable clothes. At least on these matters, he was not a patriarchal individual, but a modern, westernised man.

"You look so gorgeous and sexy when you wear a tight, low-neck top, Ira. Please don't stop wearing this, even if I die. I would love to watch you from the above." Rahul had repeated the same joke many times.

Who knew Rahul's joke would be true so soon?

While walking toward the exit, Ira's gaze fell on an older woman looking at her disapprovingly. Did the woman know she was a widow?

The cab was waiting when both mother and son came out of the restaurant. Ira consciously took the seat just behind the driver so that he couldn't stare at her through the rearview mirror. She flicked a glance at her low neckline. Why did she choose to wear the push-up bra when Varun brought this top from her wardrobe? Didn't it add spice to the peeping eyes?

Varun took her palm inside his grip and rested it on his lap with a look of assurance. Ira's heartbeat slowed down. This boy had matured within months of his dad's death.

It was only a ten-minute drive from the restaurant to her apartment. As they got off and walked on the pathway surrounded by green lawn, Ira said, "You shouldn't have uttered the word 'boyfriend' in the restaurant, that too in a loud voice. I don't know what those people might be thinking. That a widow..."

"Never utter the word 'widow,' Mum. You shouldn't remain a widow forever, and the public has no right to dictate what life you should live."

Not supposed to remain a widow forever? Did he hear Rahul's advice on his deathbed that she should remarry? But Ira had never revealed that to anyone!

As soon as they arrived at home, Ira went to her bedroom to change her clothes, but Varun stopped her.

"Mum, please stay in this clothing for a while longer. You panicked so much in the café that I couldn't take a proper photo. Please, let us pretend we are in a theatre watching a movie. You can smile better."

"Didn't I smile in the restaurant?" She adjusted her low neckline a bit just before her son clicked the camera icon on his phone.

"Another click, Mum." An innocent smile flashed on his lips. "Perfect," Varun said before putting his phone in his pocket and facing her fully. "Mum, I would like to tell you something, but promise me you won't get angry."

An unknown fear kicked Ira's heart. *Will he ask why I was in his flatmate's room? What answer would I give to him?*

A long pause hung in the air.

"Mum, I asked you something."

Shifting closer on the sofa, Varun wrapped his arm around Ira's shoulders. She had no way to stare into his eyes and guess his thoughts. Guilt whispered through her again.

No, she must be bold and tell him. Yes, she was about to sleep with Sam, but the mother inside her had taken the right step at the right time. Hugging and kissing didn't make this brief encounter an affair. But then she realized he probably wasn't going to ask about this at all. Varun wouldn't have behaved so nicely toward her had he planned to confront her.

Another thought struck her. Had Varun found a girlfriend? But that would, in fact, make her happy.

"Mum." He shook her shoulder.

Ira twisted her head to the side, looked into his eyes, and said, "All right, my boy. I promise."

"Didn't I say you shouldn't live as a widow forever?"

Ira flinched. What discussion does this boy want tonight?

Varun came down from the sofa and kneeled on the floor before Ira, holding her both palms in his grip. "Mum, you are educated and a working woman. And beautiful, too. You shouldn't be living like the ordinary, illiterate bunch."

"I don't understand, Varun. Can you be clear, please?"

"I mean, Mum," he swallowed, "you should remarry."

Her eyes narrowed at him. Rahul's voice minutes before his death appeared in the back of her mind again.

She was sure Varun wasn't there.

"Did I say something wrong, Mum?"

Ira ruffled Varun's hair as he continued sitting on the floor between her legs. "No. You don't know this, but even your dad had said so before his death. But do not underestimate the society of a country town. They won't come in a rally and shout at me. So, probably you wouldn't clearly see it. It's much more subtle, but just as hurtful. I have seen women gossip in a demeaning way."

"Who are they, Mum? Do I know them?" Varun gazed into Ira's eyes.

"That happened three years ago." Ira swallowed. "She was a teacher in the girls' school where I teach. Not from Raghupur, though. She had gotten a transfer from Toshali as her new husband got a job here. Somehow, our colleagues knew she had remarried after the marriage of her own daughter. You should have seen the reaction yourself to believe what happened to her."

"They teased her? Made rude remarks?"

"No. Whenever she would come to the teachers' common room, there would be a sullen silence suddenly. Other teachers would look at each other trying to hide their contempt behind smiles whenever she would begin a casual conversation."

"Then what?" Varun got up from the floor and sat on another sofa across from her.

"Then?" She straightened her back. "She understood. Whenever she had any leisure time, she would take a novel and sit in the garden to read."

"You didn't talk to her?" Varun's eyes were full of questions. He didn't have enough experience to understand the undercurrent of social stigma in his birth town.

"In fact, I was the only one to talk to her. And my colleagues reprimanded me. That she was polluting the society. I didn't argue with them, just ignored it. But one day I felt so suffocated, I asked, if a widower man is not polluting the society after his remarriage to a young unmarried woman, how was a widow different? Only because she is a woman? You know, Varun, women are the greatest enemies of other women."

She could hear Varun inhaling a deep breath. "Is she still working in your school? I would like to meet her."

Ira let out a suppressed smile. "No Varun, she left the job and moved back to Toshali. She even admitted to me, she was suffocating. We are in India, not in a western country."

Varun leaned forward and held his mother's hands.

"These are unforgiving people," Ira said.

"So, what, Mum? Society is not comfortable because most women don't remarry after their husband's death. They don't hate when a young and childless widow remarries. But years ago, that was also a taboo. See how the perception is changing? Someone must take the initial step, and that's a tough thing to do. Who better than a strong-willed person like you to make such a move?"

A chuckle came out from her mouth. "Varun, you are flattering me too much. You know why I'm scared? I'm in a Facebook group called 'Second chance life' created for women like us. Members often tell stories about how in-laws and even relatives almost outcast the women who even try to find a husband. These are women who have teens or grown-up children, not the young widows."

"Do you think Uncle Rohan will insult you, if you remarry?" Varun narrowed his eyes.

"Don't you think so? He is fighting against me so that I can't make a claim to your dad's share in the ancestral property. He will get a point. He'd say since I remarried, I don't have a right to my dead husband's assets." Ira looked into his eyes. "And not just Rohan. Think about my cousin, your aunt Urvi. She wouldn't miss a single chance to ridicule me."

"Can I join that group, Mum?"

"No dear. That's only for women like me."

"That's wrong, Mum. They should allow men who also are widowers or divorcees."

A tremor of discomfort ran through her. *My little boy is so mature that I'm discussing my second marriage with him.*

"Time for bed, Varun. Some other time."

Ira gave a goodnight hug to her son and trudged to the bedroom.

It's Saturday night, and we could have watched movies until late. Why did I rush to sleep? Am I not offending my only well-wisher, my son? Am I also the country-town woman who loves to live in the darkness of so-called tradition?

She stood in front of the dressing-table mirror. Her own image amused her. The low neckline on the fitted top proudly displayed her ample bust. Unknowingly, her palm started massaging her mammary glands. After so many months, this had become a forbidden zone for any man. What was the big deal if some men sitting in the restaurant were ogling her boobs?

As Ira removed her top, her push-up bra mocked her. How would another man in her life like these assets? An unknown and faceless man appeared in her fantasy and moved his palm to her chest. Heat pooled between her legs. Remarriage was a better option to protect her from a situation like she encountered with Sam.

No, how could I do this with a man when my teenage son sleeps in the next bedroom?

A moaning sound from the lounge room sneaked through her door and pounded into her ears. "Is Varun watching a movie with an intimate scene?" she asked herself.

Ira forgot that only minutes before she had pretended to feel sleepy. She opened her door slightly and said, "Varun, I'm coming back out after changing my clothes. Can we watch some Hindi movie instead?"

CHAPTER 5

That Monday morning, Ira stood in front of her dressing-table mirror and made a ponytail with her long hair—the way she always did when she went to the school. The school had strict dress codes for female teachers—no western clothing during duty hours. Ira slipped inside an orange embroidered georgette salwar suit.

It was a perfect day for Ira. All these months after Rahul's demise, she never had a reason to smile on the inside. Varun's understanding made her grateful to God. All this time she had believed only daughters were sensitive to a mother's need—a feminine need a woman couldn't discuss with males in her society. A desire she thought was dead along with Rahul. But it was very much alive and well. Was it Sam's intimacy which awoke it?

"Mum, can you please help me untangle my hair?" Varun called from his bedroom.

A giggle escaped her mouth. Varun had a soft tone, not deep enough for boys his age. Without a single hair on his face and the long hair on his head, he looked like a girl. Ira had never let it bother her. *He is still a teen, and some boys get facial hair late. Nothing unusual.*

She rushed to Varun's room. Standing in front of the mirror, he was struggling with his freshly shampooed hair.

"I have to teach you as if I'm teaching a daughter." Ira giggled. The beautiful face staring at her was in no way a boy's appearance. Her lost dream to get a daughter as the second child winked at her from the mirror.

"That's okay, Mum. You will find both a son and daughter in me."

Varun's bare chest always posed a question to Ira. His dad also had little chest hair. But her son had a clean chest, as if he had shaved it fresh like many movie stars. And his arms? Slim like a woman's hand!

"Do your friends in college mind your long hair and ear piercing?"

Varun chuckled. "No, Mum. I am not the first one to sport long hair. There are others, too."

A wave of comfort passed through Ira's heart. She often wondered if Varun was considered effeminate. No. Boys nowadays had long hair and were even tying them into buns. Pierced ears were also normal among some men. Helping a mother in the kitchen wouldn't make a boy into a girl.

No, he doesn't have a girlfriend. So what? He is still a teen.

"What are you thinking, Mum?"

Ira realised that even though she was standing behind him, he could see her facial reactions in the mirror as she helped with his hair.

"Nothing, only that you came as I've just finished my annual leave. Won't it be boring for you to stay at home the entire day alone?" Ira never dared to ask Varun why he skipped his classes to come home. How could she when her own guilt clouded her conscience?

"No, Mum. I've also got plans to meet a friend. You go to your girls' school."

Ira checked the time on her wristwatch. "Okay, my boy, I will be late. See you in the afternoon. Bye."

At Lata Devi Girls' High School, Raghupur, they were in the last class before midday recess. Ira was teaching history to year ten students—the medieval period in India.

"Long before Mughals conquered the throne of Delhi, Alauddin Khilji became Delhi's emperor in the year 1296. He was one of the cruellest emperors who mercilessly butchered many Hindu subjects and sold many beautiful young women as sex slaves."

She cast a glance around the class. Normally, the last period before the recess made girls restless. But when she began with how Alauddin tortured young women, all the ears focussed on her lecture.

"But history notices the instances of some brave women, who welcomed death rather than becoming the emperor's sex slaves. One woman was the famous beautiful queen of Chittor in Rajasthan. When her husband, King Ratnasinha, died fighting against the emperor and Khilji proceeded to the palace to capture the queen, she and a few of her close friends walked into fire just when Khilji arrived there. She displayed her utter defiance to the so-called winner of the war and Khilji admitted his defeat against the queen."

"Miss?" One girl in the class raised her hand.

"Yes, Deepa. You want to ask something?"

"Miss, is it not the cowardice to commit suicide? Didn't the queen really kill herself?"

"You are right," Ira continued, "suicide is an act of a coward. But this situation was different. Chittor's kingdom had already lost the war, and the queen, famous for her unparalleled beauty, knew Alauddin would have captured her if she tried to flee. She also wanted to teach Alauddin a lesson that women are human beings and not animals. So, given the circumstances, she thought entering fire was the best way to fight against a beast, so that he couldn't even dishonour her dead body."

"But, miss?" Another girl raised her arm.

"Yes, Mansi." Ira always made her best efforts to remember her students' names.

"Miss, what would have happened, had he gotten the queen alive?"

"Don't know." Ira continued, "But in another instance, when the king of Gujarat fled after losing the war, Alauddin's soldiers captured his queen, Kamla Devi, and took her to Delhi."

"What happened to her, miss?" Mansi widened her eyes.

"She fled to America and became their vice president," another girl said from the back bench, and the entire class burst into laughter.

Ira tried hard to control her giggle. "That was in the 13th century. And this Kamala Devi Harris, who became America's vice president, is in the 21st century. Remember, this is history class, and we are studying the medieval history of India. Not what is happening in the USA nowadays. So, Kamla Devi, the queen of Gujarat, compromised with her life and accepted the marriage proposal from the emperor. She became one of the favourite queens of Delhi sultan. Now, you guys decide who was a coward. Queen Padmini of Chittor or Queen Kamla Devi of Gujarat?"

"Miss, she was not happy with her husband and would have run away with another man, anyway. So when she had time to marry another successful man, she made her decision," a girl said from the back.

The entire class burst into laughter again.

Except Ira. She could hear someone weeping. An unease tore through her. "Can you all please stop the noise?"

Deepa, who was seated next to her, said, "Miss, she's crying because her mother ran away with another man. But that man didn't kidnap her like Alauddin did with Kamla Devi, she ran away on her own."

Another burst of laughter. It shook Ira's heart. "This is a rude and indecent joke." She stood tall and cast an angry glance around. "We are all human, and laughing at someone's loss is against humanity."

A silence descended on the class.

Suddenly, the recess bell rang. "You may all leave now," she announced.

The class dispersed quietly while Ira watched them. Sardonic smiles on most of the faces couldn't evade her notice. She sat on the chair next to the sobbing girl and gently squeezed her shoulder. "You are a brave girl," she said.

The girl raised her face. She was Divya.

"Miss, my dad died three years ago. My uncles and relatives were angry with my mum because they found her name at a matrimonial site. She was trying to find a candidate for her own marriage."

A smile came out, dancing through Ira's soul. "Your mother has done nothing wrong."

Divya's lips trembled as she met Ira's gaze. "Miss?"

33

Ira ruffled her hair. "Yes, she is a brave woman."

"My mum is not a working woman. She has no income of her own. My dad's brother has so many times tried to make advances with her. She resisted each time. He was threatening to make us starve if she didn't surrender to him. But then my dad's friend—he is a nice man. His wife died of cancer, and he has no children. Mum has gone with him to marry him. After some time, she will take me to Toshali. She didn't run away. She told me everything. My uncle is just spreading false news."

"You have any brothers or sisters?"

"No. I'm the only one. But my cousin, I mean, my uncle's son, has a girlfriend in our school. He is spreading false news through her."

"Where are you living now? In the same house as your uncle?"

"No, Miss. Mum had to move to her friend's. I am with her. But how long will her friend accommodate us? One day, we have to find something of our own."

Pain twisted through her stomach. The hypocrisy of the so-called traditional society exploded through her head.

"Miss, can I go home? I don't want to come to the school again."

"When will your mother take you to Toshali?"

"Not sure. Maybe in a week. She is afraid to come to the school to ask for a letter of transfer."

"Don't worry. You go home. I will inform the headmistress that you were not well. And if your mother wants, she can come to my home and give the application for your transfer. I will arrange all the paperwork and send it to her. All right?"

For the first time, a smile appeared on Divya's lips. "Miss, you are so nice. These girls were all my friends. But they are now taunting me."

"Don't worry about the teasing if you have done nothing wrong. Whatever your mother did is a hundred percent right. But please don't keep any ill will against your friends. They are just ignorant. One day they will realise what your mum did was right. Revenge brings nothing worthwhile."

Divya stood up. "Bye, miss."

"Best of luck." Ira flashed an assuring smile and stood there until she left. She looked at her wristwatch. It had been almost fifteen minutes of the forty-five minutes of recess. She trudged to the teacher's common room on the ground floor.

While walking through the stairway, her gaze fell on the girls dispersed over the vast garden of the school. The girls who were the symbol of a new society which would provide economic empowerment to women. But what about social empowerment? Their parents think a widow who married again has committed a sin. Why was there no curriculum in the school to teach the students that the society needs to think differently with the coming age?

She didn't realise she was already at the doors of the teachers' common room, a long hall facing the school garden partitioned into a dining room and sitting area. Ira saw some teachers eating their food from their lunch boxes and chatting among themselves. She had already finished her lunch when she had a vacant period around noon.

All Ira wanted was to talk to some teachers and vent out her frustration. She wanted to talk to some like-minded teacher who would sympathise with Divya's case. Ira glanced around for her closest colleague, Reema. She wasn't there. She might have been in the library preparing for her next class. Only five teachers were there, all in some serious discussion, in a suppressed voice.

Are these people also talking about that girl's mother? Are they also thinking that the woman who eloped with a man is a shame to the so-called honoured society?

She had been in this school for the last twenty years, shortly after her marriage with Rahul. In the beginning, colleagues avoided her because she was beautiful, stylish, and moreover, she was from Mumbai. The co-workers, most of whom were from Raghupur, had gotten inferiority complexes. But eventually she had gotten along well with them.

But there were good and bad people everywhere.

She approached cautiously and took a chair nearby. "Everything all right?" she asked Mrs. Patra.

"Oh, yes." A murmur of suppressed laughter moved through the room. "All right with us, but not with everybody."

"Comm on, Mrs. Patra. Are we making a joke of someone?"

A silence hung immediately.

Mrs. Das, a senior teacher, broke the silence. "My sister-in-law found out her son is a gay."

A murmur moved through the common room.

Gay? Ira's mind jumped from Divya's mother to another social issue which Raghupur's society would make fun of and harass another family over.

The words 'gay' and 'lesbian' were foreign terms until a few years ago, not only for Ira, but many other people. Since her childhood, she had seen eunuchs, mostly in Mumbai and rarely in Raghupur and Toshali. Disowned by their families and even the society, young boys would join with the group of old eunuchs who would castrate them and train them to dress in saree. Devoid of any social security, they would end up in the street dancing and singing for a living. Every time she came across them, her heart rebelled against the parents who threw the young boys out of their homes.

Her brain often mixed up gay, lesbian, and eunuch as one breed. She often sympathised with the people with different sexual identities but never imagined how it would be if she experienced it inside her own home. In fact, she had never come across a real gay in her life. What would she do if Varun were gay? She couldn't imagine sending him out into the streets, she'd never be able to do it. But why was she thinking like this? Varun is a normal boy. So what if he was sporting long hair? She wondered, not for the first time, if Varun really did wear her dresses sometimes, but quickly pushed the thought away.

"What are you thinking, Ira?" Mrs. Das asked.

"Does your sister-in-law live in Raghupur?" She tried to control her trembling voice.

"Unfortunately, yes." Mrs. Das looked at Ira with a smile. "They are afraid the news will spread, and they can't show their face to anyone. Anyway, the boy was effeminate since childhood."

"But Mrs. Das, in that case you should have kept that a secret. Even from us!"

Mrs. Das took her handbag from the side and placed it on her lap. "I...in fact...I never said the name of my sister-in-law. So, for you all, this is just an anonymous family."

But something inside Ira said she was not well. As if Divya's story was happening inside her own home. Or her own boy was announcing he was gay. No, this was only random, irrelevant thoughts.

Ira's head spun.

"Are you all right, Ira?" Mrs. Das asked. "You look sick."

"I guess so. I had been to Toshali on holiday to spend a week with my son, but I think I'm still tired."

Ira left the teachers' common room and texted the principal before rushing home. Varun would come back from his friend's in the evening. She must check his room, table drawers. For what, she didn't know. *God, my Varun is a boy. His dad's soul would scream in pain if Varun didn't behave.*

What else could she check? His bookcases? She would Google the traits of gay men and see if Varun has any such qualities. This town of Raghupur would make her life a hell.

Ira cast a helpless glance around. The sun pinched her skin, and the crows' cackling mocked her. She needed proof her son was not a gay, even after continuously assuring herself that sporting long hair and pierced ears was becoming common among young men.

Her home was only a ten-minute walk from the school. *Why is the road looking longer today? Am I walking slow? The heels on these shoes are too high!*

The universe had planned to be uncooperative with her when she was in a hurry. The high-heeled shoes pulled her feet back, and of course—the lift had to be out of order when she entered her apartment building! Why was God so harsh on her when she needed Him the most? She should have never prayed to this unkind God. Didn't He close His ears when she had poured her soul in her prayers when Rahul was on his deathbed?

"God, why are you so tough on me?" She barely had enough energy to climb the unfriendly stairs up to the sixth floor. By the time she arrived at the front door of her apartment, she was struggling to breathe. Unlocking the door, Ira threw the keys on the shoe rack and wrenched her feet out of the shoes.

She was about to lope inside the lounge room when a sense that someone was inside haunted her, and she stilled. Did she hear a sound? Or was it her own heart beating like a drum?

Ira took a deep breath to calm her heart and tiptoed into the living room. Her breath stopped as her gaze fell on the back side of a young woman, and her feet slammed to a complete halt.

Did a woman break into my apartment? Why is she wearing my skirt and top, the same ones I had put on when going out for dinner with Varun?

"Mum!" The young woman swung around.

Ira's eyebrows shot up. Her black push-up bra protruded through the red top without an ounce of shame.

Ira had accepted Varun having a bun on his head and earrings in his ears.

But her son wearing his mother's dress? And her lingerie? Ira remembered a few times she had suspected Varun wearing her dress secretly.

Her vision blurred. Frustration exploded through her brain and radiated from her nerves. She turned and sprinted to her bedroom. A sob came out from her throat as she tumbled on the bed, burying her face in the pillow.

Rahul was right. Varun was not normal. Why did she always protect him? Why did she never consider bringing out the boyish qualities in her son? Yes, she would love to have had another child, a daughter. Not a daughter inside her son's body.

Did Varun throw her hints of this before? She remembered the day when she helped him tie his bun and praised him for his help in household chores. Didn't he say, "Mum, I would be both a son and daughter to you?" Was it against her remark that daughters sympathise better with mothers than a son? Or it just a plain hidden confession in advance?

She lifted her head and gazed at Rahul's photo on the side wall.

"Sorry, Rahul. I should have paid heed to you. I failed to bring up your son. How would I show my face to your brother and his family?"

Rahul's upset eyes rebuked Ira from inside the photo.

This is just the beginning, Ira. Go on, watch what comes next.

Next? A pain stabbed in her heart. What else? Her son already began his new identity. He started with growing long hair and piercing his ears. And after putting on his own mother's lingerie and dress, was he planning a sex-change operation, too?

The paradigm of Ira's world had tilted dangerously. Could Rahul's soul help her?

Guilt and shame overpowered her, and she didn't have the courage to look at Rahul's picture.

Ira again plunged her head into the pillow and indulged in sobbing. Could she brush it off as another dreaded dream?

"Mum."

A soft voice and a warm hand on her back sent the emotion flooding through her. No. She wouldn't show her weakness to Varun.

Is this another instance of Varun's childishness? Would he be all right with age? Mature to become a proper man? But she was sure Varun had come to Sam's apartment when she was in his bedroom and kissing him. Didn't Varun slip out to give her privacy? Didn't her son come all the way home at the cost of missing his classes to convince her she should marry again? How much maturity should a mother expect from her son who is still a teen?

"Mum, I'm sorry."

Has Varun repented and discarded her dress? Was he back in a boy's get up? Could she again hug her darling boy?

Ira sat up.

No. Varun was still in her skirt and fitted, low-neck top. His artificial boobs still derided at her.

"I'm sorry, Mum, I had to wear your clothing. And your bra, too. Because I don't have my own." He sat on the bed facing Ira, placing his palms up on his thighs and looking into her eyes.

"Don't I buy clothes for you?" Ira lowered her gaze.

"Of course, Mum. But I feel ... at home after wearing women's clothing. It is comfortable and relaxing."

Ira's body tensed again. She couldn't understand how a woman's underwear and clothing were relaxing. Was it because she was a woman and could never guess what a boy feels inside a woman's get up?

"I never thought my boy would be a gay." Ira was still sobbing.

"Gay? No, Mum. Promise." Varun shifted closer to Ira. A feminine perfume on his dress filled her nose.

"Then what are you?" Ira was utterly confused. She wasn't aware if crossdressers became gay or gays loved to wear dresses. This was all so new to her.

She had seen the eunuchs dancing and asking for money on the streets of Mumbai, where she had grown up. Would her boy roam around wearing dresses and claim to be a woman?

"Mum, you are worrying what the society would think of you if I went out wearing this. I'm aware, Mum. I wouldn't embarrass you with my choice of clothing." Varun sat, touching his body to his mother. "I will do this in the privacy of our home. Only if you allow me. I had thought so many times about opening up with you and not hiding anything from you, Mum. But takes a long time to gather courage."

Did Varun say this to pacify her? To make her accept his new way of life?

Female clothing was relaxing. How? Was Varun stressed? Because his dad died? Was he stressed because his mother's income might not be enough to support his higher education? Or was he tense because he discovered his mother was making love with his flatmate, who was only a few years older than him? As a mother, she must find out what was disturbing him. Maybe he began this recently and felt comfort in it. She hoped her son was not similar to the eunuch she had seen in Mumbai.

She couldn't make her son rebel against her. Didn't she always take pride in having the most understanding child ever? Shouldn't she reciprocate that with her own understanding? If Varun agreed never to go out in female get up, she thought she could talk him out of this habit.

Ira inched toward him and engulfed him in a tight hug. "I love you, my child."

For the first time, she used the word *child* instead of *boy*. Did she also change with Varun?

Surprisingly, a sense of relaxation washed over Ira. She wondered if it was the same relaxation that Varun said he felt while wearing women's clothing. Strange, but cathartic.

Varun wrapped his arm around her back and buried his face in her neck. "Thank you, Mum. Are you still angry with me?" Varun released Ira from his loving wrap.

A giggle escaped from Ira's mouth. How could she ever be angry with her only child? Her heart heaved a sigh of relief. Sex change operation was not her concern.

"No, *Varuna*."

"I love this name, Mum. Please call me *Varuna*," he whispered. Light sparkled in his eyes. "Not always. But when I am in a girl's get up."

"Sure, my baby." Ira's thoughts moved back to the days and weeks before Varun's birth. "I will tell you something, if you don't disclose this."

"Is this a secret, Mum?"

"Not exactly, but it was private between your dad and me. We never did a sex determination test before your birth. And somehow, I had thought, 'I'm getting a girl.' I had thought of that name, *Varuna*."

Varuna giggled. He—no, *she* wore a girly smile. Didn't Ira see Varun's smile before? Or was it looking better since Varun became *Varuna*?

"Mum, would you come back to the lounge room? Or we could talk the entire day here, on your bed."

"You go, I'm coming."

Varuna left. Ira glanced at her gait. It looked like her daughter walking.

She got off her bed and opened her jewellery drawer. Taking out a pair of earrings, she walked to the lounge room. Varuna was awaiting her on the sofa.

She crouched before *her* and removed *her* ear piercings.

"What is this, Mum?"

"This pair is for you when you are Varuna. And those ear piercings are simple studs. Androgynous. They are for Varun."

Varuna planted a kiss on Ira's cheeks. "Love you, Mum."

"Love you, my bo...baby."

She knew she must practise addressing her son as a daughter when he became Varuna.

Ira's gaze fell on Varuna's breasts. "Where did you get those fake boobs?" A chuckle escaped her mouth.

"Online, Mum. It's made of silicon."

"And can you also choose the size, like B, C, etcetera?"

"Of course. CC."

"You naughty girl! You chose my exact size so that you can wear my bra."

Varuna giggled.

Ira settled herself on Varuna's side on the sofa, wrapping her arm over her shoulder.

"Can I ask you something, Varuna?" Ira said after planting a loving kiss on her cheeks.

"Yes, Mum. Anything you ask, I will say yes. Because you are the best mum in the world. No, universe."

"Don't flatter me so much. Okay, now listen. Do you plan to go out, I mean to the market, wearing dresses?"

Varuna closed her eyes for a moment. "Never, Mum. I will wear the dress in secret. So I can be myself at least within the four walls of a house."

"That's good, my baby."

"Mum, are you happy now?"

"Yes, my dear."

"Can I say something?"

"Go on."

"Mum, when you find a boyfriend and go on a date, I will be the one to prepare you. Just like your daughter."

Ira chuckled. "Are boyfriends for sale in the market that I can go shopping and buy one?"

42

CHAPTER 6

Ira's heart squeezed as Varun said bye, and the Toshali-Express left the bus station in Raghupur. Last week was one of the loveliest since Rahul's death. She had tried to get used to Varun's new identity—the one he lived only during evenings at home. Her girl Varuna would welcome her when she was back from school, and Ira would spend some quality time with her *daughter*.

Ira trudged to the quiet coffee shop at the far end of the corridor of the waiting area and ordered a cappuccino. It was around two in the afternoon, and she didn't wish to go back to an empty home so soon.

"Thank you, ma'am," the girl behind the counter said with a smile as she handed over the exact change. "Ten minutes, and your coffee will be ready."

Ira responded with a smile at the girl who must've been Varun's age. "Don't worry. Take your time. I'm not in a hurry." She stood aside to give way to other customers, but she realised there was no one behind her. She looked at the girl with a slight frown. She was a pretty, petite young girl with a big smile on her face. Her hair was light brown, and she had a slender nose. Her eyes were green.

"Ma'am, you don't recognise me. But I know you." The girl's head bobbed up and down when she spoke.

Ira was amused but not surprised. "Are you..."

"Ma'am, I was studying in Lata Devi Girls' High School. My name is Rupa. Last year I passed twelfth in the first division."

"Yes, Rupa. I remember now. So nice to see you. Which college are you studying at now?"

Suddenly Rupa's face fell. She looked away, tear pooling in her eyes.

"Ma'am, I will study. Just taking a break. I will go to college—" she tried to hide a sob— "after...maybe...after a few years."

Ira's heart sank. She was not ready to accept that a girl must discontinue education like this against her wishes. Rupa wanted to continue her study, but something had stopped her.

Ira again moved to the side to allow a woman to place an order. Rupa forced a smile on her face and said, "How can I help you, ma'am?"

"One burger for my son and one cappuccino for me." The lady set a heavy bag on the floor and opened her purse as the seemingly twelve-year-old boy stood by her side holding an iPad. She must have gotten off a bus or been waiting for one. "Make the burger fresh with some extra chicken," the woman commanded after paying.

Where is the word, *please*? Ira wondered.

"Sure, ma'am. Your son will love our burger."

The woman stood to the side, and Ira continued talking to Rupa.

"But, Rupa, there're so many government-run colleges here, and their fees are really nominal. Why didn't you continue to study?"

A man came from inside holding a takeaway coffee and placed it on the counter. Rupa flashed another smile. "Here is your coffee, ma'am."

Ira took the mug, but she didn't intend to go away so soon. "I hope I'm not disturbing your business," she said, looking at the man. He looked like the owner. Ira had come to this shop in the past and had seen the man managing the counter.

"Not at all, ma'am. This is the lean time. Around four p.m. and onwards until the last bus, which will leave at eight. We have the most business." The man went inside.

"I know, ma'am," Rupa continued, "but I must work to support the family."

Ira was going to take a sip but stopped. "What about your dad?"

"My papa—" Rupa swallowed. "My brother is studying engineering in a private college in Toshali. Papa was struggling to meet his tuition fees. Last year, they hiked the fees by twenty percent. Papa tried to get a bank loan but couldn't. His entire salary is going for my brother's fees and hostel expenses. How would the family survive? We have our ancestral home, thank God to my late grandfather, so we don't have to pay rent at least. But we need food, electricity, gas, and phones. So much expenditure, ma'am. But I'm happy I am just managing the cash counter, not doing any hard work in the kitchen."

The coffee mug seemed too heavy for Ira, and she placed it on the counter. A teen girl was lifting so much responsibility for the sake of the family. She was her son's age. A mother's affection bubbled in her heart.

"Ma'am, when I was in school, most girls would love to talk about you." Rupa chuckled.

"Me?"

"Yes, ma'am. You are so beautiful, and the western dresses you wear when not in the school look so beautiful on you. Girls love your sense of fashion and beauty. They say, because you were born and brought up in a city like Mumbai, you differ from other women here."

Only a few days ago Ira had seen how the girls were teasing Divya because her widow mother remarried.

"They should try to be progressive in their thinking, instead. Fashion is not that important." Ira's gaze fell on a middle-aged man who was standing on the side and staring at her. She inched to the side. "Sorry sir, I have already collected my order, your turn."

"Don't worry, I will wait," the man said without moving.

Ira lifted her coffee mug and said, "No, please place your order. I was talking to her because there was no customer."

She took a sip and moved farther to the side. She never complained about the coffee here before, but today it was too strong. Not up to her taste. Which customer would come to the stall again with this quality of beverage? She wondered.

Her gaze fell on the man as Rupa was punching the order on the machine. He was staring at her chest and licking his lips. Bitterness swelled inside her. He must be Rupa's father's age or even older. She longed to throw the hot beverage on his face and ask him to get lost. But unfortunately, that was not an option for her. She tried to take a large sip of the coffee and finish it, but she burnt her tongue instead.

"I will be back in a few minutes. Please keep my coffee ready." The man cast a flirty look at Rupa again. "I am coming here because of you. I mean your service."

The smile on Rupa's lips looked painful. "Yes, sir."

"You should never smile at him," Ira said in a low voice, coming near to Rupa.

"Ma'am..." Rupa cast a nervous glance over her and muttered, "Boss said, if a young girl stands at the counter, he will get more customers. He will ask her to leave if I don't tolerate these dirty men. But all are not like this man. There are some nice ones, too."

Now Ira understood why the owner, whom she had seen at the counter before, hired this young and good-looking girl and was managing the kitchen himself.

"Good for business, huh? Does your mother know what sort of people you have to deal with?"

"If I don't earn money, my grandmother would be angry with me, ma'am. She always thinks I am a burden on the family because I am a girl." Tears pooled in Rupa's eyes again.

Ira had just taken a large sip of coffee. "You have a grandmother? I mean, you are lucky to have a grandmother. But why does she say things like this?"

Rupa looked down. "She didn't want a girl in the family. She said my grandfather became poor because he had to pay a huge dowry to her daughter for her wedding. I know she was pressuring my father to have an abortion when she knew my mother was pregnant with a girl."

"Abortion?" Ira knew many families did this heinous sin to get rid of female embryos. Nevertheless, she struggled to digest this.

"Yes, ma'am. My mum had confided this to me. She was the one who opposed this and refused to go kill me inside her uterus."

Thank God there are women who have guts and can fight against this evil. "Is your mother educated?"

Rupa chuckled. "Yes, ma'am. She is a graduate. And she has done B. Ed. too."

Ira noticed a pride on Rupa's face when she spoke about her mother. "Then she could have gotten a teachership job easily. Like me."

"I know, ma'am. But..."

"But what? Your dad said no?"

"No, it was my grandmother. Even my grandfather was not against it. But grandma said, women who work outside the home are of loose character. She even blamed my mum because she was from another caste and my father fell in love with her. She blames it all to her education."

"Your mother could have gotten a decent job even in a girls' school, like me. But your grandma doesn't stop you from working in a stall and facing all the idiots here." Ira was from not only another caste, but she came from a difference province, too. But her mother-in-law never opposed her marriage or her job. She closed her eyes for a moment and thanked her late parents-in-law.

Rupa rolled her eyes. "She doesn't stop me, as without my salary, they would starve."

The middle-aged man came back to collect his order. The owner also came and stood near the counter, listening to what Ira was saying to Rupa.

Rupa took a cloth and started wiping the countertop, looking at Ira from the corner of her eyes, a faint smile curving the corner of her lips. She understood.

"Rupa, see you again, on another day." Throwing the half-empty coffee cup in a bin, she found her way out of the bus stop.

Rupa's mother can't apply for a teachership job in a government school because the age limit for applying is thirty, Ira thought while sitting in the cab. She couldn't even apply for a job in a private school as she had no experience even over two decades after she passed her B. Ed.

A traffic jam slowed down the cab, and Ira glanced through the window. Old houses were being demolished to widen the road. Part of a grand plan to make Raghupur a larger city. Not large like Toshali, but bigger than what it was now. Lest the heart of the people become big. A sigh came out of her mouth.

She had forgotten about Varun's absence after talking to Rupa.

"Your stop, ma'am." The cab arrived near the gate of her apartment complex. Ira climbed out of the cab and walked towards the building. The elevator door closed seconds before she could reach it, but she got a glimpse of the partly bald man and the heavy woman who walked into the elevator moments before its doors closed.

Rahul's younger brother, Rohan, and his wife, Tina. *Why are they here?* She checked her phone. There were no missed calls or texts. Were they here to meet someone else? Or did she just mistake the couple to be her brother-in-law and his wife? Anxiety whipped through her as the elevator arrived at the ground floor again and she dragged her feet inside.

Rohan and Tina were already standing in front of her door when the elevator halted with a ding and the doors slid open.

"How are you, Rohan and Tina?" She managed a smile.

"You forgot us after my brother's death. But you are our family, and shouldn't we see from time to time how you are doing?" A sly smile curved Rohan's mouth as Tina bent a little to say namaste.

"Nice to see you." Ira dug in her handbag for her keys. "Please come in," she said as she stepped inside. "So nice to see you both after so long. Please have a seat. I will make some snacks for you."

"No, *didi*." Tina had never forgotten the custom of addressing her older sister-in-law as an older sister. She slumped in the middle of the two-seater sofa, almost occupying it entirely. "We had a heavy lunch in the restaurant, and both are full now. You know I'm on a diet, and he is also trying to diet. So, no snacks please."

Rohan settled in the middle of the three-seater one.

Ira thought for a second about where she would sit. She pulled a chair off the dining table and settled in.

"Diet?" *After having a heavy lunch in a restaurant?* She struggled with what to say. "Good for your diabetes and cholesterol. Please give me some guidance on a good diet plan."

"What, *didi*? You are lucky to have that gene in your blood. Always slim and glowing. Why do you need to be dieting like us?"

Gene? Ira didn't want to tell how much time she spent exercising.

Rohan cleared his throat. "I was about to discuss the Puri Road property."

A bolt of current passed through Ira. So Rohan came for that ancestral property! Another attempt to pressure her out of Rohan's share in the goldmine? She sat straight and gazed into Rohan's eyes.

"You probably don't know that plot of land was just a garbage bin of the locality as my father didn't want to build anything there. I spent all my income building shops so that the family could earn some extra income."

"*You* spent?" Ira asked.

"That was before you or Tina came into our family. Of course, brother Rahul and our oldest brother Mehul had also contributed."

Ira didn't wish to enter unnecessary arguments. She knew her father-in-law's entire retirement savings were invested there. Besides that, Rahul and her oldest brother-in-law Mehul also invested a lot. Rohan was in a low-paying job and had hardly any savings.

"Brother Rahul and brother Mehul allowed me the entire rental income because they both have—sorry, *had* a decent income. And I lost my job. I tried so hard but couldn't get another job."

How could you get another job, Rohan? Ira thought. *You are not ready to go out of your comfort zones.* Rahul had organised work for him a few times. Raghupur, being a small town, didn't have enough opportunities. And Rohan was not ready to go out of the town.

"What do you want now?" Ira tried her best to keep her voice low and friendly.

"Brother Mehul has retired, and his daughter is also married. He has enough savings from his law profession and doesn't want to work anymore. But I understand, after brother Rahul's death, you must feel the burden of educating Varun with just one income. So, why don't you also take a share..." Rohan swallowed. "I mean, maybe ten percent of the rent? It will be a lot of pressure on my income. But we are a family and should share the burden. What do you think?"

Everything was clear to Ira now. She had demanded Rahul's share in the property, as Rohan was planning to sell it and appropriate the entirety of the money. Ira had slapped a stay order of the court through a lawyer.

"You are a lucky one, *didi*," Tina said. "You have only one son, and no daughter."

"Only assets, and no liabilities." Rohan burst into a loud laugh, which stabbed Ira's heart like an arrow.

Tina began again, "We got two daughters. Just imagine two heavy responsibilities. Not only their education, but their marriage, too."

Ira looked at Tina, and then at Rohan. "Rahul had allowed you to keep the entire rent. I'm okay if you continue doing the same. I am not asking for any of it. All I want is for you not to sell the property. Raghupur is expanding. It will become a large city in a few years, the property will appreciate by millions. You brothers are sitting over a gold mine. I know you have no job, and two children. They are like my children, too. If I want Varun to get a chance for higher education, I also would like your children to get their chances."

Rahul had always wanted to keep his brothers happy. Ira would never make his soul upset by depriving Rohan's children of a decent life because of their father's incapability. Or irresponsibility.

"But what about their wedding? You are lucky you have no daughter." Tina bent forward on the sofa and said, "We had done the ultrasounds and had planned to end them. It was you who nearly forced us to keep my pregnancy both times. Isn't it your duty to see how we manage these responsibilities?"

Bile lurched into Ira's throat. Only moments ago, Rupa was telling her how her grandmother was forcing her mother to end the female embryo. Poor girl would have died even before seeing the light of this world, and was now working hard to bring food to the same grandmother's table.

She took a long breath. "Our mum-in-law was such a wonderful woman. She never supported the killing of girl children in the mother's womb. You and brother Mehul are lucky to have girls. Rather, it was my bad luck I couldn't get another child. I had dreamt of having a girl after having Varun."

Tina didn't reply.

"Do you know how much dowry I will have to give for their weddings?" Rohan lowered his eyebrows.

Ira pulled the chair a bit closer to Tina. "Dowry? That is an outdated custom. Who is giving it nowadays? Maybe the lower-class uneducated families are still clinging to it. My father paid no money for my marriage. And Rohan, your parents never even asked my father to pay anything. My parents-in-law were both wonderful, and both were against this dirty custom. Don't you know?"

"You don't know the truth." Rohan's voice went up. "Brother Rahul fell in love with you. A girl from a different caste."

"So what? Your parents were happy to give their consent and blessings. Weren't they?"

"That's why I said you know only half the truth. Mother feared if she and father didn't agree, brother Rahul would leave the family forever to marry you. They didn't want the family to break up, so agreed for the wedding and that too with no dowry."

Ira's heart was not ready to accept this. Rohan could say anything in the names of his dead parents. Rahul would have told her had that been the case.

"Then what about you, Tina? I admit I was from another caste even though I am a Hindu, too. What about you? Same caste. Arranged marriage. Did your parents pay anything? No. I was at your wedding. I respect Rahul's parents so much. They were both years ahead of the people their age in terms of modern thinking."

"They didn't ask for dowry, I know." Tina leaned forward. "But Rohan met my father and asked to give him cash without informing his parents. And my father had to pay."

A dart of anger speared through Ira. "Rohan, you?"

Rohan looked down. "Everyone was taking. Why did my father become a saint and advise against it? And that money I invested in building those shops."

Another lie. A blatant lie.

Unable to look at Rohan any longer, Ira turned to Tina to change the subject. "Believe me, Tina. A girl child is not a burden. An hour ago, I met a girl who discontinued her studies to help her parents and is now working in a coffee shop. If you educate a girl, she will be an asset to the parents. You don't know how much I envy you and brother Mehul for the daughters you have. I would never demand a share in the rents of those shops, but please invest that money in their education."

Rohan got up and stomped to the window. Within moments, he came back and stood in the middle of the drawing room. "Girls!

Education! Look at brother Mehul's daughter, Mansi. He sent her to Delhi for higher education. She studied MBA and got a job in a multinational. And then. Found a Christian and married him."

"What is wrong with that?" Ira got up. She took a glass and poured water from the filter. "Am I not educated?"

"Yes, you are. And look at yourself in the mirror. First you trapped brother Rahul with your fashion and..."

Ira set the glass down. She felt fire coming through her eyes. "And what, Rohan?"

"Nothing." He slumped on the sofa.

"People are passing lewd comments behind your back, *didi,*" Tina said.

"About me? What? What I am wearing?"

"Yes." Tina looked down.

"What is new about that? They were commenting even when I came to Raghupur after the wedding. Slowly, they got used to it. A few years later, when you came to this family, the society had sobered up. Don't you also wear jeans? The society has accepted it."

"I was. Not now. Maybe after a few months of dieting, I can wear them again. But your case is different."

"Different? How? Because I am not fat?"

"No, *didi,* you don't understand. You are a widow. Society expects a widow to discard all the fashion items permanently from her life. You praise our mum in law so much. Didn't she abandon all her ornaments after Dad-in-law died? She stopped wearing colourful sarees even."

Ira wanted to bring a gun and shoot all those people who wanted to dictate what women should and shouldn't do. She, in fact, tried to avoid fashionable clothing where it would be an eyesore. But she was confused where she should and where not.

Ira stood up. "We are not in a Taliban country, Tina. Please grow up."

Rohan sat straight. "Grow up? That is why you brought a stay order from the court so that I can't sell the property. Because you have grown up. Even when brother Rahul studied in Mumbai. You successfully trapped him to get a nice-looking husband. And now..."

"Now what?" Ira's voice escalated.

"Now you want to divide that property and become rich overnight. Then lure another man. Why else you are going to the restaurant like a model? Thought I wouldn't get the information? I very well understand women like you."

Rohan got up and stomped out the door. Tina followed.

Ira slumped on the sofa. Rahul's photo was watching her from the opposite wall. She had never thought of disposing of the property. All she wanted was for Varun to get his share of his father's asset. And Rohan shouldn't try to sell and appropriate the money.

"Rahul, how can you tolerate your younger brother insulting your wife? But I still respect your decision to give the entire rent to him. Love you, Rahul." Tears slid down her cheeks.

CHAPTER 7

T hanks, Reema, for inviting me. Would you believe it? My social life became almost zero after Rahul died.

No, this answer would be nonsense. Reality was Ira had only a few friends in Raghupur. Reema—her school colleague—had invited her over many times before, but she avoided socialising after Rahul's death.

It was Sunday morning around eleven, and Reema's invitation for lunch at her apartment was a blessing after Varun left for Toshali yesterday. The Uber cab left the compound of Ira's apartment building for the fifteen-minute drive to Reema's apartment.

"I had to sell Rahul's car to repay the loan." Would this be a good enough reason as to why she never accepted Reema's invitations for the last several months? There were enough auto-rikshaws in Raghupur, and since last year, Uber and Ola cab services also became quite common in this sleepy country town.

Ira glanced at the new under-construction mall as the cab passed in front of it. Raghupur would be a large city in the next few years. The fact was, coming from India's largest city, Mumbai, she could never adjust to a countryside culture.

Only Rahul's unconditional love had provided her enough energy to call this place her home. Even after Rahul's death, she couldn't think of moving back to Mumbai. That would mean resigning from the state government's secured teachership job, guaranteed pension

54

after retirement. And with the age limit for applying to any government job throughout the country, she could never land another secure position. And what about the millions' worth of Rahul's share in the ancestral properties, which were going through the roof since urbanisation accelerated in Raghupur? She appreciated Mumbai, but Raghupur was her home.

From the moment the car came to a halt until she set her feet inside the lift, a strange sense engulfed her.

Reema was waiting for her, standing in her doorframe, and grabbed her in a hug. "Thank God you came this time!"

Reema was wearing a casual blue coloured blouse, which hung loosely off her shoulders, showing some of her slender shoulders, and the top buttons of her blouse were open. She wore a long, blue skirt, with a thin golden belt around her waist, which looked beautiful. Her long hair fell softly down her back.

"Reema, you look so pretty," she said.

"Me?" Reema let out a giggle. "Look who is talking! You are the beauty queen of the school. Whatever you put on compliments your slim figure. I love your sleeveless top and this slim skirt. They are beautiful. Now, let us move inside before neighbours come out and stare at this pretty woman." She wrapped her arm around Ira's waist and pulled her inside her lounge room.

Ira forced a smile. There were only a few places in Raghupur she could dress fashionably without attracting judgment—even less so now after Rohan's and Tina's visit earlier. Could she discuss her worries with her close friend and lighten her mood?

"Are you here by yourself? Where is your Dhiraj?" she asked as she settled on her sofa.

"My husband? Dhiraj loves our home in Toshali. When I started living in Raghupur after getting the schoolteacher job, he was either coming here on weekends, or I was going back to my home. But now..." Reema flashed a tight-lipped smile. "Let it go. We both will have a pleasant time today, here."

Was Reema also going through some storm? She wasn't the only one encountering one problem after another.

"Everything all right, Reema?" she asked.

Reema let out a loud laugh. "I'm always okay, Ira. We are even going to celebrate our twenty-fifth anniversary. Dhiraj has booked a five-star hotel in Toshali. And I would like to invite you."

Ira could attend the party and spend some time with Varun too. She smiled widely. "Sure, I would love to. Congratulations in advance."

"Thanks. But, Ira, I worry about you. I've seen you in a serious mood so many times in the school. Who else besides me do you have to talk to?"

Reema has noticed me in a serious mood? Can I discuss what I did with Sam? Or even my Varun being a crossdresser? No!

Ira leaned forward and cleared her throat. "You see, Reema, I supported Rahul even when he was reluctant to move to a large city for his career."

"Was he too homesick to leave the hometown?"

"No, he wanted to be near his brothers. They all live in Raghupur. But their true colours came out after Rahul's death."

"But Ira, now is the time for you to move. Start a new life in a city." The pressure cooker whistled on the stove. Reema sprung to the cooktop and simmered the flame. "Oh, my. You came to have lunch with me, and I started my blabbering."

"No, Reema. Please don't worry. I came here early so that we can spend time talking. There is still time for lunch."

Ira was in a hurry to puke out one of her many worries, only the one which wasn't a secret.

"I can't be a selfish mother. The property for which I am fighting with Rahul's brothers is worth millions. How can I ruin my son's future for my benefit?"

Ira deflated and adjusted herself on the sofa. She came to Reema's home to lighten her mood, not to discuss her husband's brothers who became her enemies.

Reema returned to the sofa. "I'm not saying you are a selfish mother. But you should plan for your future. How about a pre-lunch tea? Thank God you agreed to come."

Ira flashed a faint smile but didn't reply. Reema got up and went back to the kitchen, and Ira cast a quick glance around. A small but beautiful drawing room. Reema's taste of decoration was praiseworthy.

A nice frame with Reema's photo on the side table raised questions for her. Her own drawing room always displayed her family photo—Rahul, Varun, and herself.

Reema came out of the kitchen with two cups of steaming tea. The aroma relaxed Ira's nerves a little.

"I'm so glad you came to my place after so long." Reema sat on the adjacent sofa.

"I know, I'm sorry. I've been much too preoccupied with matters Rahul was handling." She took a sip from the cup.

"Really?"

Ira looked up to see that Reema had questions in her eyes.

"You wouldn't understand, Reema. We women see ourselves equal to men. We are earning and providing income for the family. Rahul was always consulting me before making any major household decision, especially monetary matters. And trust me, I was thinking I was equal to males in every respect."

"Rahul was so good, Ira. He could never treat you like a junior partner in the family. Would you like some snacks with the tea?"

"No, this is enough," she responded with a shy smile. "After Rahul's death, I realised so many things he was doing were outside my comfort zone."

"Like?"

"I'm sure you may also be in the same situation without realizing it."

"Don't create suspense, Ira. I am dying to hear." Reema placed her teacup on the side table and leaned forward as if she were going to say something confidential and serious.

A chuckle came out of Ira's mouth. "Do you ever manage your bank account, Reema?"

"I do. I draw cash from the ATM."

Ira blinked. "Other than that?"

Reema wore a grim look and nodded. "Yes, of course. We both had been to the bank to sign our home loan papers. That was long ago when my husband's business hadn't gone through the roof."

"Did you negotiate a loan with the bank, or did your husband do that?"

"He was doing it, but he always kept me informed."

"That's my point, Reema. When a husband is keeping us informed of all those important decisions, we consider ourselves equal. But we're still sitting inside our comfort zones. Now when I am handling everything myself, I am at least aware of how dependant I was on Rahul."

Reema's face split into a smile. "Exactly! That is my point, Ira. We women are not unequal, not because we stay in our comfort zones for such matters, but because we choose to. We love to enjoy our lives in our own feminine way, leaving all such boring jobs to husbands."

Ira didn't find Reema's smile funny. She was lifting the teacup for another sip but set it back on the table. "I had thought I was a working woman and could take on the finance matters myself. But trust me, my friend, those tasks are not only boring, but there are lots of stressors, too."

Reema's face fell. "Sorry, I didn't mean to hurt you. But that was exactly my point. You are young and beautiful..."

"I understand, and I should find another husband who can manage all these tasks Rahul was doing. Never."

"Never to remarry?"

"Yes. No, I didn't mean that. I should never depend upon a man for all the financial matters. I should have asked Rahul to pass on such tasks, and he would be there to guide me. To train me. But it was too late by the time he was counting his last days."

Reema moved close to Ira and wrapped her arm around her shoulder. "I understand your loss. In fact, when I thought about how you were passing through those dreaded days knowing that Rahul wouldn't survive, I had so much trauma that I lost sleep."

Emotion collected in Ira's throat, and tears burned behind her eyes.

"But Ira, I don't want to frighten you, and I'm sure you will learn all those boring things as you continue working through them. You are an intelligent woman..."

Ira beamed. "Like you."

"Yes." Reema laughed. "Even then, you need a man by your side. Your son is eighteen now and is living in the city for studies. You have no knowledge of where he might end up working for a living. He might even go overseas. You need the company of a man. Not only for sexual gratification but also for emotional support."

Guilt washed over Ira instantly. Whenever she thought of the words *sexual pleasure,* her mind leapt to that incident with Varun's flatmate, Samuel. She never considered that a sin. When women and men in western countries indulge in one-night stands, no one raises an eyebrow. But her son found out what his mum was up to! This might be the reason he came home with no previous plan and raised the topic of her remarriage.

"Where are you lost, Ira?" Reema was waving her fingers in front of her eyes.

"Nothing, just like..." Could she admit to Reema that her son almost caught her red-handed when she was cosying with a man only years older than him? Should she take her advice on how to handle that?

"You are right, Reema. I will think it over."

Could she also talk to her closest friend about how her son was wearing dresses, lingerie, and false boobs?

What if she laughed behind her back?

No. Let this be a secret between a mother and son. No, a mother and her *daughter.* Her special one-off *daughter.*

The doorbell rang.

"Home delivery." Reema got up.

"You ordered food from the restaurant? Then what's in the pressure cooker?"

"Yes, dear. You are visiting my home after almost a year, and I'm not sure when you will be here again. I planned to devote as much time with you as possible. I have cooked only dal here." Reema tossed her hand toward the pressure cooker in the kitchen.

Reema arranged the plates on the table, and Ira joined her for lunch. The smell of nan and Lahori chicken was enough to bring out the hunger in her stomach.

Ira would probably never admit her first attempt at her one-night stand (though it was an afternoon) to her friend.

"I have joined a Facebook group called *Second Chance Life,*" Reema announced.

"Oh wow, I'm in that group, too!" Ira's gaze skyrocketed, the spoonful of food stopped between the plate and her mouth. "You are my FB friend, but I didn't notice you. Maybe you never post anything. But it's a closed group, for widows and—"

"Don't be scared, Ira. Yes, closed group, but not locked. It's by invitation from another member. I have a friend in Toshali who added me to the group. You can see me if you visit the '*Member*' tab in the group."

"It's for encouraging members to support one another and also to encourage them to break the society's iron cordon." Ira placed the spoon on the plate and tore a piece from the nan with her fingers. "But sometimes you find depressing stories of women who have dared to try at getting another love into their life."

"I joined the group out of curiosity, but in my heart, I wish to be of help to every such woman who needs another chance in their life. Ira, how different is India from the western nations? There, no one would even care if a woman got another man in her life. Even the children are supportive when the mother goes into a live-in arrangement."

"Live-in?" Ira gasped. "Here even a woman talking about another marriage becomes taboo."

"Only because this is a small town. But I have gone through many articles, and one should follow the steps." Reema put the fork down and glanced at Ira.

She tore another piece of nan and dipped it in the curry. "Steps? Is this an exam?"

"I mean, how to convince the near and dear ones, those who are supportive, and also how to fight the rest."

Ira didn't realise she had finished her lunch. "Food was yummy, Reema." She plastered a smile and went to the bathroom to wash her hands.

Reema was looking at her wall clock when Ira came back. Ira had spent some quality time with her friend today. Even though they met regularly at school, the open-hearted discussion they had today filled many voids in her heart.

"I need to visit my cousin before her husband comes home." Ira hinted toward leaving.

"Don't go so early, mate. We will have afternoon tea together."

"No, Reema. Another time."

"You have a cousin here?"

"Yes, she is here and also is lucky to have a perfect family. I was, in fact, avoiding her. But she is being melodramatic, so I planned to visit her once in a while. You are a real supportive friend, Reema."

"Thanks. This is the type of person you should learn how to ignore, and if not how to teach them a lesson."

"But one thing, I'm so happy. My son, Varun. He is supporting me like a daughter does. Do you know last time he came from the city and spent time with me, it was only to persuade me to remarry?"

Reema stepped over and engulfed Ira in a hug. "Why are you saying this when you are leaving? You have got such a nice boy! He understands the needs of a mother like a daughter. Next time when he is with you on holiday, please tell me. I will either invite you or come to your place. To meet your lovely boy. And yes, my invitation to my twenty-fifth anniversary is for your son too. Please bring him with you."

"Sure, I will. See you again, Reema."

Ira picked her bag up and stepped towards the door. She had already booked the Uber to visit her cousin and would be there within minutes.

Ira had sent Urvi a text that she was arriving by three p.m., and in practically no time, she arrived at Urvi's place. A cloudy sky taunted Ira as she climbed out of the taxi and dragged her feet to Urvi's apartment building. Cold wind gushed and whammed Ira in the gut.

So many thoughts weighed on her mind as she got her feet moving. She didn't know what was holding her back. Urvi was also born and brought up in the multicultural city of Mumbai, like Ira, but had been living in Raghupur for over two and a half decades.

Did she envy Urvi's perfect family? Her massive, ornate flat in a luxurious building, a husband with a high-paying job, a boy and a girl? And to add to that, plenty of time to enjoy her husband's money.

She hated the way Urvi always mocked Varun for his girly features—his long hair and absence of facial hair.

"I can't believe Varun is Rahul's son," Urvi had commented one day a few years ago. "Rahul is so manly and look at this boy, he is more like a girl!"

How wrong she was when she felt only small-town people were traditional and conservative!

"Hello Ira, my dearest sister." Urvi took her into a hug as soon as she opened the door. A strong perfume hammered Ira's senses. Urvi wore a blue sari with a matching blouse. A red border adorned her sari. It was a beautiful sari and Ira noticed how she could flaunt it with grace. She had a lot of jewellery on. Necklaces, bracelets, earrings, and rings. She was looking elegant and gorgeous in a way. Her nails looked so perfect, and they matched her sari.

"Nice to see you after so long." Ira forced a smile and tried to remain inside her facade. Just a day after Rahul's death anniversary, Urvi started calling her and insisted both should meet. Ira avoided inviting Urvi to her home. She couldn't tolerate this woman enough to spend half a day with her. Rather, it was convenient to visit her home on her way back and spend an hour with her. The best way to avoid this annoying woman.

"You finally got time to meet with me, Ira?"

Was this a question, or a complaint?

The instant she sat on the sofa, Urvi said, "Did you notice our new sofa? Imported from Malaysia. You see, Ira, no one in our building has this costly lounge."

Urvi never missed a single chance to show off her wealth. Not only wealth—anything else she could boast about.

"This is beautiful." She pretended to check it out carefully and appreciatively. "Must be a rare timber."

Urvi leaned back on the sofa with one foot over the other. "You're right, this timber is not available in India. The Malaysian supplier was even reluctant to send this to us."

"Why?"

"Because they always export to the USA and Europe. I called and told him, if he sends this to me, other wealthy people in India might also become his customer, and his market would grow. But I won't give his information to anyone here. People should see we got an exclusive couch."

Ira would throw up if Urvi didn't stop. Could she change the subject?

"Are you so busy that you never get time to come to my home?" Ira threw a half smile at her cousin.

Urvi's face fell, as if a bullet hit her. She had only contacted Ira over the phone after Rahul's death.

"It was my mother-in-law, Ira. She always said never to visit a widow during the first year of her widowhood. Inauspicious. I understand this is a superstition. But what could I do? You see Ira, in our culture, we respect the elders. And I am not a working woman like you. I don't earn money on my own. I must pray to God for a long life for my husband."

A laugh was about to erupt from Ira's mouth, but she stopped it. At last, this woman—her cousin—admitted she was weak and inferior as she didn't earn money, even if in a different wording. She didn't wish to respond.

"But don't worry, Ira. Didn't I invite you for tea with me at my home? Now that one year is over, I can visit you."

"Thanks, Urvi, you are so kind to me." She slipped into her facade again and let out a smile.

"I always worry about your well-being and your reputation, Ira. I realise your in-laws are against you regarding the share of the ancestral properties. And they would find any small opportunity to belittle you and harass you. You must be careful what you say and what you wear. Here in the countryside, many people know one another, and walking on the streets would be difficult for honourable people like us."

Ira looked away to hide the disgust coming out of her eyes. How far would this woman go to find confidential matters of others? She decided not to discuss her in-laws with her. Ira didn't like Urvi's comment on her clothing, either. Was Urvi also the type of woman who believed widows should never wear fashionable clothes?

"This town was small when I shifted here after my marriage with Rahul. But with so many developments, it has grown. Many high-rises are being built. I don't even know many people in my building. Who cares what I'm doing or wearing?"

Urvi displayed a half-smile. "Try to understand, Ira. We must respect our society and their sentiments."

Ira struggled to change the topic again.

"How about your son, Urvi? He is now almost twenty-three and is earning money. Any girlfriend?"

Urvi sat straight with shoulders back. "Oh, he got a nice multinational job in Delhi and is living there. But I know my son, he is so shy, he could never find a partner on his own. But he is still in his teens, almost. Let him enjoy his freedom. He has got enough time to find a girl and marry. Maybe I will find someone for him."

"And your daughter?"

"Oh, you don't know? Didn't I share on Facebook? She is now studying management in Mumbai. As of now, only my husband and I are in this large, luxury apartment."

Ira remembered she blocked Urvi's posts on her Facebook.

"I am not really active on social media. And after Rahul passed away, my work has increased so much. How do I explain to you? God forbid, you shouldn't see such days."

"No, I won't. Don't I visit temples regularly and pray for my husband's long life with valuable offerings? Last month I even donated a gold crown to the temple deity."

Ira resisted another laugh. Since when has bribing God brought life and prosperity? Anyway, women like Urvi dwell with a different level of reasoning. She must finish the talk soon and leave this place.

After a while, Ira's glance fell on the wall clock. They had chatted for nearly an hour.

"You invited me for tea, and we have been talking for a while now. Where is the tea?"

"Oh, yes. Sorry my sister, I forgot."

Urvi took her mobile and made a home-delivery order from a restaurant.

"Please don't order any food, Urvi. I am full, just came from having a heavy lunch with a friend."

"So what? You came to my home after so long, and I'm going to serve you only tea? Are you still as figure conscious as you were before?"

"Health conscious. If that comes with a better figure, then that is just a side effect." Ira chuckled at her own comment, but it didn't go over well with the chubby Urvi.

When the restaurant delivery arrived, Urvi brought plates from her buffet and served tea with samosas and kachori. Ira lifted the teacup and took a sip. The smell from the hot and oily samosa choked her throat.

"By the way, I've seen your posts on Facebook. And it is important that I talk to you." A close-lipped smile appeared on Urvi's face. She sat on the sofa again and ate a samosa.

Ira immediately put the teacup back on the table. What did Urvi find?

"I saw your posts in *Second Chance Life* group." Urvi twisted her lips, the half-eaten samosa still in her mouth.

Ira swallowed. "But that is a closed group! Only for single women." She regretted never checking to see which friends were in that group.

"I am not a child, Ira." Urvi grabbed another samosa and put it in her mouth. "I admit I am not a working woman and not earning money, but don't forget I too am a graduate, like you. This is not a closed group, rather an invitation only by any member. Anyone who is a member of the group can invite another. Who knows if I am a single woman?"

Urvi was right.

"Also, I was curious to know if you were a part of it. And you are." Urvi takes a prim sip of tea.

Ira sat up straight. In fact, after Varun talked to her about remarriage, she had posted, 'What do you ladies think of widows remarrying?' Did Urvi notice this?

"Yes, there are many women who suffer a lot after nasty divorces. Also, widows without their own income need mental support from other women in the group. I love to support as many women as possible."

"That is a commendable job. But what about your post asking members for advice about widows remarrying?"

Ira felt like throwing the hot teacup on Urvi's face and leaving. Did she owe an explanation to this woman?

"Don't take it the wrong way, my sister," Urvi said. "I also support widows remarrying, but only those who are young and childless. You are now old enough to simply dream of romance. We are not in a western country. We are proud of our own Indian traditions and cultures. In fact, romance shouldn't even come to mind at this age."

Ira couldn't digest Urvi's last sentence. *At this age?* Did her age stop her from romancing with Samuel?

How could she bring such a secret to a woman who was an expert in spreading gossip?

Silence was the best weapon for Ira, the protection from Urvi's bullying.

"Remember, your son is eighteen and any day now he might introduce his own girlfriend."

So what? Can't I get the love of a man if my son finds romance?

"What are you thinking, Ira? Oh, my, I am so stupid!"

"Stupid?"

"Did I say your Varun will get a girlfriend?"

"Yes. What is wrong with that? He is going to the college. There are girls there. He can develop friendships with anyone he likes. I will support him as his mother."

Urvi burst into a loud laugh, and Ira didn't understand the joke.

"I forgot your son is almost like a girl."

Ira pressed her lips together. "Open your eyes, Urvi. So many men nowadays are sporting long hair and pierced ears. They are still men."

Will Urvi also say Varun has no facial hair?

"Anyway, I hope Varun remains a boy." Urvi's gaze fell on the snack plate. "You have touched none of the samosa, Ira. Or even the tea."

"No, I have acidity and don't think I can touch any of these."

The tea was almost cold. Didn't Urvi give her enough food for thought which she could never digest?

"I must leave, Urvi. I have so many exam papers to evaluate, I need to work late tonight. But I'm happy for your perfect family. Your son and daughter both are doing so well, and a husband to look after you. Please go to the temple more frequently, and if possible, pray for this cousin of yours."

She snatched her handbag and trudged toward the door, burying her eyes in the Uber app of her phone.

Urvi slammed the door behind her.

Instead of getting off in front of her apartment building, Ira asked the cab driver to drop her off at the market instead. The small market had only a few shops, including one boutique fashion store.

"Can you please show me that frock in another size?" Ira asked the man, whom she thought might be the owner. Ira was the only customer in the store, as people would normally do their shopping in the evening. "You had a girl here, didn't she come in today?" Ira had bought the skirt and top from this store only a month ago from the girl.

"Ma'am, she left. I am the only one now. Looking for another girl. What can I do? She was managing the lingerie section while I was tending to general customers. But don't worry, ma'am, I am the dress designer. I have seen you here before. I have many repeat customers." The man flashed a salesperson smile at her and brought a dress from the pile.

"For you, ma'am?"

"No, my daughter, an inch taller than me."

"And slim like you?"

"Yes, almost." She wondered how much the man knew about her. Did he know Ira had only a son?

"This should be the right size, ma'am. You made a fine choice. This skirt and top you are wearing fit perfectly on you. Who would believe you have a daughter who is taller than you? How old is she? Eighteen?"

"Yes. Exactly."

"Ma'am, you can check this in the trial room. If this fits you, it will also fit your daughter."

After checking the dress, she came out of the cabin.

"Can you show me some lingerie, please? Size xxx."

The man stopped. His gaze focused on Ira's chest, but only for a few moments.

"Ma'am, please don't mind, but that size bra may not fit you."

Could this man just look at a woman's top and know her size? Ira didn't feel flattered by the unwanted attention. She should have gone to a supermarket instead. Nobody would have asked about the size or who would be wearing it. But she loved the dress she found there. Her *Varuna* would love it, too.

How could she say this was for her son, who sometimes dressed up like a girl?

"Ma'am, do I get a bra in your size?"

"No, I need that for my son, s... sorry, for my daughter."

CHAPTER 8

I ra got into the bus at Raghupur intercity bus station and occupied the right-hand window seat of the fourth row. The brilliant Friday morning marked a one-week annual leave, which Ira had gotten sanctioned by the school authorities. She looked at her watch—eight in the morning. Passengers were still entering the bus and looking for their allotted seats.

"Four-B!" A middle-aged woman holding a ticket stood near her seat. "I think this one!"

"Yes, ma'am." Ira flashed a grin at the woman and sat straight, making space for her.

The woman placed her bag in the overhead luggage compartment and seated herself next to Ira. She inhaled a sharp breath and drank some water from her bottle. "Thank God," she said with a smiling face. "I thought I would miss the bus. Traffic jam. But it looks like the bus won't leave on time. Passengers are still arriving."

"Non-stop bus. Raghupur to Toshali should be roughly two hours. Only if there's no busy traffic."

"You live in Toshali?"

"No, going to spend a week with my son. He is in the uni, living in a shared apartment."

"Oh, I see." The woman took out a magazine from her handbag to read.

Shared apartment. The two words hammered Ira's heart. Why can't there be a rewind button in life? Or an eraser! Sam's masculine scent pinched her nerves. That tainted afternoon with Sam? Erase it. At least Ira wanted to. And her promise never to visit Varun in Sam's flat? Sam's courteous phone call melted it.

"You are a wonderful mother, Ira. Varuna is so lucky. I'm sad that my mother is not as affectionate as you," Sam had said when he called on her mobile.

Varuna? Sam addressed Varun as Varuna?

One more person on this earth knew her son was a crossdresser!

Ira had replied with only a meek 'thanks.' She couldn't even say, 'you are my son's friend, and I am like a mother to you.'

How could she?

"Welcome on board, ladies and gentlemen," the bus driver announced.

Ira sat straight as the bus left the Raghupur bus station and crawled through the heavy morning traffic. She looked at the woman sitting on her side. She was eating a sandwich. Ira remembered she also should have something for breakfast and pulled out a protein bar from her handbag. But she put it back inside the bag. She didn't feel like eating anything.

Ira was getting rather hungry for a man in her life. The hunger which couldn't be fed was more of a problem. She wanted to break the shackle of the so-called tradition of her small conservative town and run to find her love.

She unlocked her phone, touched the Facebook icon, and scrolled through the posts. One post forced her to halt and take a closer look—Urvi's son Amit announcing he was gay, and the comments thereafter: some supportive but mostly insulting. Ira couldn't believe what she just found. She tried to find if Urvi had commented. Nothing. How would she react to a break in her perfect family?

She typed *'congrats'* but soon deleted it, just touched the *like* icon instead.

The bus stopped at the traffic signal, and Ira's thoughts also came to a halt. She glanced through the window at the busy market—the traffic police directing the errant auto-rikshaws with a piercing whistle, a cacophony of a different kind. The air was heavy with a mixture of dust and soot from the exhaust fumes of the passing traffic. But Ira was safe behind the windowpane of the luxury air-conditioned express bus. The bus started again, and within minutes, the driver swung it around and entered the freeway.

"Welcome, Mum." Varuna opened the door as soon as Ira pressed the calling bell. *She* looked stunning in the beautiful dress she had sent for *her*.

All her cells shuddered. She said, "You are my charming daughter, Varuna."

"Hello, Ira," Samuel greeted when she hugged Varuna. "You have a lovely and beautiful daughter."

"Thank you, Sam." Ira flashed a smile. "And how are you?"

"Fine. Varuna was missing the best mother in the world."

A void crept into Ira's heart. She could neither be a mother figure nor a girlfriend to Samuel.

"Your travel must have been tiring, Ira. Please get some rest in Varuna's room. I am making tea for all of us if you don't mind."

Was Samuel trying to be closer to her? She was unaware of the relationship between Varuna and Sam after he found out Varun was crossdressing. Ira had no intention of hurting his feelings. Wasn't she, as the older of the two, more responsible? Sam had not forced her to his bed!

Life was throwing fresh surprises at Ira. First it was Varun in girl's clothing, and next, Urvi's son coming out as gay. Did life watch her reactions?

But she didn't know how life was revealing itself, and if she should fear it.

Even though marriage wasn't a priority for her, deep inside, she was dreaming of a warm bed with someone.

Varuna had just gone to the toilet when Samuel knocked on the bedroom door.

"Ira, would you like to have your tea in the room, or would mother and daughter like to come and sit in the lounge?"

She let out a chuckle at Samuel. "You also love when Varun cross-dresses?"

Sam smiled his approval as she made her way into the lounge.

"Varuna, let's have our tea with Sam," she said when Varuna came out of the bathroom. "And later I will cook dinner for both of you."

Varuna came and sat on the sofa, leaning on her. Her gaze fell on the door of Sam's bedroom. The old wound immediately became raw inside her. She sucked in a deep breath and let out a smile. Sam placed three cups of steaming tea on the coffee table and sat by them on the sofa.

Ira was sure she could have never been comfortable had Varun been there. Because when Varun became Varuna, she found herself on a different level of her comfort zone. Was it because she always wanted a daughter?

"Ira, I am sure you had wanted a girl before Varun's birth," Sam said.

"Yes, unfortunately, that was not possible. But I'm happy I have got a boy and girl in the same individual." She took a sip from her cup.

"But you can still produce another baby."

A shock passed through her.

"I am the mother of an eighteen-year-old, Sam, and also a widow."

"So what? My mother had another baby when I was twenty. From her second husband."

"You have a step sibling?" Varuna twisted towards him and said, "and you have never told me?"

"Why would he tell every personal bit to you, Varun? That's okay. He didn't get the occasion to bring it up." Then she looked at Sam and asked, "A boy or a girl?"

"Girl, but I haven't seen her. Mum never came back here after her marriage. She never even invites me to visit her place. I think it is her husband." A distressing wave crossed Sam's face.

"That's sad. How can a mother forget her first born even after she gets another life partner?"

A pause hung in the room for a while. Ira needed to break the ice.

"You guys talk to each other; I will cook for you." She got up and walked into the kitchen.

"Mum, I will help you. Like a dutiful daughter."

"If you mother and daughter don't mind, can I also help you?"

"Why can't both mum and daughter share the bed tonight, Varuna? After all, this is a queen bed. Wide enough for both of us," Ira asked when they retreated to Varun's bedroom at around ten that night.

Varuna chuckled. "Mum, last time I slept on the couch. I mean, your son slept on the couch. Why are you so partial to your daughter?"

Ira chuckled.

"I like the new dresses you bought for me. And sleep wear, too."

Ira realized that it didn't feel odd when she stripped down to her undergarments before slipping into her night wear in Varuna's presence. *She* was a *girl* anyway. At least she believed so.

"Are you sleepy, Varuna?" she asked as she climbed on the bed and stretched.

"No, mum. This is the time we are spending together," Varuna muttered and sat near her.

"My colleague at the school is having a party here, in the city. She has invited both of us. You remember Reema?"

"Yes. But is she in Raghupur?"

"Yes, her entire family lives here though. She is there because of her job and manages weekly travel to her family."

"Why me, Mum?"

"She told me many times; I must bring you."

"Are you sure?"

Something tingled inside Ira, and she let out a chuckle. "Sorry dear, not you. She said I must bring my son to the party."

"Now you are right," Varuna tittered. "So, ask when your son comes tomorrow."

Ira read a book while lying on her back as Varuna placed an arm on her tummy.

After a while, she closed the book and turned to face her.

"Varuna, you know your aunt Urvi's son Amit, who is living in Delhi?"

"Yes."

"He is a gay. He has posted on his Facebook."

"I saw it, Mum. He is on my Facebook too, and I noticed you liked it."

"I shouldn't have. I should have thought of how his mother would react. But this Urvi, you don't know the type of woman she is."

"Did she do something?"

"Yes. I had made some comments in the *second chance life* Facebook group. That woman has somehow become a member and was following my posts. She asked me if I am looking to marry again and insulted me as if I am of a poor character."

"Didn't you tell her it was I who convinced you?"

"No. She even commented about you because you have long hair and no facial hair. And was proud she has a perfect family."

"That's okay, Mum. If you listen to every so-called well-wisher relative, you can't have a life of your own. I love you and will be with you no matter what."

The new generation rushed much faster than Ira could've imagined. Varun's crossdressing, Amit being gay.

She was not against the gay and lesbian culture, but she had a preference of her own.

"Varuna, I want to talk to you about something, if you don't mind."

"Okay."

Ira swallowed. How long could she pretend Varuna knew nothing? She had been getting nightmares about what she did.

"Varuna, would you ever mind if your mother were in a bedroom with a man? I mean, a man who is not your father?"

"No, Mum. Why else would I say my mother must find another man?"

"I didn't mean that. To find another man, and marry him, those are all in future tense. I mean..." She wasn't sure if she should discuss that.

"Mum, I don't understand. But I will always love you as you are, not what you did or would do in the future."

Ira loved this sort of assurance.

"That day," she inhaled a sharp breath, "you were in college."

Pause.

"Mum. Tell me."

"You were in college and Sam came back early. I was feeling, I mean, I felt a bit..." How could she say she was horny? "It was like a void in life after your dad passed away, and Sam touched me."

Varuna's arm wrapped around her waist and passed a shock wave through her. But she must spill out everything before Varuna becomes a boy again.

"I went inside his bedroom and forgot that he is only a few years older than you. He was also lonely as he had no girlfriend. We both became close."

"It's cool, Mum." Varuna planted a kiss on her cheeks. "And I love you. You were with him. I just slipped away to give you total privacy. Mum, that happens. As long as you are safe—I mean, use..."

"No Varuna. It wasn't what you're thinking. Yes, I went to his room, but we didn't go all the way. I wanted to come clean with you. You must be thinking Mum needed to fulfill her carnal desire, but I am a responsible woman and a mother too. But I am not blaming your flatmate. I am the older person, and I am responsible for everything."

"But I trust you, Mum. My mother is the strongest woman on this earth."

These were words children used to describe their fathers.

A sigh slipped through her lips. A heavy weight lifted from Ira's mind. Her child was the only one she cared for in the entire world.

Ira tried to close her eyes and fall asleep. But Samuel's eyes still flashed in her memory. How could she forget the way his gaze mesmerised her that day?

Sam shot the same gaze at Varuna this evening. Was Samuel bisexual?

Who knew Urvi's manly looking son would declare himself a gay and become a female partner to a man?

What if Samuel convinced Varuna to be his girlfriend?

"Varuna," she whispered.

"Yes, Mum."

"Sorry baby, did I wake you up?"

"No, Mum."

"Can I ask you something?"

Varuna moved closer to her and wrapped her arms around Ira's shoulder. "What?"

Ira struggled to coin the words. But she must ask her now. She inhaled a deep breath.

"Do you have a boyfriend, Varuna?"

"Boyfriend? Mum, what are you asking? I wear dresses only inside the four walls of this apartment. Outside I am the same Varun."

"But for Samuel, you are a young and beautiful woman. Does he..."

"Mum, can I sleep? Please, Mum."

Ira didn't have courage to insist further. She didn't want more surprises, not so soon.

The next evening, Ira and Varun got out of the taxi at the party venue. A five-star hotel.

Varuna became a fine young man, Varun, just before they left. And Ira, a hot young woman.

She wore her new outfit which matched her personality perfectly. It was a soft, black sleeveless one. A deep, dark red blouse matched the skirt. The skirt ended just below the knee. A matching belt tied in a knot. Her hair was styled into a neat, tight bun at the back of her head. She had smoky eyeshadow and pink lipstick. Varun was wearing a shirt with a V neckline, which revealed the outline of his chest. His black trousers hung on his hips. He was wearing dark sunglasses and a smile on his face. He wore his hair brushed back from his forehead.

"Mum, I will address you as Ira, is that all right?"

"Why, Varun?"

"Because no one will believe you are the mother of an adult young man."

"Adult? Young man? Varun, you just turned eighteen. You're still a child!"

"But Mum, look at yourself in the mirror. You appear stunning in this skirt and the top. Did you buy this in Raghupur?"

Ira smoothed down her pencil skirt and flicked a peek at her low-neck string top. "Raghupur? Still in the stone age. I got it online."

"People might think I am your younger brother." Varun said as they entered the hotel lobby. *Bhandari Couple 25th Anniversary Party – Jashn Hall, 13th Floor*—a notice board smiled at them.

Ira let out a giggle and pinched his arm when Varun pressed the button for the lift. "But if I have to introduce you, I will say you are my son."

"But Ira, what if you find a man at the party? I mean, someone suitable for you?"

"You are so naughty!" she said as they stepped inside the lift. "Why do you think single men would look for women like me, and that too at the first party I am attending after your dad..."

"Come on, Ira. Please don't spoil the mood. I was just joking."

The lift stopped at the thirteenth floor. Reema and Dhiraj were welcoming the guests at the entrance of the party hall.

"Happy twenty-fifth anniversary, Reema, Dhiraj." Ira shook hands with both Reema and her husband after handing over the gift. Reema wore a shimmery purple dress. The dress hugged her figure like a second skin. It was cut to accentuate her slender waist and her long, elegant legs. The colour matched her eyes. She had twisted her hair into a braid that reached down her back. She wore high heels, and her makeup was minimal.

"Thanks for coming, Ira. And this is Varun?" Reema gasped.

"Yes."

"Lovely. I had seen him last, when? Almost five years ago? He has grown up. A young man now!"

A proud parent inside Ira watched Varun smile back.

"And Ira, you are dazzling! Raghupur people would go mad if you wore this there. What would I say? You're Varun's sister?"

Ira and Varun both chuckled.

"And Varun, my boy," Reema winked, "will you please address this gorgeous woman with her first name, here? At least until the party finishes."

"Already started. She is just Ira. Not even my sister. A beautiful young woman."

"Yes, you are right. She will be the attraction of the celebration in this stunning outfit."

Ira stole a glance at Dhiraj, Reema's husband. His gaze was digging into her chest, sending a warning signal. She flinched.

"Thanks, Reema. I must spare you to greet your other guests, and please let me know if I can be of any help to you."

"You are already, by adding to the glamour of the party." Reema let out a chuckle. "And you both are at table number seventeen."

Table number seventeen.

One gentleman was already there.

Harry, the name tag placed in front of him read.

Ira and Varun sat at their nametags, opposite Harry's chair.

"Hello Ira, and hello young man." Harry extended his hand to Ira. "I arrived too early, and thank God I'm not the only one at this table."

A silence hung in the air as Ira waited and glanced around. She was curious to see which guests entering the hall could be the other occupants of the ten-seater table. Guests with families headed to other tables around her.

She spotted Reema sitting on a chair near a huge, circular marble fountain. The entire hall was decorated in stone figurines of ancient temples of Konark and Khajuraho. There were no walls, and it was open on all sides. The whole hall seemed to be a room inside a room. The room was decorated with floral paintings and an enormous poster of Reema and Dhiraj. The ceiling was covered in floral arrangements. The dance floor looked like a stage on a sun-chariot, ready to fly to the sky, with twelve wheels representing twelve months and seven horses for seven days of the week—designed after the concept of the thirteenth century Sun temple of Konark.

The fountain was surrounded by an arched gallery filled with huge round tables and chairs. An enormous table held drinks, food, and cake. People were sitting at the table, chatting and drinking.

"Ira, thank you for bringing me here," Varun muttered to her. "You friend is so wealthy. Look at the arrangements."

Ira nodded and looked around again.

She wondered why there were hardly any women in saree. Then she remembered the dress code Reema had mentioned in her invitation card—casual cocktail for ladies and smart casual for men.

Ira poured some water from the bottle into a glass and flicked a quick glance at Harry, wondering why he was not with his family. It was possible his wife worked in another city. Didn't Reema live in Raghupur for her work, and her husband here in this Toshali City?

Harry must be a man of around forty or forty-five. And his wife? Ira's thoughts moved around the only man at her table, as she didn't know anyone else at the party. One couple finally approached the table, and a wave of comfort passed through Ira.

"Oh, this is table seventeen?" the husband exclaimed. "Ours is twenty-seven. Sorry."

Ira controlled a sigh and released a faint smile. She took a sip from her glass.

"The couple who would have been here with us didn't come. Some urgent work came," Harry said, breaking the ice between them.

"Oh, I see. So, we are just three at this table?" Ira said. She set the glass on the table.

"Yes, unless Reema moves someone else here. But unlikely, as they have already decided tables for each guest."

"And your family?" Varun asked while pouring some cold drink in a glass.

"My daughter, she is studying in Delhi."

"And wife?"

Harry's face fell. "Unfortunately," he sucked in a long breath, "she passed away two years ago."

Oh, no. Poor man, Ira thought. "Sorry to hear about your wife, Harry." Ira nudged Varun with her elbow. He was asking too many questions.

"How about some wine, Ira?" Harry opened the wine bottle that had been sitting idle and grabbed a wineglass.

"Thanks, Harry."

Harry poured a glass for Ira.

"And you, young man? Are you eighteen?"

"Yes, but I wouldn't drink."

"That's all right. Anyway, you appear like a sixteen-year-old." His voice reflected a genuine appreciation. "I had a son who would have been eighteen last month," Harry said after taking a sip.

"You had?" Ira's glass suddenly slipped away from her lips.

"Sorry to discuss only the sad news here," Harry chuckled, "that was a long time ago. He was just two then."

"That's okay, Harry. My dad also passed away last year. Ira is a single woman now. But let's be happy and enjoy the party."

"Ira?" Harry exclaimed.

"I decided not to call her Mum today, especially at a party. People are mistaking her as my sister."

A smile seemed to cause her face to glow from the inside, but Ira pinched Varun's thigh. "You are talking too much."

"He is right, Ira. You don't look like you are a mother, even. You look like a girl just out of the college. Sorry, I am not trying to flatter you. An honest compliment."

Ira felt her face blushing. However, the cacophony from the party laid a protective layer over their conversation. But she couldn't sit idle for the entire party.

"But I am not a single woman—" she added a mild complaint to her voice— "widow would be the right term."

"Maybe." Harry's gaze met hers. "But using that term sometimes brings out sorrow from the past. I never say I am a widower unless someone asks about my wife. Life has to move on."

"Ladies and gentlemen!" A hustle-bustle spread across the hall at the announcement as the guests moved their chairs to look at the stage. "Welcome everyone to the twenty-fifth anniversary of Mr. Dhiraj Bhandari and his better half, Mrs. Reema Bhandari."

"The hall is almost full except for ours and another table," Varun whispered to her.

A server came and placed two types of appetizers on the table.

"As many of you might know," the female moderator continued, "Mr. Bhandari had come to this Toshali City thirty years ago with only a few thousand rupees and struggled hard to set up a business..."

"Can I serve some food on your plate, please?" Ira's gaze swung over; Harry was about to place a chicken tikka masala on her plate.

"Thanks." Ira glanced around. People were busy enjoying the starters while paying little attention to the MC and her speech. She looked at the MC on the stage while eating the starter.

"As you all would appreciate, our Toshali City is lucky to have a successful businessman like Mr. Dhiraj Bhandari."

"I didn't hear a single line of appreciation for Mrs. Reema Bhandari." The unwanted comment slipped from Ira's mouth.

"That's awful," Harry said. "Obviously the MC appreciates the amount of money Mr. Bhandari has paid her. I know little about him."

"Oh, I thought you're also a businessman and know Mr. Bhandari well."

"No, I am Reema's guest."

A male voice on the speaker system drew Ira's attention again. Mr. Bhandari delivered a speech praising his own business accomplishments while Reema was standing by his side, appearing like she forced the smile on her face.

"Boring," Varun muttered.

Harry chuckled. "Don't worry, focus on the appetizers."

Neither the appetizer nor the main course could appease Ira's taste buds. Something in the air told Ira that time was moving too fast, and she wanted to hold on to it.

Varun had gone to bring a sweet dish when Harry's gaze moved to hers, and the air in her lungs froze. She tried to say something, but her lips twitched.

"Ira, would you mind if I ask for your mobile number?"

Surprise hunted Ira. She bent down to pick up her handbag sitting on the side of her chair and slowly unzipped it, thinking again and again. Harry's request seemed harmless. How could she say no to such a gentleman? "Sure. 98..."

"Thanks, Ira. I appreciate it." Harry punched the numbers in his address book.

Varun came back with three sweet dish plates. "The queue is too long as there's just one counter," he said and placed the plates before Ira and Harry.

"You guys free tomorrow evening?" Harry asked.

Ira held Harry's gaze for another moment. Suddenly Varun said, "Of course. Tomorrow is Sunday and Ira is on holiday, anyway. We are in."

Ira swallowed. "Varun, you have exams coming." *Was it all right to accept the invitation of a man just after the first introduction?*

"It's okay, Ira. You can go alone; you have no exams," Varun said.

Guest had started leaving. Varun looked at his mobile and said, "The Uber will arrive in a few minutes, we better hurry."

Harry also got up to leave. "Okay, let's meet tomorrow evening then. I will text you the address." He shook hands with Ira.

A tingle passed through her skin. The way he said that, 'text me the address' and 'tomorrow evening,' was so casual. It was like they were friends.

Ira dragged her feet to the curb side when the cab arrived. Why did the party last only four hours?

"I don't know why I didn't say no to his invitation for tomorrow. I only have this party dress here. I had brought it for Reema's anniversary celebration," she said after sitting inside the cab.

"That's all right, Ira," Varun said. "Tomorrow we will go to the supermarket and buy another party dress for you. Sexier than this one."

"Shut up, Varun." Ira added a fake anger to her voice. "The party has finished. Now you should call me Mum."

"But I am still in a party mood."

"So, what? Didn't Harry know I am your mother even though you addressed me with my name?"

"But he almost fell for you. I saw the way he was stealing glances at you."

"Varun!" More fake anger.

"Tomorrow, first thing in the morning, we both will go shopping for a dress for you. And in the evening, I will spend time with Sam while you meet with Harry."

Ira's mind jumped straight to Samuel and his suggestive glances towards Varuna. Why else would Varun have ignored her question about a boyfriend last night?

Ira was modern enough to accept Varun's crossdressing but still too traditional regarding same-sex relationships.

"And why would you stay with Sam? What would you do with him?"

"Nothing, Mum. I meant you are going alone with Harry, and I will be in the apartment. What will I do then? I will study and...and occasional chitchat with the flatmate."

Ira spun to the side and glared at Varun. "Why would I visit with Harry alone? Why not you, too? I just pretended you have exams."

"Mum, I am a grown-up man. And you are going on a date. A date means only two individuals, a man and a woman."

"Date? Harry invited *us* for dinner. That's all."

"Mum, try to understand. Didn't we both agree you should re-marry? How? Would aspiring men find you online and come to you asking for your hand? This is an opportunity to find a man. He is good looking and a wealthy businessman. Make him your boyfriend and then marry."

"Make boyfriend and marry." Ira imitated Varun's voice mockingly.

Varun laughed but didn't reply. A silence hung inside the cab for a while. Something was wrong. Her gut had been sending tense signals ever since she sat inside the cab. Something churned her stomach. Was it too good to be true that she would find someone so quickly?

Ira's phone buzzed. She pulled it out of her bag and looked at it. Her heartbeat stuttered. Rohan's name glared at her from the screen.

This was the man who overnight became Ira's enemy after Rahul died. She didn't wish to answer the call, so the mobile continued to buzz on her lap.

S A SPENCER

Why was this man after her like a ghost? What did he want?

The ring stopped.

"You didn't answer."

"It was a call from your uncle Rohan."

"But you should have taken it. So what if he is against us? After all, he is a family member."

The mobile screamed again. Ira tapped to answer the call with a shaking finger.

"You have now shown your actual face, you loose-character!" Rohan shouted from the other end.

"What happened Rohan? What did I do?"

"Don't act innocent. You don't know what you did? On the one hand, you're saying you are the daughter-in-law in our family and have a share in the property. And at the same time, you are going to a five-star hotel and dining with your lover? Don't think you can hide from me."

Ira pulled the phone from her ear and harped at the red button to disconnect.

Was Rohan at the party?

Her vision blurred and spiralled.

"Mum, we have arrived."

Ira's energy started to fade. She yanked her feet from the cab and followed Varun into the apartment.

CHAPTER 9

Ira checked her mobile—six in the morning, time to get up. But her headache was agonising. Rohan's humiliating phone call yesterday evening still pounded inside her head. She rolled over to see that Varuna had already left the bed.

"Is it my fault I became a widow? Don't I have the right to see better days after Rahul's death?" Tears rolled down her cheeks. Thank God Varun was not there.

Last night was the longest and most painful one for Ira. A widow had no right to live a blissful life. Why did she tell herself she was strong and positive?

She wiped her tears and kept staring at the ceiling fan until Varuna came back from the bathroom.

"Mum, your body is hot," Varuna said when she returned. "You've got a fever."

"I have? I am feeling sick, but didn't realise my body is hot. I'm sure you don't have a thermometer with you."

"You must rest, Mum. At around eleven, we will go to the mall. I will also buy a thermometer."

"Mall? Why?"

"Did you forget? You are going to meet Harry."

"Don't daydream, Varuna. How can I go when I am not feeling well? I already sent him a text that I am not coming."

"When? Why?" Varuna sat on the bed at her side.

"You were in the bathroom. And he texted back."

"Is he all right? Okay with that?"

"Yes, Varuna. Why he shouldn't be?"

Varuna placed her arm on Ira's waist.

"I really wanted you to meet Harry tonight, Mum."

"Don't be too serious about this, Varuna. Yes, we met this man. He seems to be a nice gentleman, and we should honour his invitation. But we can meet him another time. So what?"

"Mum, since Uncle Rohan called last night, you've sounded miserable. I'm sure he made some remark or something, and you are hurt. We don't care about that property, Mum. We have an apartment, and you are a career woman. Uncle has almost no income after he lost his job years ago. That's why he is clinging to those ancestral properties. We must wash our hands of that."

"It's not about the ancestral land." Ira sat up in the bed.

"What then?"

Ira paused. Her throat was tight. "Last night, someone had seen me walking alongside Harry when the party ended. It might have been when we came out of the hotel, and you had been to the shop to buy chocolate. We both were chatting, standing together. Someone had seen me and has told him. He is calling me a woman of loose character."

"Did he? How dare he? Let me ask him." She jumped up and snatched her mobile phone from the side table.

"No, Varuna." Ira's voice went up. "Sit down, here."

Varuna didn't sit. For a moment, Ira saw a boy's glare in girl's clothing.

"Mum."

"He is your uncle. And remember, I will deal with him. Not you. You got me?"

Varuna came and sat by her side. "Okay, Mum. Can I request something?"

"Yes, my baby."

"You have school holidays. Can you stay a few more days with me? I know it would bore you when I go to the college, and you are here alone in the flat. But I'm sure in the evening when I'm back, we will have a great time."

The suggestion sounded attractive to Ira. She must stay close to her child as long as possible. A smile slipped out of her mouth.

"I would have been alone at home there also during the holidays. I will stay here until my it is over."

"Thanks, Mum. And I won't go to college today."

"Why?"

"Because you are sick."

"This is nothing, Varuna. I will take a few paracetamol tablets and be all right. You shouldn't miss your classes. Please change your clothes. Time to become Varun and go to the college. I am going to make breakfast for you."

Varuna hugged her. "You are the best mum."

She let out a hearty smile. Yes, she would be all right now.

Ira's heart bounced inside her ribs when Samuel came home early from his office. Did he work it out this time so that he could get another chance with her?

She glanced at the clock. Three p.m. Varun would take at least two more hours to come home.

"Hello, Ira."

"Office finished early?" Ira's smile broke through her anxiety.

"I had a meeting in this part of the city and finished earlier than planned. Boss allowed me to go home."

Was this a prearranged answer? That day he gave a similar explanation.

What next? Start praising her about how young she looks?

"Ira, would you like to have a cappuccino? There is a coffee shop across the road, and I feel like having one. If you don't mind..."

The sickness Ira was feeling that morning was still not over.

"Thanks Sam, I would love to have one. And here is the money." She opened her purse.

"No, Ira. Please. Can't I buy coffee for you?"

"Sure, you can. But I am the mother of your flatmate and the older person here. So..."

Sam flashed an understanding smile and took the money.

This was her first step in controlling a man who tried to enter inside her modesty. She wished to get another life partner, not a lover boy.

Ira remembered she was still wearing her sleep wear as she was resting on the bed after lunch. She walked into the bedroom and put on decent clothing.

Sam would take at least fifteen to twenty minutes to come back. Ira went to the balcony to get some fresh air—the place where she loved holding a book and immersing herself in an imaginary world of stories when she was alone in Varun's apartment.

A clapping sound broke her attention. Her gaze fell on the road. A group of sari-clad eunuchs had surrounded a man and was harassing him for money.

"Hey my hero, hey handsome. You pay us money and God will bless you."

"No, another day, please," the man said. "I have no money with me."

"We know, we know that. But we will give you a chance. How much can you give us?"

The man looked at the eunuchs with disdain. "Don't know."

He was obviously in a hurry to get away, but the eunuchs were adamant. "Hey handsome." One of them forcibly hugged the man and planted a kiss on his cheek. "You want more lipstick marks on your face? Pay us or else."

Her heart bled when she thought of the word *eunuch*—castrated men dressed as women. She had heard several stories about them. Families disowned young boys who loved to dress as girls. And they had no place to live other than the street. Easy recruits for the eunuchs to expand their tribe.

She got up to come inside the drawing room. This was not Varun's future. No, never. This was a fetish; he might overcome it when he grew older. She had read blogs on the Internet.

"Ira, I'm back with coffee."

"Thanks, Sam." She sat down on the sofa. Sam sat on the adjacent lounge.

Ira took the coffee cup to her lips, and a burnt odour filled the air. She stopped, the coffee still at her lips.

Sam startled. "What happened?" he asked.

"Nothing." She forced a smile and took another sip. The bitter taste of the coffee filled her mouth. She closed her eyes, and the heat of the liquid burned the back of her throat. "It's fine. Really." Her eyes darted away from him.

"This isn't like the coffee I always get from this shop," he said, his voice softening.

She took another sip. "I'm fine, Sam." She wanted to begin chatting with him, but didn't know what about. She decided to bring up the topic of his mother. "Do you ever visit your mother, Sam?"

Sam's face fell. "Never. I have no contact with her. Not even on the phone."

"Are you upset because she married again?"

"No, Ira. Nothing like that. My dad married a younger woman after divorcing Mum. Why couldn't she? But her marriage was an enormous loss for me. I lost her after that. She was sending money as long as I was a student. But whenever I thought of visiting her during school or college holidays, she would avoid me."

"Avoid you?" Ira noticed a cloud engulfing Sam's mood.

"Yes, and her husband doesn't like me to be there. Maybe his family is there, and they think my mother had no children from her earlier marriage, so his lies would come out if I visited. She pretended to be busy with her new baby."

Ira must keep this in mind for her son, Varun. She would never let him get the life Sam was experiencing now. "I'm sorry about what happened to you."

"Yes, I am so lonely. There's nobody for me."

"So whom do you visit when you go to your native town?"

"My grandmother. Father's mother. She is living with my uncle. But Dad has no contact with them."

How could parents be so insensitive after marrying a second time?

"But Ira, I am glad Varun is my flatmate. And I appreciate that you are supportive of her crossdressing. I look forward to the times when Varun becomes Varuna after coming back from the college."

A fire loomed in Sam's eyes, and a dark memory smoked into Ira's mind.

That one moment of lust. His desire to make her his girlfriend. Was it worth it, anyway? Did she really need that affirmation?

"How much do you like Varun? I mean, as a friend?"

"Oh, *she* is a nice *girl*. So caring and thoughtful."

"*She*?"

"I mean, I love when Varun changes into female clothing. I would love if *she* came with me to the market, but *she* never wears those dresses outside our home."

"Yes, that was our agreement when I discovered he loved crossdressing. After all, he is a boy. I support him if he wants to wear a dress sometimes. I have read many online articles. Some men love occasional female moments. There is nothing wrong with that."

"You are such a thoughtful mother, Ira. Varuna is so lucky."

"Please refer to him as Varun. I call her Varuna only when he becomes *she,* wearing a dress."

For the first time, Ira regretted seeing a girl in her son. She had loved to imagine she had a daughter. But Sam could be a ticking time bomb between Varun and her. She had seen enough clues.

Ira never understood how Urvi's macho looking son found men attractive. Even though she hated the way Urvi treated her, she never wished her cousin's perfect family to have a crack in it.

But Ira had lost that ideal family after Rahul's death!

"Sam, can I ask you something if you don't mind? I mean, something personal?"

Sam gazed into her eyes. Something was going through his brain.

A tension hung in the air. The sight of the eunuchs stabbed Ira's conscious.

His eyes were full of many questions, but only one came out. "What?"

"Do you and Varun, I mean, do you get close to Varun?"

His eyes dazzled with a smile. "Yes, we are good friends."

"No, do you guys sleep together?"

Sam turned his face away. Ira noticed he was hiding a grin.

I ra sat on the balcony and watched the busy afternoon traffic. The slow breeze—warm and soft—stirred her hair, and she enjoyed the peacefulness of the moment. A flock of birds—blue wagtails—flew around the fountain that marked the entrance to the building. The sun was shining, and the sky was a deep blue. Peace—it was a rare occurrence in her life, but today it was something she felt.

Sam had left for the market after they drank coffee together. She glanced at her wristwatch. It was already past five, and Varun should be home anytime. And Sam should also be back from the market soon.

She got up and ambled into the bedroom.

Varuna was there and flashed a beaming smile, wearing the red dress she had bought for her from Raghupur.

"Mum, how do I look?" she asked while applying lipstick.

"When did you come?"

"I thought you were resting, so I opened the door with the least amount of noise as possible. How are you now?"

"Much better."

"And the headache?"

How would Ira say another headache had replaced the one she suffered this morning? She wanted a quiet evening with her son. At least a place where Sam wouldn't be with them. Her desire to keep Varun away from Sam was so strong, she was considering something she'd never considered before.

"Varun, can we go to the market? I need to do some shopping, and we can have dinner outside."

"Mum, I am in a dress now, and you should address me as Varuna."

"Sorry, my baby, I forgot. Yes, Varuna. And this dress is so lovely on you."

"Thanks. But you should have told me a while ago. I have already changed into female clothing, applied lipstick, and now I have to become a boy again."

She was right. But Ira wished to slip away before Sam was back.

"This is a big city, Varuna. And you look so pretty. Nobody will think there is a boy inside. Let's go as mother and daughter. I am bored to death sitting all day at home and have been looking forward to you coming home."

I love you, Mum." Varuna stepped forward and took her in a tight hug.

She knew Varuna would love her suggestion.

Relief streamed through Ira when she stood in front of the lift with Varuna, as if a mother had snatched away a little girl from the clutches of a violent rapist. Or a deer from a lion's cave. But for how long? The deer and the lion coexisted in the same den, anyway. Release from one tension soon gave way to another. Varuna was standing at her side after pressing the lift button. Her son in a girl's costume was about to make their first venture outside the home.

"Toshali is a large city, and hardly anyone knows us," she said.

"Are you afraid because I'm wearing a dress?"

Ira let out a nervous chuckle. "Remember what we had agreed. Not to wear a dress in public. This is the first and last time."

Varuna nodded in affirmation.

As soon as they entered the lift, a woman inside smiled at Varuna. Varuna responded to the woman's smile. Ira cast her a sideways glance.

"She knows you?" Ira asked as soon as they came out of the lift and walked onto the street for the cab.

"Yes, she lives on a higher floor."

Ira's heart sprinted. "Did she recognise you in the dress? I mean, she knows you as a boy, not a girl."

"I'm not sure. I don't understand why she smiled at me. It's possible she recognised the eyes. Anyway, she doesn't really know me, I'm just a known face to her in the same building. We have never spoken to each other, so why does it matter?"

Varun's voice was soft. Nobody would know if it was a girl's or boy's tone.

A sigh spilled from Ira as they sat in the cab.

Ira intentionally walked behind Varuna as they arrived at the mall and entered.

"Varuna," she muttered, approaching close to her.

"Mm, hmm?"

"Your gait is so womanly. Do you walk like this when you dress as a boy? And when did you learn this?"

"Mum, so many questions at a time! Yes, I was practising even when I was in school, in front of the mirror at home. When neither you nor dad were at home."

"I am confused. Do you still walk like a boy at other times?"

"No, Mum. I walk like a young man. I am now eighteen plus. Don't you look at me when I walk?"

"I didn't notice, my child. But you are so beautiful, men are ogling you."

"No, Ira. They are ogling you. You are a single, young woman. An eligible bride."

"Varuna, I will slap you when we get home. I'm your mother. Not a bride to anyone." She blended an anger into her voice.

They were passing by a lingerie shop. Varuna was staring at the dummies wearing sexy, lacy underclothing. Ira pinched her arm. A chuckle escaped from her mouth.

"Now, a boy is staring at what? Women's undergarments!"

Varuna also giggled. "No, Ira. Not a boy. A young woman is thinking of buying a pair of lingerie for her friend, who is also her mother."

Ira's mind flew back to her younger days. Her mother was always taking her lingerie shopping, but never when her brother accompanied them.

"Come, I will also buy a pair for you."

After buying two sets and paying at the counter, Varuna said, "Sam has texted that there's an excellent restaurant here, and we should visit it if we are in this area."

"Sam? How did he know we were here?"

"He asked me where we are, and I told him. When you were inside the dressing room."

She was overthinking. But she didn't want another surprise.

"What else do you talk about with Sam, Varuna?"

"Not a lot. But what's wrong with a man giving some information? I told him we made a new friend called Harry at the party last evening, and Sam also knows him."

A flash of disquiet passed through Ira as she stepped into the passage. Had Varuna become so close to Sam, that she was sharing each minute detail with him?

"Did you tell him Harry had invited us for dinner?"

"Not us, you. Only you."

"No, Varuna. I am not going on a date with any man just after meeting him. That too a brief one at a party! I am not a modern, western woman. Still a woman from a small town. With a teenage boy and orthodox in-laws."

"Chill, Ira. Please. Sam doesn't care. Look, his mother has also remarried and has another child from her second husband. And Sam was twenty when that child was born. You're thinking only on the negative side. Didn't you accept that I love to be in female clothing? How many Indian mothers can accept that?"

Ira inhaled deeply. Yes, she was thinking too much, even more so after getting the abusive call yesterday from her brother-in-law.

"Can we get a restaurant with a bar, Varuna? I don't want to finish my dinner and go back to your apartment so early. Rather, I would love to pass some time sipping..."

"Fantastic idea, Ira." Varuna scanned her smart phone to select a bar cum restaurant around the area.

Ira had never been to a pub in Raghupur, where pubs were only for men. Drinking had always been in the privacy of her home.

"Found one, Butterfly Pub. Good rating."

"How far is that from here?"

"Inside this mall, another floor."

As soon as they arrived at the pub and both were settled at a table, Varuna brought a wine and a soft drink from the counter. Mum and daughter both cheered.

"I love this place," Ira said as she took a sip from her wine glass. "Nice one. Love it." A satisfaction brewed inside her that they didn't go to the restaurant Sam had suggested. But could she stop Varuna from sleeping with that man again?

"Sam had a pleasant choice of restaurants," Varuna commented.

"You don't like that I wanted to come to this restaurant instead?"

"No, Ira. This is the same place he had said. And this one has the best reviews."

The wine in her mouth stopped at her throat. She swallowed and inhaled a deep breath.

"Are you all right, Mum?" Varuna asked. "You seem upset."

"Yes, I am."

"Why? Because Sam suggested it? Okay. We can go to another place after finishing this one drink. There are plenty of restaurants nearby with bars."

Ira was about to say something, but her gaze fell on a man entering the pub.

Harry! Why was he here? Was it a trap for her?

She noticed a waiter directing him to a single table, and he sat there alone.

Guilt washed through Ira. This morning only, she had texted him her inability join him for dinner as she was not well. How could she convince him she really was sick and felt better only this afternoon?

She had never dreamed of an awkward situation like this. Should she stop drinking and ask Varuna to leave the place? Harry had seen Varun last evening. Wouldn't it be humiliating when he'd find the same boy here wearing a dress?

Her brain stopped working. The wine struggled to pass through her throat. Harry was sitting only one row away, and anything she said to Varuna could fall on his ears.

Varuna got up to go to the counter and pay the bill.

Ira held the glass to her lips so that she could take a big gulp.

"Hello, Ira."

She raised her head. Harry was standing near the table with a smile on his face.

Ira's heart dropped to her stomach as she plastered a smile on her face. "Evening, Harry. What a surprise!"

She couldn't think what to say about her sickness. And how would she introduce Varun again in a dress? She closed her eyes, and an inscrutable pain messed up her brain.

"You still look unwell, Ira. Why did you come out?"

Ira raised her head and looked at him. There was no scrutiny or judgment in his eyes.

"I had no plans. But sitting alone the whole day in the flat was boring. So when I felt a little better, I asked Varun if we could go shopping." She glanced at the shopping bags at her side.

"I understand."

"We just came for a drink. No plans to have dinner here." The lie sprang from her mouth since Varun was paying for their drinks. Now she could change their plans and go back home instead, buying takeout.

But how would she hide Varun's woman avatar?

"I had no plans to come out for dinner either," Harry said, "but my cook didn't come this evening. I came here for a drink and dinner, as this is near my home. In fact, I had plans to invite you to a better restaurant. Not this one."

That was enough explanation for Ira.

She smiled and heaved. But how would Harry react to Varun's feminine look?

Embarrassment hit Ira. Could Varun just run away before coming there?

She took out her mobile to compose a text for him. Never again would she come with him like this. Varun was a boy and should roam out as a boy only. The female clothing must stay inside the home.

Before she could type the message, Varun came back.

"Hello, Harry," Varuna said.

Everything went dark for Ira. She had never faced such humiliation in her life.

Harry's gaze remained fixed on Varun for a few beats. But he let out a gentle smile and said, "Why don't you both join me for dinner here?"

Ira was about to say a polite 'No,' but Varun said, "Okay, Harry. We would love to."

What is this boy is doing? Has he no shame? This man would be the second person outside her home to know her son was a crossdresser.

"Can we all move to the cubicle there? We will have some privacy." Harry suggested to the waiter.

Ira got up and dragged her feet to the cubicle, along with Varun and Harry.

After tonight, I will keep no contact with this man. Ever, she promised herself as she took a seat opposite Harry and beside Varun.

"You met Varun last evening," she said, lowering her gaze. Shock rustled through her, and she swallowed. "Sometimes I love to treat him as a girl. In fact, I always wanted to have a g—"

"I understand, Ira. You don't have to be apologetic."

Ira looked up with mouth agape. An assuring smile flashed across Harry's face. Harry was not making fun of this situation.

"I arranged for us to come inside this cubicle as I wanted full privacy for all of us. And believe me, last evening I had already noticed a woman in Varun's eyes. And I suggest you address her as Varuna when she is in dress."

Relief washed through Ira.

"That's what Mum is doing!" Varuna chuckled.

"I haven't told you what else I do besides managing my business."

Ira failed to understand how this applied to their talk or even the dinner.

Harry ordered a few more drinks and began. "I am with an NGO. In fact, I'm one of the founding directors of that NGO. They provide psychological support to gay and lesbians. And to crossdressers, too."

Possible. She had read articles supporting people with different sexual preference. Ira met Harry's eyes. She had never seen an individual as understanding and cool-headed as Harry. A powerful and amazing feeling tethered them together. *Is this too good to be true?* She wished to jump over the table and give him a big hug.

"But my Varuna is still an occasional boy. Straight. Not a gay."

Varuna looked away.

The drinks arrived with starters. The waiter served them in three glasses and left.

"This is for Varuna, the beautiful young woman." Harry raised the glass. "You are now eighteen and can drink."

A chuckle came out from Ira's mouth. A heavy weight had lifted off her shoulders. Slow music was playing in the restaurant. Soothing.

"I will tell you about why I started that charity," Harry said.

"Do you have someone like..."

Harry snatched Varuna's sentence. "Yes. I had a brother."

"Had? Gay?"

"Don't know. But he loved to wear our mother's and sister's dresses. Secretly, of course. I had been to Delhi for higher studies and was staying in a hostel there. Those days there was no mobile. Telephones were in a stone-age in India. Making a long distant call would cost a fortune, and I was from a lower middle-class family. Not enough money with me."

Ira noticed the brightness on Harry's face fade.

"Was he caught? Family didn't accept?"

"I could have made everything right, but I wasn't there. He couldn't bear the humiliation and hung himself." Harry's eyes got misty. "He was a wonderful brother. But no one understood him. He didn't do any sin. He did something which made him smile. If we can drink here thinking this is helping us enjoy life, why can't a person do something harmless if he gets a little pleasure?"

"I'm sorry for your loss, Harry." A sob was gathering in Ira's throat, but she was holding it back.

"My mother is incredible, Harry. She is the best mum in this world."

"I know. How many mothers would take their sons outside dressed as daughters?"

Ira was almost on another planet when the dinner came. The pleasant aroma of garlic nan and chicken tikka masala engulfed her soul. She pondered why an hour ago she was planning to escape this man. Her heart expanded, and she couldn't hide her smile throughout dinner.

She stole a few glances at Harry while he was busy eating. Tall, robust and sexy, with large and caring eyes.

She felt beneath his wide chest lay a heart large enough for both she and her son to fit comfortably.

No, Ira. No. Don't behave like a college girl. Don't give your heart at the slightest hint of love. You are a mature woman. And what about his religion? He is a Christian and you are a Hindu. Control your emotions.

They finished dinner, and the time came to say goodnight to Harry.

"Can I say something to you, Ira, if you don't mind?" Harry said as they walked to the street.

Within no time, Ira's heart came into her mouth. What would Harry ask? Wouldn't this be shameful with her son there?

She didn't answer, but stopped and eyed him.

"What?" A faint and timid voice struggled through her mouth.

"Can I be a friend to you?" Harry asked.

Her eyes widened. "A friend?" she asked, unable to believe he was asking her that.

"Yes. A friend," he repeated. "You're a good woman, Ira. You've been through a lot."

She felt her face light up.

Varuna moved closer and held her hand.

"I promise I will stay within the limits and will never come to your hometown to meet you."

She cast a sideways glance at Varuna. Her eyes were dazzling with enthusiasm.

"Yes, Harry. We are already friends." A chuckle came out of her mouth. "And thanks for the drink and dinner. It was amazing."

CHAPTER 10

The luxury intercity bus passed the signpost that read *Goodbye, See You Again, Toshali Municipal Council* and entered the freeway. Seated at a window seat, Ira smiled inside. Last week in Toshali was a wonderful period for her. *How did life move so fast?*

Ira glanced around—most passengers were asleep in their seats, and others were reading books or newspapers. The elderly lady sitting to her side was dozing.

"Your weeklong holiday was over in the twinkling of an eye, Mum." Varun had come to the bus depot to see her off.

"Next holiday, for sure. I will be here the entire fortnight."

During the past couple of days, she had witnessed a new world. A world where tolerance and acceptance were the mantra of living. The evenings after Varun came back from his college and became Varuna were amazing to her.

"You should have gone on a date with Harry." Varun was after her like a small child insisting the parents buy toys.

"He is a busy man, Varun. Do I run after him when he flies to Delhi for business?" she had argued.

The only two evenings she had been with Harry, she had seen a glint in his eyes, but did not know what that meant. Harry offered friendship, and she was okay with that.

Daydreaming was not a good idea for a woman who already had a teenager. And Harry was such a fine, good-looking, and wealthy man—even young women of twenty-five would die to become his life partner. He was not only rich, but also understanding. Ira should never expect too much.

"You going to meet someone in Raghupur?" the lady on her side asked. The woman had finished her nap and started reading a magazine, *Femina*.

"I work there." Ira returned a smile.

The bus reached the highway and moved at a brisk pace. Ira closed her eyes for a few moments. She could see the hills of Toshali receding in the distance.

"You missing someone?" the lady asked again.

"Yes, my son. He is studying at Uni in Toshali. I had been with him for the last couple of days. And you?"

"I was in Toshali for my sister's wedding. She was a divorcee. Now married to her ex-husband's friend. She also has a college-going son."

"How lovely!" A tingle passed through her soul. *The universe is blissful.*

Ira glanced out the window. The distant hills, the trees on the roadside, and the lush green meadows mesmerised her. Ira smiled. She had forgotten how beautiful life was. Her past was gone now. It had been a long time since she had felt so free and happy.

The bus stopped at a rest area for a break, and most passengers disembarked. Ira also got off along with the lady.

"I'm sure your sister will live a wonderful life from now on. God is great," she said to the woman.

"Thank you, she deserves some happiness after what had happened to her."

The air around her suddenly became pure and friendly, and she drank its coolness into her lungs. An aroma–the scent of clean earth, freshly cut grass, and something else–filled her nostrils, and she felt a sense of peace as she breathed it in. The air itself seemed to be alive and whispering a secret to her. She heard birdsong, which she had never heard before, and felt a gentle breeze caress her face and hair.

The bus started again after a few minutes. As it entered Raghupur, she came down to her own world. She would see her cousin again, who would remind her every moment that she was a widow and needed to maintain a *decent* way of living. And the in-laws! They would spy on her and find out whom she was meeting.

Life in Toshali was a lot more accepting than the society in Raghupur.

"Can't you live in Toshali forever, Mum?" Varun had asked that silly question one evening, and Ira had just ignored it.

Hometown? It was Rahul's decision. Ira's unconditional love. He liked his parents' birthplace. His brothers lived there.

Could she move to the city permanently? If she sold her apartment in Raghupur, she couldn't even buy another apartment half the size in Toshali. But the first thing she could do would be to request a job transfer out of Raghupur.

Yes, Ira should apply for a transfer to Toshali City, rent an apartment. Varun would be with her during his studies.

She stepped off the bus as it stopped in front of her apartment building.

As soon as she unlocked her door and entered, her landline rang.

Nowadays, she hardly received calls on the land phone.

Ira threw her bag on the sofa and ran to lift the receiver.

"Hello Ira, Mehul calling. Finally, you are back at home? I have tried a few times."

"Y...yes."

Mehul, Rahul's older brother. He didn't have her mobile number. Her hand was shaking.

The younger brother, Rohan, had humiliated her only last week over her meeting with Harry. And now the older brother. What did he want?

"Can I come and meet with you? This evening at six?"

Ira glanced at the wall clock. It was almost five.

"I am going to Delhi to see my daughter tomorrow morning. So, if you can spare a few minutes this evening..."

A request sounded in Mehul's voice—a tone that wasn't demanding like Rohan's was. But who knew how much poison was hiding beneath those sweet words?

"P...please come."

She called Varun as soon as she hung up.

"Take it easy, Mum." That was Varun's first sentence.

She couldn't imagine what Mehul would discuss with her.

Had anyone spied on her when she and Varuna were enjoying dinner with Harry? Was it now open that her son was a crossdresser?

So many thoughts crowded her emotions. Why did she ask Varun to venture out wearing female clothing? Didn't she make him agree to keep such fantasies inside the four walls of the safety of a home?

Ira recollected the day when news came from Mehul's daughter Mansi announcing she was marrying her college sweetheart. A storm passed over the Ray family. Not because the girl chose her own life partner, but because the boy was a Christian.

She recollected how Rahul was the only one who had supported the marriage. Even Ira was not comfortable.

"You know, Rahul," she had muttered to him when they were on the way to brother Mehul's home. "When I told my parents about you, they were relieved that you were from the same religion—Hindu."

Rahul was laughing. "There are many Christians in India who bear Hindu names. Converted Christians. I don't recollect you asking me my religion when we became boyfriend and girlfriend. Do you think, when that boy said 'I love you' to Mansi, she would have first asked, 'Are you a Hindu? Oh, I love you too.'"

Ira also laughed at the joke.

When they arrived at Mehul's home, they could hear the screaming of Rohan. "This is the price when people send their daughters outside for higher education. Brother Mehul, you should disown her. She is a dark spot on our family's reputation. You should treat her as dead from now on."

Ira had witnessed a father's dilemma. On the one hand, he was not ready to accept his daughter marrying a Christian, and on the other, he couldn't let her go from his life.

Ira didn't stop at the lounge room of Mehul. She went to the bedroom where his wife, Nirmala, was sitting, burying her head between her knees.

"*Didi*," Ira said, always addressing her as an older sister, "I understand your pain. But..."

"She had told me." A sobbing Nirmala lifted her head. "And I don't want to lose my only child. Let her marry that boy if she loves him. He has a Hindu name, and no one here will even know. Unless Rohan and Tina open their mouths."

Ira understood. The boy belonging to another religion didn't matter. It was the family honour.

"I respect your decision, *didi*. Rahul and I will come with you to attend the wedding. What is there to do if she is already in love with the boy?"

Ira was not that modern yet to be happy with such a union, but not that conservative to keep religion above love. Finally, it was the love that won.

Ira glanced at the wall clock. It had been almost fifteen minutes since Mehul called, and he must be on his way. Another fifteen minutes, maybe, for him to arrive. *Time flies so fast*, Ira thought. How quickly two years had passed since she and Rahul went to Delhi with Mehul and Nirmala to celebrate the wedding! And Rohan, even though he didn't attend, had kept his mouth shut about the inter-religion marriage. Relatives in Raghupur knew the boy's Hindu sounding name only.

But the same Mehul and Nirmala showed an unfamiliar face when, within a month of Rahul's death, Ira continued wearing all the fashionable clothes she was used to.

"Why do I beat the drum to announce to the world that my husband has died?" she had said when Nirmala had suggested Ira should live like a widow. And Mehul had stomped out of his house when Ira went to talk to him about the property dispute.

Was he coming here to advise that a widow shouldn't have dinner with an outside male? Did Rohan tell him about her meeting with Harry after adding spices?

The clock moved at a super-fast speed, and the doorbell rang.

"Were you out, Ira?" Mehul asked even before Ira offered for him to sit on the lounge.

Mehul sounded like he had memorised what to say to her—no smile, and his hands in his pockets. Eyes roving around like he was trying to study everything in the room. Ira took a deep breath and tried to remain calm.

"Yes, school holidays. Spent time with Varun, in Toshali."

"Good for you. He is not far away, so you can spend time with him." Mehul slumped on the sofa. "And look at me. I have to visit Mansi, and she is in Delhi. Thirty-hour train journey. What can I do? Only child. She is insisting again and again that I spend time with her."

"That is so nice of you." Ira ventured a faint smile.

"Can you please make a tea for me, Ira?"

Ira sprang up from the sofa as a bolt of consciousness washed through her. "Sorry, I'm so rude. I haven't even asked you, out of courtesy."

She trudged to the kitchen and took a deep breath. Putting the kettle on the gas burner, she poured water into it.

But Rohan's humiliation echoed in her mind. A shriek began in her soul.

Why is this society after women only? Why is it wrong if a widow talks to another man? Hadn't Rahul's widower uncle remarried when his own daughter was almost twenty-five?

She must plan a strategy to face additional humiliation. She must take the bull by the horns.

"Here is your tea." She placed a steaming teacup in front of Mehul and sat on another sofa with a teacup for herself. She could either drink it or use it as a weapon if required.

"This tea is good." Mehul smiled as he sipped from his cup. "I am sorry Rohan called you last week and spoke nonsense, Ira."

The teacup stopped before Ira could take the first sip. She lifted her head and gazed into his eyes.

What is there to discuss now? Rub salts into the wound?

"I didn't know until this afternoon. His daughters told Mansi, and she called me. When I asked Rohan, he acted proud of what he had done to you. But I silenced him. That was shameless behaviour. I am so ashamed of my younger brother's actions; I decided to come here and apologize."

Mansi? The only family member outside Ira's home who always sympathised with her. Mansi was always supportive of her. Maybe she was witnessing a different world in a multicultural city, Delhi. It was like pouring water on a burning heart for Ira. She didn't wish to discuss it further.

"Why would you apologize for another man's actions? No, this is not right."

"He is so adamant, he still thinks he has done the right thing. What do I do?"

Ira inhaled another deep breath. Thank God it was not about her having dinner with Harry or even Varun's new way of life.

"My daughter is only a few years younger than you, even though you are my sister-in-law."

The glint of compassion in Mehul's eyes touched Ira's heart. That one sentence made a tremendous difference to her perception. She hoped this was not another trap for the property dispute. She hoped Mehul had really changed, thanks to Mansi.

"I know. You and Rahul had a wide age gap. He always considered you a father figure, even though you were the oldest brother."

"Yes. And I wish the same for you as I would for my daughter."

Ira gazed into Mehul's eyes. She had always respected this older brother of her husband before Rahul's death. She didn't know why there was so much tension over the ancestral property after Rahul left this world. Had Mehul come there to convince her not to ask for a share in the tens of millions of rupees worth of lands?

"You know I was a lawyer before retiring," Mehul said. "Rohan is unnecessarily creating problems. I am trying to settle this out of court. And now he is saying because my daughter is married to a Christian; I shouldn't get a share as per law governing Hindu families. What nonsense! Who is a lawyer, he, or I? You would not get a share because your husband died, and I wouldn't get one as my daughter married a Christian. Those laws simply do not exist."

"Out of court settlement is good," Ira said. "Even if you and I have valid reasons to get our shares, the court proceedings in India take fifteen or twenty years."

The property's value flashed in Ira's mind. She could afford to buy an apartment in the city in the next few months!

"You certainly need a better life, Ira," Mehul said again.

"Yes." She didn't know how to answer.

Mehul cleared his throat and shifted on the sofa. "I mentioned that I wish for you the same as I wish for my daughter. I would want my daughter to remarry in your situation."

Ira pressed her eyes closed and inhaled a deep breath. She was not having a daydream. Rahul's own brother was suggesting what the so-called small-town society hated! Now she was sure it was Mansi who was talking through her father. She was the only one in the family who had told her over the phone one day, "Aunt Ira, I would have looked for another husband had I been in your situation." And Ira had laughed that away, saying it might be normal in Delhi but a daydream in Raghupur.

"You are right, *Bhai*." Ira had forgotten she had always addressed him as *Bhai* as if he were her own older brother. "But I have an eighteen-year-old son. This is not a western society, where forty-plus-year-old women remarry."

Did she indirectly say she was looking for another partner? So what?

"You are right, Ira. In our society, people try to find a life partner inside their own community. Their own caste and even religion. But frankly, one should go beyond this. A man who wishes to give you company irrespective of your situation is the person you should select. And believe me, I will support you with all my heart, even if the other person doesn't belong to our caste or religion."

Mehul looked at his watch. "It's already late, Ira. I didn't look at the clock. Let me go. See you again when I am back from Delhi."

Mehul left.

Am I in a dream?

Ira said a silent *thanks* to her niece Mansi.

107

CHAPTER 11

I ra woke up to the scream of her phone. A shudder passed through her. She rubbed her eyes and looked at the glowing wall clock. Three a.m. The ring stopped. *Must be some wrong number,* she thought and pulled the sheet to cover her face. Still three hours left for the dawn to arrive.

Another buzz. She hoped it would stop again. Someone was determined to reach her at this uncivilised hour. Was it Varun? Many negative feelings clogged her mind. She reached for her cell phone off the side-table and stared at it. A number outside her phone book.

"Hello, who is this?"

A female voice sounded through it. "Is this Mrs. Ira Ray? Teacher in Lata Devi Girls' High School?"

Ira stilled for a moment. Should she answer 'yes'?

"Ma'am," the caller continued without awaiting her answer, "I am a police inspector from Kaliwadi police station. I got your number from your principal."

Ira sprang up in her bed. Police? At this hour of the night? Why did the principal give them her number? "Yes, this is Ira. What is this about?"

"Ma'am, you know Divya, one of your students?"

"Divya?" How could she forget this name? Divya's weeping face flashed in her mind. "Yes, she is a student in my class. Is everything all right with her?"

"Ma'am, she is in hospital. Kaliwadi Government Hospital. We suspect she has consumed some sort of poison. Might be a suicide attempt. She was babbling your name. So, we had to find your number."

Ira remembered the day in the school when the girls were teasing Divya. But this she didn't know. How could she help the police?

"Is her mother there?" Divya had said her mum had been to Toshali and would come back to take her after marrying the man she had chosen.

"No, ma'am. There is a man. He says he is the husband of Divya's mother's friend, and she was living with them temporarily. Can you please come here in the morning, ma'am? I think she could gain consciousness and talk."

"Should I come to the hospital now? How is she?" Ira felt she was sweating.

"No, Divya is out of danger and is sleeping peacefully, so it would be best if you came in the morning."

"I will come in the morning, after six. Is that okay?"

"Sure, ma'am.

Ira had lost her sleep. She brought Varun's number to the screen, but stilled when she was about to dial him. He was a child, what could he do?

Divya was a sensible girl. What could have happened to her that she took such a drastic step? She felt like running to the hospital to be by her side.

She deposited the phone on her side table and pushed herself under the sheet after switching off the bed light. She tossed and turned in her bed and grew strained with every passing moment. For a while she'd feel hot, then she'd throw off the covers and grow cold and repeated the process.

She thought over and over—who in Raghupur could she talk to? She couldn't approach her in-laws for sure. Mehul has left for Delhi. Reema? No. Her family also lives in Toshali.

The only name that came to her mind was Harry. She planned to get some sleep and call him first thing in the morning.

After changing sides again and again, she sat up to grab the water bottle from the side table in the darkness. Instead, her hand fell on the cell phone, and she pulled it to her. What was wrong with sending a text to Harry requesting him to call her in the morning? Ira typed a text. *A student of mine has consumed poison, maybe a suicide attempt. Babbling my name and the police are asking me to come to the hospital. Please call me when you wake up. I am scared and don't know whom to turn to for help.*

She felt an enormous burden vanish from her chest. Setting the cell phone on the side table, she drank some water and switched off the light. As soon as she pulled the sheet over her, she felt her limbs relax. A cool wave passed through her chest.

The phone buzzed again, and Ira jumped from the bed. *Police? Again? Didn't she tell me I can come in the morning? Which woman in Raghupur City would venture out in the night's darkness?* Ira grabbed her cell phone from the side table.

Harry? Oh no. Why did I send the text? I could have waited until the morning. She swiped the answer icon and brought out a sweet and apologising voice.

"I'm sorry..."

"How are you, Ira? Are you at home or on your way to the hospital?"

Did I send an incomplete text? "No, I am home. I need to go in the morning. Sorry, I thought your phone must be on silent mode at night."

Harry chuckled from the other side. "It is. But the *favourite numbers* can reach me anytime."

Favourite? My number is in the favourite list in Harry's phone?

"Ira, are you there?"

"Ye...yes."

"Okay, listen to me. Did the girl at any time tell you her personal situation?"

Ira flinched. "Only once, in the classroom. Other girls were teasing her as her mum planned to remarry. You know remarriage for a woman having a teen is still a taboo here in Raghupur. Her mother had been to Toshali so that she could marry her man and was supposed to come back to take the daughter with her. I don't know what happened in between. She never came back to me after that one instance."

"Don't worry, when you meet the police in the morning, don't tell them so many things. You talk to many students and are unable to remember each minor incident at the school. The superintendent of police of Raghupur is a friend of mine and I will talk to him in the morning."

"That is so nice of you, Harry." Ira struggled to find words to praise him. This personal connection of Harry with a senior cop would help in Divya's case. "Can I call you when I meet the police? I'm sorry I disturbed you at night."

"Don't worry. Call me anytime. Now, please don't worry about what is going to happen in the morning and go to sleep. Goodnight."

Ira kept staring at the phone for a few beats after Harry hung up. Then she slid inside the blanket, curling her hand tightly around the phone and pressing it to her chest. The little device seemed to be the only solace in this unforgiving world.

"Ma'am," the woman at the customer service counter said when Ira arrived at the Kaliwadi Government Hospital at around six in the morning, "second floor, room number sixteen."

"Thanks." Ira headed towards the elevator. *Government hospitals in Raghupur began keeping receptionists?*

She didn't take time to find the room. A female police officer was sitting on a chair on the veranda near the doors, surfing through her smartphone.

"Hello, officer." Ira didn't know if it was the same police who had called her last night.

The policewoman winced and stood up.

"I am Mrs. Ira Ray. Teacher in Lata Devi Girls' High School. How is Divya?"

The officer slipped her mobile into her pocket. "She is better. Regained consciousness this morning, and the doctor said she is out of danger. Thank God the woman she lives with could tell something was happening in her room and called the ambulance immediately."

Ira knew Divya's mother had moved to her friend's house as a stop-gap arrangement and was supposed to move out after her marriage.

Ira glanced around. "Where is she? I mean, the woman?"

"She was here the whole night and went back this morning. Doctors might relieve the girl today, and she will come to take her home. But ma'am, the girl is not ready to give any information. You may try to find out what happened to her."

Ira walked into the room. Divya was lying on her side, facing the door. She gazed at Ira with a faint smile on her face.

"How are you, Divya?" Ira gently touched her hair.

"Miss, I... I am..." Her gaze was on the door.

Ira closed the door and came back, sat on the bedside.

"I will take care of you, believe me." Ira muttered to her. "When is your mum coming back?"

"Don't know. She has been to Agra with my new dad. She said she would come back next week."

Ira wanted to ask if she took poison, but resisted.

Divya propped herself up on one elbow on the bed.

"You don't have to, my child. Please lie down if you need."

"No, miss. I am tired of sleeping." She got up and sat against the headboard.

"Divya—" Ira looked into her eyes— "you are like my child. I have a son who is older than you. You can trust me."

"I do, miss." Another faint but painful smile.

Ira swallowed. "You can tell me what is troubling you now or during the last few days."

Divya's lip trembled. Tears rolled down her cheeks.

Ira's heart sank. "Your mum's friend, I mean the family you are living with. Any problem there?"

"No." Divya shook her head. "They are good. But..."

Something had been troubling the girl so much that she had decided her life had no value.

"I know there are demons out on the street—" Ira's voice was still low but firmer than before— "but remember, I have contacts with top police officers. If anyone is trying to cause harm to you, I can protect you." She gently squeezed Divya's shoulder. If Harry said he had contacts, he would never let her down.

Divya glanced up. "Uncle came when there was no one at home."

A shiver passed through Ira's bones. "Uncle? You mean your late dad's brother?"

"Yes."

"Did he come alone?" Ira's heart started beating against her ribs. "How did he know there was no one home?"

"Mum's friend went out and then he came. He was probably waiting outside and keeping an eye."

"What did he say?"

Divya looked away.

Ira waited for a few beats. "Divya, my child, I am here to help you out. I will do anything for you. Trust me." She sucked in a deep breath.

"Miss, I have done nothing. Believe me." Divya wept.

Ira moved closer, pulled her against her chest, and patted her back. "I believe you. Only you."

"He...uncle...he has photos. Mine. Bathroom. In his house."

Ira understood. Before moving out, Divya's mum was sharing the house with her brother-in-law. Joint family. Did he take forbidden photos when she was in the bathroom?

"Did he threaten you?"

"Mum has changed mobile numbers because he was calling her and harassing."

"What was his demand?"

"He was asking Mum to sign some papers."

Ira understood. Same joint property. Harass the vulnerable woman and grab everything. She got up and gave her a hug. "I will be back soon."

"Miss!" Panic sounded in Divya's voice. "Please don't tell the police. Uncle might release the photos."

Ira swung around. "I won't. I know how to manage."

She gently closed the door after coming out of the room. The police guard outside the room asked, "All well, ma'am?"

"I think so. Please take care that her uncle doesn't come here. You should check the ID of anyone before allowing them inside, especially if the visitor is a man." She loped towards the elevator before the guard could ask any questions.

As soon as she came out from the lift and walked towards the main gate, she noticed a man coming alongside. Not unusual in a busy place, like a hospital. But the man seemed to be watching her. A disquiet washed through Ira, but she kept walking. The coffee shop just outside the gate looked like a sanctuary. She needed a coffee badly before she could talk to Harry.

"Ma'am." The man approached to her.

Ira's heart lurched into her throat. She stopped and looked at him. He looked like he might be in his early forties. Smells from his dirty clothes pinched her nose. Scars on his forehead made him look like a walking ghost. "What?"

"Ma'am, how is my niece?" A sly smile curved his mouth.

Ira felt her fists tightening. "Your niece? Who?"

"Divya is my niece. Ma'am, my daughter is a student in your school, where Divya is studying. I know you."

Ira inhaled a deep breath. "Why don't you see yourself? After all, she is your niece. Who is stopping you?" Ira hoped he wouldn't call her bluff and try to go to Divya's room. The police should stop him, but what if they didn't?

"Ma'am, after all, this is a police case. I...but..."

Ira understood. The man had seen the police sitting outside the door of Divya's cabin and sneaked away.

"Look, Mister." Ira's voice was rough but low. "I came here as I am her class teacher. I mean, we assign each teacher a class and section in the school, and we know each student in that class personally. Beyond that, I have nothing further to do with this. She is your niece, and this is your family matter. I suggest you deal with your own issues." She started walking towards the coffee shop.

"Ma'am, please wait." The man inched alongside her. "You didn't understand. I am asking you..."

Ira stilled. The man's voice sounded threatening.

"Ma'am, you don't know me. I am not only Divya's uncle, I am also something else."

"Something else, meaning...?"

"Meaning, I can make your life miserable if I want. I know your husband is dead and your in-laws are against you. And there is no man at your home, other than your teen son. So, please be careful about what you are doing. Yes, you are right. This is my family's business, and I will deal with this. But you shouldn't meddle in my family affair. Got it? Namaste. Have a good day." The man swung around and vanished into the crowd.

Ira stood there for a while, frozen. She had no man in her home to protect her. *Who said we are in the twenty-first century? Does every woman need a man for safety?*

Taking the cell phone from her handbag, she dialled Harry's number. Harry listened patiently and said, "You wait there, I'm coming."

Ira walked into the coffee shop and ordered a coffee.

"Rush time, ma'am. May take fifteen to twenty minutes," the counter girl said and attended to the other customers without waiting for Ira's reply.

Ira glanced around. It was around seven, and she couldn't believe so many people would be there when most of the markets nearby would open after nine. Possibly because this was a public hospital. But at least it was a safe place where it would be difficult for anyone to assault her.

Toshali to Raghupur was approximately two hours when Ira travelled by non-stop bus. Harry would come by his car and would take less time. Maybe he would arrive in one and a half hours. That too only if he started immediately after he spoke to her. Ira wished she could ask him if he was already in the car. But that would be inappropriate. She had already disturbed him by texting during the early morning when he was in bed. No doubt he was a nice gentleman. But there must be a boundary line which she should honour. Divya's uncle literally left her with no option. He was right. There is no man at her home to protect her. So what? She has a friend who is a gentleman. Regardless, it was not about a man or a woman. She needed a person who had contacts, and Harry had them.

"Mrs. Ira Ray," the girl at the counter shouted, "your coffee is ready."

Ira walked up to the counter to collect her cup and then found a seat.

"Can I take this seat, please?" she asked a man who was the only occupant at a table, as no table was fully vacant for her.

"Yes, ma'am." The man said with a smile and continued savouring a piece of toast.

Ira sat with her coffee cup and looked at the wall clock. Almost twenty-five minutes since she called Harry. She should order some breakfast after finishing her coffee to kill time. But she wasn't hungry. How could she be? There were so many incidents since early this morning, and she would take time to digest all of them.

Ira's gaze went to a part of the lawn where a chopper with an ambulance logo descended. *Air ambulance in Raghupur?* She didn't know Raghupur's infrastructures moved ahead to modernisation at such a fast pace. Yes, she had noticed roads being widened with multiple lanes and new, massive shopping malls coming up at each viable location, but choppers?

Everything was developing in Raghupur except the mindset of its people towards the women.

Another chopper with the ambulance logo descended onto the helipad that had the capacity for multiple helicopters. A silent smile escaped from her mouth, and she could feel it. She looked at the wall clock. Still half of her coffee left and almost forty minutes since she had spoken to Harry. Impatience bubbled in her heart.

The first chopper rose in the air. Her attention shot to the second one, where paramedics were bringing a patient on a stretcher out of it. Another chopper had just landed. But this was not an ambulance. She kept her eyes peeled for any patient coming out. Her cell phone chimed inside her bag, and she fished it out. A text message from Harry: *where do I find you?*

Is Harry driving or is he coming with a driver? Anxiety laced through Ira. How careless could he be? No one should text while driving.

Ira's stomach swooped. She was used to this feeling when Rahul would text her while driving. Why was she thinking of Harry like this?

I am waiting for you in the coffee shop, which is just outside the main gate of the hospital, she texted back and looked at the chopper, having nothing else to do.

Ira's gaze shot at a known gait walking out of the heliport. Someone like Harry. Impossible. Ira twirled her cup. There was still some coffee left, and she could kill more time if she sipped it slowly. Then she could go leisurely to the counter again and order her breakfast. The man who was at the table left a newspaper. She could read through it while waiting. By the time she would finish breakfast, Harry might have arrived.

"How are you, Ira?" She jumped at the familiar voice. Harry was standing before her.

"You? So soon? I thought the drive to Raghupur would be two hours at least!"

Harry chuckled and pointed at the sky. "You are right. But much less through air route."

Harry! Chopper! Is this his own? Ira stopped herself from biting her lip.

But a colossal weight came down on her chest. Was she getting a similar vibe like she would get with Rahul? No, Rahul was her husband. How could she compare Rahul with any man on this earth, or even the universe?

"Are you all right?"

Ira came out of her thoughts. "Yes, but..."

"Okay, can we go to another place? We can have breakfast and also have a quick chat."

"Where? Oh!" Ira remembered this was her town, and she was supposed to guide Harry to some place where they could get breakfast. After all, Harry came for the first time to meet her in her hometown, and it was her duty to become a host. "Let's go out." She let out a smile, and both walked alongside each other out of the coffee shop.

While Ira was surfing through her smartphone for an excellent restaurant nearby, a man with a white uniform came and saluted Harry. "Sir, the car is ready. Please come with me."

An Audi Q7 was waiting for them in the hospital parking lot. The driver opened the rear door, and Harry signalled Ira to climb in. He got into the car after her.

Ira continued to scan her mobile for a restaurant when the car moved out of the hospital parking.

"Sir, to the Oberoi Hotel?"

"Oberoi?" The word jumped out of her mouth even though she wished otherwise. *Breakfast in a five-star hotel?* She tried to cover up her surprise.

"Yes," Harry said to the driver and then turned his head towards Ira. "I think that place would be better to have a confidential discussion." Ira put her phone away.

The Oberoi Hotel was only a five minutes' drive from the hospital.

Ira and Harry walked into the restaurant. Ira glanced at her dress. She was clad in a simple salwar kameez. She wondered if it would be appropriate for a five-star hotel. She had come here a few times with Rahul for parties, but always in smart western clothing.

A server showed them to the table Harry had reserved and gave them a menu card. Ira took a seat opposite Harry and cast a quick look at him. He was in a kurta and jeans.

"We have one more person arriving. We will place our order after that." Harry said to the server. "Do you want some tea or coffee, Ira?"

"No, I already had coffee. I will wait."

The server left.

"Who is joining us?" Ira asked while surfing through the menu and without making an eye contact. The turn of events since last night overwhelmed her. What was she worth that she would deal with a person of Harry's status?

"Commissioner of Police. Jugal Mohanty. He is my friend."

His sentence had hardly come to a stop when a tall man with civilian clothes arrived. "How are you, Harry?"

"You're here!" Harry smiled and shook his hand. "Meet Mrs. Ira Ray. She is a teacher in Lata Devi Girls' High School."

Ira flashed a warm smile and shook his hand. "Please sit down."

"I'm hungry. Can we order something quickly?" Harry said to Jugal and Ira as the server approached.

"Sure. One Egg Benedict and coffee for me. And ma'am?" Jugal said without even looking at the menu. He probably knew what was available for breakfast at this place.

"Only water," Ira said.

"Oh, come on Ira. I am also going to order Eggs on Toast. It will look like two voracious eaters are sitting with a figure-conscious, model-looking woman." Harry let out a laugh at his own joke, and Jugal also joined in.

"Okay, one plate of Idli for me, and a green tea."

"We got him." Jugal said immediately after the server retreated.

"So quickly?" Harry asked.

"Yes, he was loitering at the hospital gate, and my men took him. Difficult to obtain bail for alleged sexual offence against a minor girl. He won't come out of the prison for a long time. We have also got evidence from his mobile phone. Concrete evidence."

They couldn't be talking about Divya's uncle, could they? Already?

"He can't threaten to you, ma'am." Jugal said. "In fact, the police were following him since last night when the girl took admission in the hospital."

A cool wave washed through Ira. Who else other than Harry could have helped her out of this situation?

"I'm happy this case came under control before it got too nasty. Even the media has not gotten hints of it, so far," Jugal said. "The girl is in a better condition. The substance she had consumed was very little, so in a way, it's good there wasn't much harm to her."

The server came with three plates and set them on the table. The aroma of Idli dipped in the steaming sambar curry cooled Ira's nerves. "I am coming back with coffee and green tea," he said.

"Her mother had been to Agra for her honeymoon with her new husband. The woman with whom the girl lived told us. She is coming back this evening to Toshali by plane. Her new husband lives in Toshali," Commissioner Mohanty said and pushed a forkful into his mouth.

Harry rested his fork against his plate. "That's good. If you can talk to her mother, and if she gives permission, I can take her with me to

Toshali and give her to her mother when she comes back this evening," Harry said.

"I think it's a good idea," Jugal replied.

Harry just took a horrible situation and fixed it in a way she never could've done on her own. Gratitude bubbled in Ira's heart.

I ra walked with Divya to the chopper along with her mother's friend, who had brought two suitcases with her clothes and books. Divya's mother had faxed an authority letter to the police so that she could accompany Harry to Toshali.

Divya stopped just before arriving at the chopper and held Ira's hand. "Miss, you are not coming with me?"

"No, my child. Your mum and new dad are coming back by afternoon flight, and Mr. Harry will take you to the airport. You will receive them. Of course, I will come to Toshali eventually. My son studies there. I go there from time to time to stay with him. I will meet you there. All right? And you also have my mobile number. We can talk any time you like."

"Thanks, Miss. But I will miss you in my new school. Why don't you also leave Raghupur and join my new school in Toshali? Your son will be with you all the time."

Harry and Ira both laughed. "No, my child. My home is here. How can I leave my home?"

Will I be that lucky to join a school in Toshali?

Ira said bye to Divya as she climbed into the helicopter along with Harry.

"Thanks, Harry. This was a great help." Ira's soul was full of gratitude.

"See you in Toshali. Please call me when you come there." His gaze held hers, a current pulsating tangibly between them.

"Sure." Ira looked down, a smile touched her mouth.

The woman was listening to the conversation.

"That gentleman Harry, he's your friend?"

Ira didn't know how to answer. Did the woman notice how Harry looked at her? But there was nothing between the two except plain friendship. Any wrong answer might circulate in Raghupur like spicy gossips, and it wouldn't take long to reach the people who were close to her.

"He..." Ira paused. "The Superintendent of Police is his friend. I met him for the first time. But he is a thorough gentleman. He was behaving as if he's known me for a long time." *Is lying a sin in all circumstances? This should be an exception. I didn't lie, only gave irrelevant information!*

"He must be a wealthy business owner." The woman paced to walk alongside Ira. "That must be his own helicopter."

Nausea churned in Ira's stomach. She avoided the woman's gaze.

They had already come to the road. Before the woman could ask more, Ira said, "Look, I am in a hurry. I need to go to the school. Talk to you some other time. Thanks for all you did for Divya."

She pretended as if her cab was about to arrive and parted ways as soon as possible. Luckily, she had already booked the Uber, and the app notified it was about to arrive.

Ira resisted the urge to look at the woman while climbing in the taxi.

"Good morning, ma'am." The cab driver looked over his shoulder and smiled. "Is everything all right?"

"Yes, why?" Ira settled on the seat.

"No, ma'am. You had come to the hospital, so I asked. I am seeing you again for the first time since Mr. Ray died. It was so sad, ma'am."

Ira felt as if she would throw up. So many people in Raghupur knew her. The irony of a small town. When Raghupur would grow, and she could hide...

"How do you know me?"

"Ma'am, I was a driver in Mr. Ray's office and have seen you with him many times. I left that job and started my Uber business. Ma'am, so many industries are coming to our small town, one day it will become a large city like Toshali. I have a decent income and am even planning on buying two more cars for the taxi business. It was Mr. Ray's idea, and I took his advice."

Pride swelled in Ira's chest hearing the praise of the man she always loved.

"That would be so nice if our small town develops. So many people would get jobs and they would get no time to meddle in other people's lives." She shouldn't have said the last sentence.

The driver continued chatting. Ira occasionally responded with monosyllables until finally the cab entered her apartment complex.

"Your stop, ma'am."

"Thanks." Ira climbed down and hobbled to the elevator. She hadn't slept since almost three last night, and tiredness had crawled through her muscles and nerves. She unlocked her door and slumped on the sofa. She must hurry to the bathroom for a shower and dress up for the school. *Oh no. Not today.*

She grabbed her phone from the handbag and typed a text for the principal, with briefings of what happened to Divya, that she was extremely tired and would need a day off. Sick leave.

Don't worry, the head teacher texted back with minutes, *you did a commendable job. Take a rest.*

She stretched her legs on the sofa.

That afternoon, Ira woke up to a chime on her phone. She stretched to grab the cell phone from the side table.

It was a text from Harry.

Received Divya's parents from the airport and sent Divya with them to his home. Told them I can organise counselling for the girl.

Thanks, Harry. Hope everything will be fine for her now, she texted back and sat up on the sofa. It was around one in the afternoon. She felt a lot better than when she came back after sending off Divya with Harry. But soon boredom began sinking into her. She missed the lively environment of the school.

Ira must wait until the next morning for another day at her work. Or catch the next bus to Toshali. No, that was not an option. Indecent to ask for so many leaves. But what was wrong if she spent some time in the bus station and watch the crowd?

Ira punched the destination into the Uber app.

Burying her head in a fiction book called *The Pink Mutiny,* Ira had settled in a lonely corner of the waiting room of Raghupur Inter-city Bus Station. The lead character of the nineteenth century historical romance cum thriller Amelia was alone in Sultanpur after her friend Sehnaz abandoned her. Amelia' plight, first in the hands of her abusive husband and then when she tried to escape from him during a civil war, made her blood race. *Amelia is a strong woman; she would overcome the obstacles by the end.* Ira raised her head.

Passengers were embarking and disembarking from the buses outside, and a few of them came to the waiting area and headed straight to the food stalls. Her gaze shot to the corner where she had met Rupa the other day in the coffee shop. A man was attending the counter when she walked in front of the stall. Perhaps Rupa would start in the afternoon, or she might have taken the day off. Rupa would grow into another strong woman, she believed. She won't be sorry for her discontinuance of study. Her conscience told her this girl will be an example to those who even remotely think of aborting the girl foetus.

She buried her face in *The Pink Mutiny* again. *Amelia noticed her husband's security guard, Chetan, and thought the man was following her. She was trying to escape when an old but charismatic woman stops her.* Would this woman be an angel or another villain?

"Miss." A girl's voice tingled her senses. She didn't expect to meet anyone here, just enjoy the liveliness of the place.

"Miss, is your son arriving today?"

Ira raised her head. Rupa was standing there. A beautiful smile curved her lips. Ira folded the book and set it on her lap.

"How are you, Rupa? I thought you were off today."

"No off day, Miss. The shop opens all seven days a week, and an off day means less money."

Ira wished to ask Rupa to sit down with her and talk. But that seemed impossible. She must report to her boss. "So, you will begin your shift now?"

"No, miss. I came an hour early. Our neighbour's daughter was coming to this side in her scooty. She offered me a lift, so I came as per her time. Can I sit down with you for a while?"

A chuckle escaped Ira's mouth. She looked at the huge wall clock hanging from the roof in the middle of the large waiting hall. It was two p.m. Her stomach growled.

Rupa sat in the chair opposite her.

"You had your lunch at home?" she asked.

"Me?" Rupa paused. "I...I had a heavy breakfast."

"No, that won't do. Wait here, I am coming back in two minutes." She set the book on the chair and strode through the crowd to the food stalls. What could she get quickly so that she could spend some quality time with Rupa? Ira's gaze went to the pizza and kebab stall.

"Three large chicken pizza slices, please. Please give me two paper plates." Ira took out her credit card to swipe at the machine.

"One minute, ma'am." The man at the counter said. Ira swung around and glanced at Rupa through the crowd. Dressed in a cream-coloured top and a denim skirt, she looked like a strong woman in the making. Or so she imagined.

"Here is your order, ma'am."

"Thanks." Ira took the plates in both her hands and strode to Rupa.

"I forgot to ask you, Rupa, but I brought chicken pizza. Take this plate." She gave the plate with two slices to her.

"Miss, why two for me? I said..."

"You are young, Rupa. When will you have your next meal? Does the owner allow you a dinner break?"

"No, Miss. I will start at three. Until about ten there will be such a rush, and I will handle them all myself. And then I finish and go home. Mum will make roti and veggies for me. I love the food she cooks." Rupa took a slice into her mouth. "Thanks, Miss."

"I took a day off, but felt bored sitting at home, so came here to spend some time." Ira stopped eating. The events from early morning flashed in her eyes.

"Miss, are you all right? I supposed you were here to receive your son. But..."

Ira needed someone whom she might share with.

"Something happened this morning." Ira swallowed. "A girl from the school. Divya..." She shouldn't have said the name even though there was a remote chance Rupa might know her.

"Divya? Poor girl..."

Ira stilled, staring at Rupa, the pizza slice still in her hand.

"I live only two houses away from her house."

"Her house?" Ira still didn't know much about Divya except the fact that her mother remarried after her dad's death.

"They lived in a joint family, the ancestral house. Divya's parents and her uncle's family."

"And the uncle tortured them after the older brother's death?"

Rupa glanced around and lowered her voice. "Miss, Divya won't like that I have told this to you. If you can..."

"I will keep everything a secret." Ira gazed into Rupa's eyes. "Rest assured."

"The uncle is a rogue. She had confided in me. It was her uncle and no other man."

"What?"

"I mean, Divya was pregnant. Her mum knew. She left the house and moved in with her friend. And she had to spend lots of money to abort the child."

"She didn't complain to the police? The girl is a minor. Not even sixteen!"

"Police? She was scared her uncle would blackmail her."

A shock wave passed through Ira's nerves. Abortion? What a golden chance Divya's mother lost fearing the so-called society! The DNA test could have revealed everything, and the *uncle* could have been in prison long before this morning.

"Her uncle forced Divya's mother to sign papers forsaking the claim for the property. She said no. Then..."

"Then what?"

"When the mother went to Toshali, leaving Divya alone with her friend, her aunt spread the false news that some schoolboy had made her pregnant. So, she ate the rat poison." Rupa's eyes moistened.

Ira wanted to pull Rupa and press her to her chest.

"I hope things will be better for Divya. She will no longer live in Raghupur. And her mother should never forsake her claim to the property."

"Right, Miss. Her uncle thinks they shouldn't ask for a share as Divya's mum doesn't have a son."

"He must think again, and he will have ample time in the prison. This morning he has been arrested."

Rupa's eyes dazzled.

A woman holding a takeaway coffee cup came and sat on their side. Rupa got up.

"This reminded me my shift is about to start." Rupa pointed her chin towards the coffee cup.

"It was nice to see you, Rupa. I might spend a bit more time here and will come to buy coffee from your shop in about an hour before going back."

"Would love to see you again, Miss." Rupa took her bag and left. Ira opened her book again, but her eyes followed as Rupa walked to the coffee shop.

CHAPTER 12

Days passed by as they always did in Raghupur. Ira went to Lata Devi Girls' School in the morning and came home in the afternoon as she routinely did. Divya's absence in her class tormented her for a while, but she was happy she escaped from the unfriendly society and would have time to lead a better life with her mother and stepfather in Toshali.

Another Friday morning arrived, and Ira was on her way to the school. Her cell phone buzzed. She took out the phone from her bag while continuing to walk. An unknown number flashed on the mobile screen.

"Who is this?" Ira had made it a practice never to utter her own name for unknown numbers.

"Mrs. Ray? I am Leela, Divya's mother."

Ira stilled. What happened to Divya? She hadn't enquired about her since the last message she had received from Harry.

"Oh, Divya's mum? Is Divya all right?"

"Yes, Mrs. Ray. And thanks a lot. She has told me about you. You saved her life. And Mr. Harry. He is like a God to us. He helped us get admission into a decent school here. I am sorry, I should have called you to say thanks much sooner."

Harry's name brought a tingle to Ira's mind.

"Divya is doing well?"

"Yes, Mrs. Ray. And Mr. Harry said you come to Toshali sometimes. Please let me know, Divya would like to meet with you. She talks of you all the time. You are the only teacher in the school she will remember always."

A smile slipped from Ira's mouth. "That's so nice of her and you. Sure, I will save this number and will come to meet you and Divya when I'm in Toshali. See you."

She had just deposited her cell phone in her handbag and *zip*—it buzzed again. She took it out and saw Harry's name flashing on the screen. In a moment, the world stilled for her.

"Hello Ira, how are you?"

Her heart swelled a couple of sizes. She was afraid her voice would break if she tried to speak.

"Ira, are you there?"

"I'm good, Harry. On my way to the school."

"Did I call you at a wrong time?"

Ira waited at a pedestrian crossing for the green signal. "No, I'm fine. How are you?"

"Fine. Thanks. Guess what Ira, I am going to Delhi tomorrow for business."

"That's good, Harry. And you will be with your daughter too. How long will you be there?"

"Little more than a week, I think. I haven't booked my return journey yet. It all depends on my business needs."

"Have a delightful journey and a pleasant stay in Delhi, Harry. Please call me when possible."

"Sure. I will. Thanks. Bye."

The pedestrian traffic signal flashed green. Ira slipped the phone inside her bag and crossed the road. *Did I ask him to call me from Delhi? Wouldn't he think I am becoming too friendly? Usually, women love to befriend wealthy men. But I'm not that cheap.*

By the time Ira arrived, she was ten minutes late. Maybe for the first time in her career. She thought of taking the day off instead, but she was already inside the school and walking to the office to collect the attendance register.

"Principal wants to see you, ma'am," the clerk in the school office told her instead of giving her the register.

"Principal?" Ira felt like a student getting summoned for disciplinary action for coming late to the school. Principal's office was the next room. She wondered if she would be sent home instead of going to the class.

"May I come in, ma'am?" Ira peeked in, pushing the door slightly, her heart beating.

"Please come in, Mrs. Ray." The soft voice of the elderly principal cooled down Ira's nerves. She was not a habitual latecomer like a few other teachers in the school and deserved leniency.

"Good morning." Ira stood before her, awaiting further instruction.

"Please take a seat." Principal madam smiled at her. "You know Mrs. Ray, Mrs. Shah was going to attend the interstate history workshop in Delhi."

Ira swallowed. "Yes. I know. I am taking a few of her classes in her absence."

"Right. But Mrs. Shah had to change plans as her husband is sick and in the hospital."

Ira didn't understand what she had to do with this. "How is he?"

"Better. But he will be there for a couple of days. Unfortunately, she will miss the workshop."

"Oh, I see."

"Mrs. Ray, you are the next senior history teacher in the school. I have recommended your name to attend the workshop. If you are okay with this, we will book a ticket for you tomorrow morning on a flight from Toshali and cancel Mrs. Shah's ticket. The school will also transfer her hotel booking to your name."

What a coincidence! Harry was also going to Delhi. All the cells of Ira's heart vibrated, but she managed to say, "Yes, I am happy to attend, if Mrs. Shah can't." Should she be happy with her colleague's bad luck? She sent a quick prayer for Mr. Shah's speedy recovery.

Next morning.

"Mrs. Ira Ray?" The airhostess approached Ira even before the other passengers were settled.

"Yes, I'm Ira Ray." Surprise stung Ira. Was something wrong? Did she occupy a wrong seat? She fished out her boarding pass and checked.

"Ma'am," the airhostess said again, "can I see your boarding pass?"

"Yes, why? I think I've occupied the right seat." She handed over the pass and craned her neck to check the row number.

The lady chuckled. "Ma'am, I will give you another pass. You need to change your seat, ma'am."

Unease feathered softly into Ira's chest. "What was wrong with my boarding pass?"

"Ma'am, you have gotten an upgrade to business class! Here is your new pass. Please bring your cabin bag and come with me."

Ira knew sometimes airlines gave free upgrades when they had excess passengers in economy and vacant seats in business class. She got up and opened the overhead locker to take out the cabin bag and followed the air hostess.

"Here is your seat, ma'am, the window seat there," the airhostess said, "and enjoy your journey."

Ira didn't expect to see Harry sitting there and smiling at her. Why did she forget Harry was also supposed to travel in the morning? But there were so many flights to Delhi, and how would she know they both would be on the same plane?

"You, here?" An irritation flushed through her. She had appreciated Harry bringing his chopper to Raghupur to help Divya. But she was an independent and enlightened woman. She didn't expect any man other than her husband to spend money on her. "So, you have paid for my upgrade? I thought... Please don't, Harry. I don't want you to spend money on me."

Harry furrowed his brows. "You are standing in the aisle, and the plane will begin leaving soon. Others are watching. Please take your seat, and I will give the explanation."

Harry was in the aisle seat, so Ira manoeuvred herself to the window seat. The plane had started rolling on the runway.

'Ladies and gentlemen,' the inflight announcement thundered, *'the captain has turned on the Fasten Seat Belt sign. If you haven't already done so, please stow your carry-on luggage underneath the seat in front of you or in an overhead bin. Please take your seat and fasten your seat belt. And also make sure your seat back and folding trays are in their full upright position.'*

"Once the plane is in the air," Ira said, keeping her voice low, "I would love to go back to the economy class."

"You are right, Ira. I shouldn't throw money on you. In fact, I didn't. You know I travel a lot for my business and have gained lots of air-miles. Some of them were about to lapse since for the last few months I haven't travelled. So, instead of the airlines getting the benefit, I upgraded your ticket. What is wrong with that?"

Nothing is wrong with that. Ira didn't travel frequently, and she never had a frequent flier account. She didn't even know if the frequent flier miles lapsed.

"But how did you know I am on this flight? Are you spying on me?"

Harry chuckled. "No. You know I lost my son when he was a baby. I have found a boy who would be my son's age had he been alive. And he is a lovely boy. He said his mum is travelling to Delhi. I think you know I had booked my ticket long before they booked your ticket yesterday. Doesn't it prove I didn't plan to be on the same flight as you?"

'Ladies and gentlemen, now we request your full attention as the flight attendants demonstrate the safety features of this aircraft.'

Harry was right. When he had called to inform about his travel yesterday, Ira didn't even know she would fly to Delhi for the workshop. But if he was trying to get close to her through her son, he was definitely the most intelligent man on this earth. He knew well Varun was Ira's life. She closed her eyes and felt the aircraft leaving the ground and jumping into the sky. Her heart also began flying along with the plane.

A few minutes passed.

'Ladies and gentlemen, the captain has turned off the Fasten Seat Belt sign, and you may now move around the cabin. However, we always recommend keeping your seat belt fastened while you're seated.'

Ira opened her eyes and glanced out the window. The sky was clear, and the plane was flying above a band of white clouds.

"Thanks, Harry. Sorry I was rude," she said.

"That's all right. No worries."

'In a few moments, the flight attendants will pass around the cabin to offer you hot or cold drinks, as well as breakfast.'

Ira's stomach growled. All she had since this morning was a cup of coffee after the security check. She knew it took a long time between the announcement for the snacks and the actual time they were served. But the airhostess arrived in the row shortly after they made the announcement.

This is business class, not economy, Ira thought. She chose Upma for her breakfast, along with a cup of coffee.

"What about you, sir?" the airhostess asked Harry.

"Same, like this lady with me. Upma and a coffee."

The airhostess served their food and moved on to another row.

"Where are you staying?" Harry asked after taking just one spoon of the upma.

"Don't remember the hotel name. The workshop is in JNU, Jawaharlal Nehru University, a few minutes from the airport. I was told my hotel is somewhere near it. The hotel has pick up service."

"I know JNU. I will be in hotel Marriott, near the airport. You have plans this evening?"

Ira was wondering if she should visit Mansi while in Delhi. Mehul and Nirmala would be with her, and as her aunt, she must let her know she was in Delhi. *Not today,* she thought.

"Won't you see your daughter?"

"Joanna? She has some party with her friends. I am there for a full week, so we will meet. Not tonight, though. Can I invite you for dinner tonight?"

Ira replied with a smile.

Is this a date? Ira was wearing a black western shirt with a short skirt. She wore a pair of high heels and a silver necklace. Her hair was tied into a knot at the back of her neck. The bottom of her skirt came to mid-thigh, exposing the luscious curves of her perfect figure. She looked into the mirror in her room in Hotel La Sapphire. She knew Harry would be there during her one-week stay. Did she subconsciously know she would meet Harry in Delhi and he might invite her for dinner someday, and that's why she packed these clothes for a simple teacher conference?

Ira looked at her watch. Harry would be there soon to pick her up. But this was not Toshali where Rohan could spy on who she was having dinner with. Not even Raghupur, where the whole town would know her movement. A silent giggle erupted from her mouth. The only person who knew about her dinner with Harry was Varun. He was the first and only one Ira told about tonight's plan.

"That would be so fantastic, Mum." Ira could feel the thrill in Varun's voice.

"It's just a dinner, why are you so happy?"

"I...my...Mum, Harry is a sort of family friend. And you will get time to know him better."

"Know him better? What do you think I would do *knowing him?*" The word 'date' was taboo in Raghupur in the context of a widow or divorcee, and it had settled in Ira's subconscious. She couldn't imagine how freely she was dating Rahul long ago in Mumbai, even though the word *date* was never in Indian vocabulary until now. The popularity of Hollywood cinema amongst young Indians brought a massive change.

Her cell phone buzzed. Harry must have arrived at the hotel lobby.

JW Lounge—the elegant restaurant in the JW Marriott Hotel. Harry had already booked a table overlooking a pool.

"Thank God, this is Delhi, not our Raghupur," Ira said after cheering her vodka cocktail with Harry's scotch drink.

Harry flashed her a smile. "Why are you so scared of what people would think?"

Ira took a sip and placed the glass on the table. "People in Raghupur think if a woman is having dinner with a man, that might be ..." Ira bit her lips. *Was she going to utter the word 'date'?*

"What?" Harry narrowed his eyes.

"Nothing." A weak chuckle escaped Ira's mouth. She tried to hide her emotions by holding the glass in front of her face and pretending to drink.

"I think people of Raghupur are getting smarter with the growth of their place—going from a small country town to a city. That's good. But why do you care what they think?"

Ira twirled the glass for a while. "Because...because you are not a woman like me—a widow, a teen son, and surrounded by in-laws who are still living two centuries behind." Ira looked out the misted window and felt how her freedom had been curtailed under the weight of the traditions of Raghupur.

She smelt and inhaled *liberation* during the two hours she spent with Harry in the restaurant, drinking and having dinner. Memories of her time with Rahul when both were going to restaurants in Mumbai came alive. It was true, Rahul didn't have that much money then, and both were going to cheap restaurants and looking at the menu for the cheapest drink again and again. But those days were lovely, full of freedom.

"Thanks Harry, for the drinks and dinner," Ira said as they stepped out of the restaurant to the lawn.

"Daddy, surprise!"

Ira was stunned as a charming young woman strode to Harry and hugged him.

"Oh, my girl, is your party over now?" Harry planted a kiss on her forehead.

"Yes, and I came to see who your friend is." Then, looking at Ira, she said, "Hello, I am Joanna, Harry's daughter. You must be Ira."

Ira noticed a proud father in Harry's eyes. "Joanna knew I was here having dinner with you."

"Daddy, your date is so beautiful. I adore her."

Ira felt she was blushing. *Did Harry tell his daughter he was with her for a date? But neither she nor Harry ever planned for a date.*

"We are just friends, Joanna." Harry chuckled.

"Right, but don't remain 'just friends' for long. Okay, Daddy. I will go for another drink with my friends. They are waiting outside. Bye, see you again, Ira."

I should have such a lovely daughter. Ira kept looking after Joanna long after she left.

CHAPTER 13

The next evening, Ira stood near the front door of her niece Mansi's twelfth-floor apartment in Delhi's posh Friends' Colony for a few moments after pressing the doorbell. Two decades' old Bollywood hits blaring through Mansi's front door made Ira slide back to her own past with Rahul. His absence suddenly whispered through her.

"Aunt Ira, so nice to see you after so long." Mansi came forward after opening the door to hug her, but stilled. "Are you all right, Aunt?"

Ira flew back to the present, stepped forward, and took Mansi into a tight embrace. "I am good, tired after an entire day of workshops and this Delhi traffic."

Throwing her handbag on the lamp table, Ira slumped on the sofa when her sister-in-law Nirmala appeared from a bedroom. Ira got up. "Namaste, *didi*. How is your stay in your daughter's home? And where is brother Mehul?"

"He has so many friends in Delhi, when does he stay at home? A friend has invited him for dinner, he will come later," Nirmala said with a smile and sat on the adjacent lounge.

"You didn't go with him?"

"All male gathering, what would I do there?" She let out a loud laugh, and Mansi and Ira laughed along.

"Aunt, let me make some tea for you," Mansi said.

"So nice of you. And where is your husband? What is his name?"

"Karen," Nirmala said before Mansi replied. A playful smile ran across her face. "You know Ira, Karen's mother, she has got a boyfriend."

"Boyfriend? Was she not married?" Ira sat straight and shot her a look.

"She had. But she divorced her husband and moved in with this man. Can you imagine this happening in Raghupur?"

"Mum," Mansi said from the kitchen bench-top, "she was having regular fights with her husband. She fell in love with another man and planned to live with him. Soon they both will marry. What is strange about this?"

"Your father also fights with me. Do you think I could even dream of leaving him for another man?"

"Because you financially depend on him. And also, you live in a town where 'divorce' and 'remarriage' are still a taboo. But time is changing fast, Mum."

Mansi poured hot tea into three cups and brought them to the coffee table. Seated beside Ira, she asked, "Aunt, why don't you stay here for dinner?"

Ira was lifting the teacup to her lips, but stilled. "No Mansi. I am afraid of the traffic. I just wanted to spend some time with you. That's all. By the way, is Karen not back from the office yet?"

Nirmala giggled. "He has gone to help his mother move furniture to her new home."

Mansi suppressed her chuckle. "Mum, why is her remarriage becoming an item of gossip? Just because she has a thirty-year-old son?"

Nirmala sat straight and stared at her daughter. "You said she dared to remarry because she is financially independent. In that case, Ira is also earning money. She can also find another husband if she likes."

Ira didn't respond. Only a few days ago, brother Mehul had come to her apartment before travelling to Delhi. He even advised Ira to find another man, even from another community. Did Nirmala know this from her husband? Was her meeting with Harry just a coincidence? No. Harry invited her only for dinner. It was never a date. A courtesy dinner meeting only.

"Look at her silence," Nirmala commented, "Ira, are you seriously thinking of marrying again?"

Ira inhaled deeply and set her teacup on the coffee table. "Raghupur is neither Delhi nor Mumbai. You don't understand how severely people there would react if a middle-aged woman thought of getting another life partner." She closed her eyes. The weight of society's cruelty was horrendous. "I had a student, Divya, whose father died last year. Her mother found another man and married him. But this poor girl had to leave not only the school but also Raghupur. So much teasing and bullying!"

"I see," Nirmala said quietly. "What she did is great. But we are living in a society and should compromise to their norms, because not everyone has guts to face the consequences. Mehul and I both were so scared when Mansi chose a Christian boy. Thankfully, with a Hindu sounding name, we could..."

"I have an idea!" Mansi left her seat and sat opposite Ira, holding her hands. "Aunt, you are independent and good looking, too. Why do you care what people in Raghupur think of you? You should ask for a transfer to Toshali and find another man. Don't worry about Raghupur. I'm with you."

"Don't mislead your aunt, Mansi. You are from a new generation, different than ours." Nirmala stood up and went to the toilet.

Ira's cell phone buzzed in her bag. She got her handbag from the side table and pulled out her phone. "Varun, how are you? I am sitting in Friends' Colony, with Mansi." She put it on speakerphone so that Varun could say hello to Mansi.

"All right, Mum. Did you meet Harry again after that dinner?"

Ira felt she was blushing. "Varun, can I talk with you later? Okay, bye."

"Aunt, who is this Harry?" Mansi teased.

"Harry? Which Harry?" A current of electricity raced up and down her spine.

A smile pulled across Mansi's mouth, rendering Ira in an awkward situation. Mansi, being her niece, was still a child to Ira, and the culture commanded that elders shouldn't discuss their love life with children or the equivalent.

"Aunt, you are blushing. Don't worry, I won't tell Mum. I know she loves gossiping," Mansi whispered, a flash or something in her expression that Ira couldn't identify before it vanished.

"He is just a friend. I had met him at a party in Toshali. Nothing serious. No need to daydream." Ira tried to maintain a stern face.

"I understand, Aunt. Everything starts with a good friend. Then moves ahead. I can see bright days for you ahead."

Ira looked at her watch. "Mansi, I will get delayed. God knows how much time I will take to go back to my hotel in this Delhi traffic."

She grabbed her handbag and got to her feet, without even waiting for Nirmala to return from the toilet.

CHAPTER 14

Ira's gaze fell on the unusual poster just outside the building gate as soon as she climbed out of the Uber Saturday morning. Her own photo, along with Harry and the chopper in the background, made her breath stop somewhere in her throat. She had seen posters of Bollywood movies on the walls of Raghupur despite *No posters please* signs. She dared to cast another quick glance to avoid the attention of the building security guard. The slanderous sentence just beneath the picture: *My rate is a hundred thousand rupees per night. Only billionaires are welcome to romance with me.*

She felt like throwing up.

For a moment, Ira blamed it all on the early morning flight from Delhi to Toshali and the subsequent bus journey. She had gotten less sleep last night and was exhausted. She rubbed her eyes and looked at the building. But it was still there. The work of Divya's uncle, no doubt. She wished she were tall enough to rip the poster down. Even so, if she were caught, it would only add to the gossip surrounding her.

The security guard had kept the gates open for her. "Good morning, ma'am." He saluted.

Avoiding his gaze, Ira stomped toward the lift. Tears pooled in her eyes when the elevator doors opened and then closed, wrapping Ira inside. The air around her felt stuffy. Thank God none of her neighbours were inside. As she dragged her luggage out of the elevator when she arrived at her floor, her maid, Shanti, was standing near her door.

"*Madamji*," Shanti said with a smile that looked too artificial. "I thought you were already back."

Ira tried to reply with another smile, but couldn't. She digged out the keys from her handbag and unlocked the door.

"*Madamji*, give me your luggage."

"No, Shanti. I can..." She tried her best to control her sob. Why did Shanti have to come as soon as she arrived? She would have run to her bedroom and cried to her heart's content, digging her face into the pillow. Shanti would take at least an hour to clean the apartment. She tried to trudge to her bedroom, but Shanti stood in her way.

"No poster on the walls yesterday, *madamji*. It's wrong to insult women of decent families like you. But, *madamji*, the posters are affixed only on the walls of this building."

Ira didn't reply. She simply slumped on the sofa, and sobs flooded out. Shanti sat near her with her hands on her back. "Don't weep, *madamji*. It's Saturday morning, and many people are still not out of their home. If you want, I will call my husband. He will come with a ladder and water bucket and remove all of them."

What will happen? Ira thought, head still buried. Those who have already seen it must have taken photos, and they'll circulate them through WhatsApp. It would be viral news in Raghupur. Would she call Harry and tell him this? What could he do? Take her out of Raghupur? Not possible. Raghupur was her workplace.

"Shanti." Ira sat up, tears still rolling on her cheeks. "Can you please open all the windows?"

The apartment was locked for an entire week, and the air inside stunk. Fresh air gushed in as Shanti opened the windows. She came back and stood before Ira.

"Someone is trying to tarnish my image." Ira glanced up and met Shanti's gaze. "Can your husband come now? I will pay him money."

"Yes, *madamji*." Shanti took out her mobile from the pocket of her purse and dialled her husband.

Life must go on, and Ira grew more determined than before. A warm shower in the bathroom energised Ira, and her confidence started building again. She had done nothing wrong. The only time she met Harry in Delhi was just a courtesy dinner together. They both still talked like friends, rather than lovers or a couple. Harry had planned to spend time with his daughter, and the day after she met him, both father and daughter headed to Jaipur. Had he known Ira would be in Delhi, he could have planned differently.

How certain could she be that one day she would be Harry's girlfriend?

A knock sounded on the door. Shanti's husband was standing, displaying a smile, when she opened the door.

"*Madamji*, I finished peeling off all the posters. I also checked the nearby buildings, but there was nothing. Only this building."

Ira forced a smile. She had set aside the exact amount negotiated with Shanti and handed it over to him. "Thanks. You may go now."

"Thank you, *madamji*. Any work, just tell Shanti. I will be happy to help." He headed to the elevator and within a second the elevator bell donged.

Mrs. Gupta spilled out. "Hello, Mrs. Ray! Nice to see you again after a week."

Ira couldn't shut the door even if she wished. She continued forcing a smile on her face.

Mrs. Gupta kept staring at the man as he entered the elevator. "Sorry to see the posters. I'm sure someone is trying to settle scores with you."

Was she supposed to give an explanation?

"I know the man behind this." A confidence bloomed in her voice. "I was trying to help the man's niece against his wishes, and he is trying to take revenge even from the prison."

"I know," Mrs. Gupta said, "you were originally from Mumbai. And I, from Kolkata. Nobody bothers you in our cities if you talk to a man. But this is Raghupur, so even if you fart, the neighbours find out. I am here because of my husband's job. He's been trying to get a transfer out and is finally successful after many years. We will go back to Kolkata. I'm so happy!" A smile swept across her face.

Ira could finally let out a chuckle. "Congrats, Mrs. Gupta."

"Thanks. Why don't you try, Mrs. Ray? Your son is in Toshali. If you can get a posting in Toshali, he would be so happy."

"I will." She shut the door.

Ira would write an application now, requesting to get a transfer to Toshali.

CHAPTER 15

An unknown fear halved Ira's confidence by Monday morning when she prepared to go to the school after an entire week. An eerie feeling that something was brewing in her absence and was going to surprise her badly made her nauseous.

For the last two days, she hadn't come out of her apartment, fearing to face the people who might have seen the libellous posters. If she could, she would jump into an intercity bus and go to Toshali permanently. But that was not an option for Ira. She was the sole bread earner of the family and responsible for the higher education of her only son.

Instead of walking to the school as she always did, she booked an Uber and came to the building gate when the cab was about to arrive. She even took the stairs instead of the elevator as on weekday mornings, many people would go to the office from her building. Pretending to be in a hurry, she tried not to look at anyone as she climbed into the cab.

"Good morning, ma'am," the driver said as he started the car.

Ira didn't respond. She kept her head buried in a book which she wasn't even reading. What would happen if the Uber driver knew her and had seen the offending poster?

Within minutes, the cab was at the school gate. "Please drive up to the school building," she pleaded.

When Ira climbed out of the cab and walked into the school office, an assistant teacher who had just come out said, "Principal ma'am wants to meet you."

"Me? Now?" She knew she must see the principal as she would ask about the workshop in Delhi. But was that so urgent? Couldn't it wait until she had no class?

"May I come in?" she asked, approaching the principal's door and peeking inside. Two more teachers were standing near the principal and talking to her.

"Please come in and have a seat."

The teachers left but threw a glance at her. Ira felt as if they all knew what had happened.

"I have a class, ma'am," Ira said as soon as she was the only one with the principal. "Can I come and report to you about the workshop when I have a free period?"

The principal gazed into her eyes for several seconds, and each moment hammered Ira's heart.

"The workshop report can wait," she said. "But this is the time all teachers are in the class. And I have already arranged for another teacher to take your class, so you have some free time with me."

Ira felt her body sweating. She took out her kerchief and wiped her face.

"Someone called and told me about the posters on the school walls yesterday. Thank God it was a Sunday, so no staff might have seen. I managed to clear them last evening. Do you know about them?"

Ira felt her jaw drop, and the universe tilted.

She inhaled a breath and thought for a moment. She could feign ignorance, but it was difficult for her to spill a lie. That was not in her character. And why would she hide anything?

"I know, ma'am. As Divya's uncle was harassing her and her mother, I helped her. I knew this man Harry through a common friend." She swallowed. The common friend was none other than another teacher at the same school, Reema. *Come on Ira, this is not lying. Just don't spill out Reema's name.*

145

"I understand. He is a wealthy man. He came here to help you and the girl. But remember, you are young and beautiful. And wealthy men love to keep mistresses. You must be careful."

"But ma'am—"

A clerk came into the office without even knocking.

"You may go now and prepare for the next class." The principal turned to the clerk, dismissing Ira completely.

Ira lost the golden chance to explain to the principal that she was in no way romantically involved with Harry.

Feeling defeated, Ira got up and headed for the teacher's common room. The hall was empty, as it was first period and all the teachers were in their classes. She pulled up a chair and took a few deep breaths. She closed her eyes. The school felt stuffy, as all the oxygen had drained away. After Rahul's death, she suddenly became an alien in Raghupur. An unwanted person, even for her own extended family. Walking on the road with her head upright would be tough for her now. Could she run away somewhere, forgetting that her absence would mar Varun's education? An educated person like the school principal thought her meeting with Harry was inappropriate. How could she stay away from a man who was the only source of air for her tired lungs? Her knees felt weak.

You will be all right, Ira. Everything is happening for the better. She opened her handbag to take out her cell phone and noticed the folded paper. Her application requesting a transfer. She must give this to the principal to forward to the higher authorities with a recommendation.

Determinedly, Ira got up and headed to the principal's office, hoping nobody would be with her.

In fact, the principal was alone.

She glanced up. "Are you all right, Mrs. Ray?"

"Yes, ma'am. Can I take a seat?"

"Sure."

Ira sat and took out the folded paper. "You are right, ma'am. What you advised me. But I have a request for you."

Surprised, the principal gazed into her eyes. "Tell me."

"Ma'am, you know, after Rahul's death, I've been the sole earning member of the family, and it is really tough to meet my son's education expenses with just one income. I was thinking if I can shift to some school in Toshali, Varun can stay with me, thus saving a lot of money."

The principal snorted softly. "So, you have brought an application requesting a transfer to Toshali, and you want my recommendation?"

"Yes, ma'am." Ira unfolded the paper along with a copy and placed it before her.

The principal read through it and then placed it on the table. "You know, Mrs. Ray, a scam was in the news a few months ago."

Ira leaned back. The news was everywhere. Something inside Ira said she was asking for the impossible.

"Some teachers paid bribes for their favourite placements, and someone spilled the beans. The investigation is now on, and until further notice, the board has stopped all transfers." The principal glanced up at Ira, whose shoulders were deflating. "And this is not the only reason. High School exam is only a few months away. In the past, we have waited for months to get a replacement teacher. What will happen to you if you find some influential person and get yourself a posting in Toshali? Students here will suffer. Who am I to ruin the career of the current twelfth year batch? Mrs. Ray, I am sure you will appreciate my situation."

"I do, ma'am." Ira closed her eyes for a moment and inhaled a quick breath. She must hold back her tears.

"I would have been happy if I could have helped you, Mrs. Ray." The principal looked up, holding the application. "Be care—" She ceased abruptly, avoiding eye contact.

Ira stood up and took the paper from her. Folding the application, she slowly left the room. Ira headed straight to the school garden and settled beneath a flowering Gulmohar, the Royal Poinciana tree. The garden was silent. No one played there. No one laughed, and no one cried. There were no children running around and no one talking in hushed voices. The only sound was the gurgling of the fountain. It was a sad place.

An idea struck her mind. She had only fifteen minutes left for the next class, and the chances the principal would still be alone were slimming. She loped to meet the principal again.

"May I come in, ma'am?" Ira peeked into the room.

"Come in." The principal flashed a confused smile.

"I have come up with an idea." Ira stood in front of her.

"First, take a seat."

"Thanks." Confidence bloomed in her. "Ma'am, my son's education is not the only reason for my request. There's something else, but I didn't want to show that." She knew the principal, even though being a successful career woman, was still a product of the old beliefs. She needed something in her own language to be convinced.

The principal gazed at her without saying a word.

"The other reason is I have no male member at home and am vulnerable. I didn't think to mention that. Some people think they can exploit my situation. I was confident I would pull through. But after what happened yesterday, I am shaky. But I understand your problem, ma'am. Without a replacement teacher, the career of the year twelve students is at stake. You are right. What I suggest, if you can recommend my supplication subject to a substitute, that would be great. I have devoted so much time and energy to my pupils. No disadvantage should affect them because of me. I would also like to stay here until another teacher can come into my position."

A smile appeared on the principal's face as she extended her hand to take the application from Ira. "I will not hold back your application. I will recommend you and send it to the Board of Secondary Education anyway. Then it all depends on your luck. Please deposit this in the school office and take acknowledgement." The principal scratched a note on it and handed it back to Ira with a soft smile.

Ira could barely contain her own grin as she stood and received the paper. "Thank you, ma'am."

Ira didn't wish to open her lunch box during the recess, instead heading straight to the teachers' common room. She was hungry for a bit of mental peace, not food.

The weight of every eye was on her as she entered the hall. Was it because she went to Delhi for the workshop, or because they were aware of the posters?

She wished to share the news with someone, but not with anyone. All her plans could be ruined even if one of her colleagues became jealous and played spoilsport. But was it a cause for celebration? She didn't know if her application would succeed in providing her a Toshali placement. But at least it could pass through the first and toughest hurdle. She could at least talk to Reema.

Ira cast a glance around to find Reema. She had no communication with her since the day Harry helped Divya, and she wondered why she didn't think of talking to her sooner. Did she fear Reema would suspect she was flirting with her friend?

"How was the workshop in Delhi, Mrs. Ray?" Mrs. Das asked as Ira settled on a chair.

"It was good, learned a lot," Ira said flatly.

"Mrs. Ray," Mrs. Patra said, "the entire school is talking about how you helped Divya. You have such good contacts! You even organised a chopper to carry her? Who is Harry?"

Ira blinked at Mrs. Patra's shining face. She couldn't say Harry was Reema's friend. She couldn't bring her friend into their dirty gossip. It was not a sin to lie to save her own or someone else's reputation—an innocent lie which wouldn't harm anyone.

Ira swallowed. "In fact, Mr. Harry—" she was still thinking what to say— "one of my friend's husband who lives in Toshali. He is close to Harry. That morning, I called my friend and asked her for help, as I knew she had contacts. Her husband contacted Mr. Harry. It was a coincidence he was coming here for business and helped to take the girl. Divya's mother was coming back from Agra the same afternoon, and Divya joined her mother."

She glanced around, hoping there wouldn't be more questions.

"I heard Divya's mother remarried to a guy in Toshali?"

Ira nodded slowly. "I also heard the same. Not from Divya, though. She was too weak to talk. Anyway, this is her personal matter. I only wanted the girl to remain safe from the family dispute."

Ira hoped she had answered everything diplomatically. She looked at the wall clock and said, "Oh my God, I need to prepare for my class. I need to go to the library!" Then she scurried off.

Confidence was back in Ira when the school finished at four p.m. She began her walk home when she heard, "Mrs. Ray."

Ira looked back. It was Mrs. Das.

"Mrs. Ray? I think your walking route to your home is through the *Purana Bazar* market, right?"

"Yes, Mrs. Das."

"Good, can I come with you?" She was breathing heavily. "I usually take a cab home. But lately I started walking part of the distance and the rest by taxi. Exercise, you know?" She let out a chuckle. "I will come with you up to the market and take a taxi from there."

"Of course, Mrs. Das." Ira smiled. "Your place is farther than mine. Wise decision."

Ira and Mrs. Das crossed the school gate to the Biju Road.

"You see, Mrs. Ray? You maintain such a perfect figure, all the other teachers think it's because you walk a lot. You never take a cab or autorickshaw to or from the school."

Ira replied with a chuckle. Then both turned left to the *Purana Bazar* market Road. Suddenly, a motor bike stopped in front of them. A man got off and pushed up his helmet visor. Ira's jaw dropped. That was Divya's uncle.

"How are you, Mrs. Ray?" he sneered.

Ira stilled. She wondered how this man, who was in the police custody, had gotten out. Must have gotten bail. Mrs. Das stared between her and the man.

"Do you understand what I can do to someone who meddles in my family affair?"

Ira felt faint.

The man stepped closer and lowered his voice. "The posters you saw are like the trailer of a movie. Just the beginning. The next will be movie posters. Heroine Ira Ray—price five thousand rupees per hour and twenty thousand per night. Full satisfaction guaranteed. Take care." He jumped on his motor bike and sped off.

Ira's body started shaking. She slumped down on the footpath.

"Mrs. Ray, are you all right? Who was this man?"

"He...he is...uncle. Divya." Her voice was shuddering.

"It's not safe for us women to walk on the streets of Raghupur." Mrs. Das stopped a taxi on the road. "Mrs. Ray, let's take this cab, I will drop you off on the way and then go home."

Ira stood and climbed into the cab.

"And it's my advice, Mrs. Ray," Mrs. Das said when the cab moved, "take a few days off and go to Toshali tomorrow morning. For your own safety. Please spend time with your son. I will tell everything to the principal. You can email your leave application to her."

Mrs. Das dropped Ira off in front of her building's gate. As soon as Ira entered the compound, the watchman said, "Ma'am!"

A foul, sweaty smell filled Ira's nose. She shot a glimpse at the guard. This was not his routine. He usually stayed inside his cabin unless some unknown person came. Ira stopped. A few minutes ago, she faced the unthinkable on the streets of Raghupur. She would love to slip into the safety of the four walls of her apartment without wasting more time.

"Ma'am," the watchman said, "a man had come and was looking for you."

Ira staggered backwards, placing a hand over her heart. "A man? Who? When?" The unpleasant experience a few minutes ago came back and slammed Ira hard. Her breath stalled.

"He didn't tell his name. Around an hour ago. I said Ira Ma'am would come back from the school and he should wait. But he went away on his motorbike. He sounded angry."

Ira understood. Divya's uncle had come to her apartment building and then met her on the way.

"Please, tell nothing about me to unknown people." She heard the threat in her head again. '*The posters you saw are like the trailer of a movie. Just the beginning...*'

"Sorry, ma'am." The guard looked down. "I won't. I thought you knew him. I understand you are alone, without a male member at home. I will take care of it, ma'am."

Ira didn't have patience to reply. She loped towards the elevator. Tomorrow morning might be too late. She must pack her bags and leave Raghupur immediately. NOW.

"There is one last bus to Toshali," the booking clerk said as Ira approached for a ticket. "At eight p.m."

Ira flicked a glance at the wall clock. It was half-past six. She would wait. Her gaze fell on the CCTV cameras pointed in various directions. The crowded bus station looked safer than her own apartment. She booked a ticket and headed for the waiting area.

Her cell phone beeped a notification as soon as she took a seat and set the bag on the side. Retrieving the phone from her handbag, Ira swiped it open. Varun had sent a photo in a new dress in WhatsApp. Ira typed a smiley symbol and sent it to him. She then typed a brief message that she would arrive soon in Toshali. Since the incident happened, she had been working like a machine and hadn't had time to talk to her son. Varun's girly photo, possibly taken a few moments ago, smiled at her. She didn't think it appropriate to spoil his moments by offloading her tensions onto him. She kept pressing the erase button until all the words she had typed vanished from the screen.

"Good evening, Miss." A soft female voice alerted her. Ira raised her head.

She smiled widely. "Rupa, how are you? Again, the evening shift?"

Rupa flashed a weak smile and stood closer. "Miss, I started my shift at two p.m. today, the two-to-ten shift. But I was not feeling well and asked the boss if I could finish early. He agreed and let me go."

Concern aroused in Ira's heart. She would love to have a daughter like this girl. "Everything all right?"

"Miss, nothing serious. I get stomach pain during my period," Rupa said after casting a careful glance around and lowering her voice. "And it was difficult to stand at the counter for long."

"How would you go home now?"

"I will take a town-bus."

"I will book an Uber for you; can you spend some time with me here? Only if you have no urgency to go home."

"No need to book an Uber, Miss. Why would you spend money? I am used to..."

"You are like my child, Rupa. I would love to see you be comfortable."

Rupa sat on a chair facing Ira.

"Chai, ten rupees only, chai." Ira's attention went to a hawker announcing his product near her.

"Rupa, would you like some tea? I left home in such a hurry I didn't even get time to have my afternoon tea." Then, without waiting for Rupa's reply, she asked the hawker, "Two cups, please." She took the exact change from her handbag.

The hawker immediately poured the hot beverage into two disposable clay cups from the large thermos he was carrying. The aroma of the hot drink soothed Ira's brain.

"Thank you, ma'am." The man left with a smile.

"These hawkers," Rupa said when the man left, "are no longer allowed inside the bus station once the new depot with food stalls began operation last year. The police will fine him if they see this man selling tea like this."

Ira had already taken a sip. She angled her head. The man had vanished into the crowd. "These people are so poor that they can't afford to rent a stall for their businesses. How do they survive when we change everything so rapidly in the name of development?"

"Stall owners here pay money to the police to keep these vendors out of the premises. Do you remember Nilu, Miss? She was my classmate."

"Nilu?" Ira tried to scratch her brain. How could she remember the names of the thousands of students she had taught? "No."

"Her father had a street stall near this bus station. He lost his business when the new bus terminal was built, and the police forced him and many others to move away."

A sigh came out of Ira's heart. Raghupur was full of misery, and she was not the only one suffering.

"Miss, I have some news."

Ira glanced up at her sharply. A buzz began in her mind.

"Divya's uncle was in police lockup, but he has gotten bail."

"I know." The foul threats the man had fired at her this afternoon were still raw inside her. *Do you understand what I can do to someone who meddles in my family affair?*

"Miss, he is a dangerous man. You must be careful with him."

Ira couldn't rewind what she had done to help Divya. She couldn't afford to take unlimited leave. Once her leave balance was finished, she must risk her life to work in the school or remain without income. How would she sustain herself and Varun's study expenses? Her stomach churned. She fought the urge to flee somewhere. That was not possible. She must find ways to fight against everything for her survival.

An announcement came over the PA. "Attention, passengers. There is an earlier special bus to Toshali. Those who have booked for the eight p.m. bus can shift to this bus. Please approach the ticket counter to exchange your tickets."

"I am booking the Uber for you." Ira took her cell phone and swiped the Uber app on her screen. "What is your address?"

Once Rupa was on her way in the Uber and Ira was seated comfortably on the bus, she texted a message to Varun when the bus started rolling. *I am arriving in Toshali by nine p.m. See you soon.*

CHAPTER 16

Ira was reading the *Toshali Press* newspaper and sipping tea the next morning in the lounge room of Varun's shared apartment. Sam had already left for his office.

"I will skip classes today and stay with you. I think…"

Ira looked up. "Why Varun?"

A look flitted through his eyes. "Mum, you might be under stress with what happened yesterday."

Ira breathed deeply. She had told Varun everything last evening.

She sprayed some confidence in her smile and placed the newspaper on the coffee table. "I'm your mother, Varun. Not the other way around. I know this is a problem, and yes, I was scared. But that doesn't mean I will run away from Raghupur forever. I will find a way out. And I don't want you to miss your classes."

Concern rode in Varun's eyes. But he hooked his backpack around his shoulder and got to his feet. "Okay, see you in the evening." He left the apartment.

Ira took the newspaper again and began reading. But her mind was wandering everywhere other than the piece of paper she was holding before her eyes.

"I have the *balls* to fight with anybody to protect you." Rahul's voice when Ira came to Raghupur after her wedding buzzed in her brain. Her Mumbai lifestyle had become an eyesore to some people in that small town. '*Rahul has brought a fashion model from Mumbai, not a wife. Wait and see, she will run away with someone in no time.*'

"Do I need balls to fight all the challenges coming my way?" Ira laughed at her own thought. How could a woman have balls? That didn't mean she couldn't fight.

Ira took another sip from the teacup. It was already cold. She ambled to the kitchen to make another tea.

Her cell phone buzzed. Reema's name flashed on the screen.

Reema. Her only close friend among all the colleagues at the school. She knew Reema was on leave, and she hadn't had time to tell her about Divya and how Harry helped her. It was she who had introduced her to Harry, and she would eventually know that Harry had come with his chopper on a mere phone call from Ira.

"Hi, Reema." Ira filled the electric kettle with water. "How are you?"

"I am fine." Her voice was weak. "I was thinking of going back to Raghupur and start working, but my sister insisted on taking a few more days off. I might go there this afternoon."

Sister? Isn't Reema with her husband?

"Are you in Toshali?"

"Yes, why?"

"No, just asking."

"Are you all right, Ira? Where are you? Toshali?"

How does Reema know I am in Toshali?

"Ira, are you there?"

"Yeah. My... I..."

"Mrs. Das called me and told me about the man who threatened you yesterday."

Ira sounded a mirthless laugh. "Price of helping a girl. This is a man's world anyway, you know."

"Don't worry, Ira. Everything will be all right. I will talk to you when you are back at the school."

Ira dipped a tea bag in the cup and added some milk. She could have visited Reema, but Reema was planning to go back to Raghupur this afternoon.

After their call ended, she went to the lounge room again and slumped onto the sofa, setting the cup on the coffee table. Then she opened WhatsApp and started surfing through it. Harry had sent a few photos of his travel to Jaipur with his daughter Joanna. One photo was of herself with Harry in front of the hotel they had dined in while in Delhi. Joanna had taken the shot. Her comment sounded in her mind, "Daddy, your date is so beautiful. I adore her."

Did Joanna really think she was her dad's girlfriend? Her pulse danced inside her ribcage.

No, it was odd. Harry was just a good friend. She shouldn't day-dream.

The phone buzzed again. Harry was on the other end.

"Hi Ira, I noticed you are online and not in the class. A free period?"

Harry's bass voice made vibrations in Ira's heart, but she managed to let out a mild chuckle. "No Harry, I'm not in school. I'm in Varun's apartment."

"You in Toshali? Another holiday?"

She let out a mirthless laugh. "No. Are you still in Delhi, or are you back here?" She weighed if she should share all her problems with a man just because he was helping in nature. Wasn't it unjust to ask for help again and again?

"I am back in Toshali. Is everything all right, Ira?"

"Not that bad. But I... I will tell you when we meet. I don't wish to disturb you when you are in the office. I'm sure you are missing Joanna."

"Ira, believe me, I am free. I have hired many people to work for me so that I can have free time. I can come there to pick you up."

Ira thought for a moment. She didn't feel comfortable with Harry picking her up, as if someone from Raghupur were watching her every movement.

"What if you just let me know the address of your office, and I take a cab there?"

"As you like. Okay, I'm texting the address and you text me as soon as you are in the taxi. All right?"

"Yes."

"See you soon." Harry hung up.

The teacup was still sitting idle on the table. She thought for a moment to finish the beverage and then dress up. But Harry was a hundred million times more important than anything else in the world. She breezed into the bedroom.

Ira stared at the building after getting out of the cab. A small, two-storied building on a quiet street with a few shops around. No signboard of Harry's company. She unlocked her cell phone to check the address again from Harry's text, and typed the address into Google Maps. The taxi could have dropped her off at a wrong place, and Google Maps was definitely more reliable.

A BMW stopped nearby in front of a restaurant called Dine and Wine. A couple climbed out of it and walked inside. Next to the restaurant was a beauty parlour.

Her gaze fell on the house number. 39 Hope Street. As she approached the main door, it opened automatically and closed behind her when she stepped into a lobby. A pleasant perfume was in the air. She glanced around, but there was nobody. *What type of office is this?* Unknown fear rose in her belly, and she turned around to leave, but saw Harry coming out of a room and stopping in front of her with a broad grin.

"Welcome to my office, Ira. Please come with me."

Floral perfume washed over Ira as she walked with Harry into his office. With the Orchid plants along the back wall and frilly curtains on the windows, the entire room looked as if it was anything but a regular office. She glanced around—only sofas, no office table or chairs. And not a single employee around.

"Let's sit here." Harry lowered onto a sofa.

"What type of office is this? No employees!" Ira still couldn't believe she was in fact inside Harry's office.

"This was my workplace when the company was small. It moved to a larger building. But I am keeping this as a memory. Sometimes I hold meetings here and sometimes I spend some time here quietly for introspection. One attendant helps me when I come here alone, but today he is on holiday. Please, get comfortable."

Ira was still speechless. She didn't know what to say or where to start.

"Can I get some water?" she said, seating herself on a matching sofa.

"Oh, sure." He got up and brought her a water bottle from the fridge. Then sitting on the side of the sofa, he asked, "Anything else? Coffee?"

"Not now." Ira took a few gulps of the water and placed the bottle on the side table.

"So, spent some quality time with your daughter?" She brought a smile to her face, still wondering if she should bring up her personal problems.

"I did." Harry closed his eyes for a moment. "But I want to know what happened when you were in Raghupur. Did that horrible man come to you?"

Tear pooled in Ira's eyes, but she managed to hold them back. "He came and warned me of the consequences. That's why I came running here, to figure out how to deal with this."

Ira's cell phone buzzed inside her bag. She flicked a look at the handbag but avoided taking the call. Time with Harry was more important than anything else.

The phone shrilled again and again.

"Please take the call. Might be important," Harry said.

Ira fished out the phone. "Oh my, call from the principal." She swiped it to answer mode. "Hello, ma'am."

"Mrs. Ray, how are you?" The principal's voice was soft and full of concern.

"Thanks, ma'am, for asking. I am fine."

"You can't be fine. Mrs. Das told me about the incident. I am really sorry about what happened. You have done what you could do for the harassed student at our school, but this is not what we expect."

Ira let out a sigh.

"Mrs. Ray," the principal said again, "I have mentioned the incident on your transfer application and sent it to the Board of Secondary Education with a strong recommendation and as a special case. Hopefully, you will be lucky. Until then, I advise, stay on leave. For your own safety."

Soft solace washed through her. "Thanks, ma'am."

"Okay, take care. Bye."

Ira put the phone back in her bag and gazed into Harry's eyes. "I was going to tell you."

"I could hear everything. I will do my best to keep that bastard behind bars. And also, I will try with my contacts in the education ministry for your quick transfer to some high school in Toshali."

Ira tried to say something, but she couldn't control her tears, which she'd been holding back until now. She got up and took Harry into a tight hug. Then, burying her head in his chest, she sobbed.

Harry moved his palm on her back and caressed. "Everything will be all right, Ira. This is only for a short period, and you will overcome."

Ira released Harry from the hug, but Harry's arms were still around her. He gazed into her eyes. Harry pulled her in again and planted a kiss on her lips. For a few moments, both were lip locked. But then Ira came back to her senses. This was not Rahul's kiss. Guilt overflowed her emotions, and she released herself immediately from his arms.

"I am sorry, I shouldn't have done this." She yanked her handbag and loped toward the door.

Harry caught her hand and stopped her. "Don't worry, Ira, this is my private place, and nobody would notice us."

Each of Harry's words sounded genuine to her. She didn't wish to hurt the only person whose presence lighted positivity inside her soul. Ira stilled, and then returned to the sofa. The air around her was relaxing and she could spend hours here with Harry. She wanted to enjoy every moment of this life and she knew that she needed to stop dwelling on the past. She felt happy and carefree as she inhaled the fresh, clean, air. It was a feeling that she hadn't experienced for a long time. It felt wonderful. She wondered if Harry was still just a friend or if this was turning into something more. A smile escaped her lips. "Thank you."

CHAPTER 17

"**M**y application must pass through all the red tapes of the bureaucracy of the education department," Ira replied to Varun.

"Why, Mum? Can't we use social media and get sympathy from the public?" Varun said while eating his breakfast at the dining table. For the last few days Ira had been in Toshali, she had cooked breakfast and dinner for both Varun and Sam. Sam had already left for his office.

"Because you are not the only one who knows the benefits of social media. People also use it to spread malicious propaganda."

A WhatsApp notification pinged on her cell phone. Ira swiped across the screen. A sexy joke from Harry. She typed a smiley image and sent it back. Harry was like a young boy in the matters of romance. Then she realised she was in the middle of something with Varun.

"Yes, as I was saying, those same people who would sympathize for me would also use social media to harass someone they don't like. Don't you think the posters on the school buildings are still circulating in photos taken of them? They will use those to counter your FB posts. Then what?"

"But, Mum..."

"No *but,* Varun. The principal has written a strong recommendation citing harassment for me. Harry will do his best to push the application through the red tape. We need to be patient and wait."

Varun went into the washroom after finishing breakfast, and Ira's phone rang. For the past two days after she met Harry in his private office, she had received several calls from him. Even though they had discussed nothing about love, the talks were on shallow subjects. But Ira had enjoyed everything that Harry had said. His voice on the phone always brought a thrill and made her day. She could've spent her entire life just listening to Harry's talks.

"Harry, how are you?" Ira lowered her voice so that Varun wouldn't hear. She was like a teen who talked to her boyfriend secretly from the overprotective parents.

Varun came out of the washroom. She thought about slipping inside the privacy of her bedroom and talk to Harry. But a mother hiding from her son?

"Harry, can I.... Varun is about to go to his college."

"Mum, don't worry. Please continue to talk." He rushed to his bedroom to get his backpack.

"Ira, will it be okay if we go somewhere this evening for a proper date?"

"Date?" Ira glanced around, and Varun stood there with a naughty smile on his face. Her eyes rounded and widened. "Today's date is...can I call you later?" She killed the call.

"Mum, was he asking for a date? So nice of him. Please go, Mum. He is such a nice man."

"Varun, where did you learn about these *date* things? Watching English movies? Remember, we are not in a western country," Ira said, blending in as much fake anger as she could, but her nerves made everything inside her vibrate.

"Come on, Mum. Don't pretend. Dad was dating you in Mumbai. You became a changed woman after living in Raghupur. Remember, Toshali is nothing less than your Mumbai or any European or American city."

"But on a date? Yes, we had gone out together, but that wasn't..."

"Same thing, even if you didn't use the word *date* then."

A sigh leaked from her mouth. "No Varun, this evening..."

"Mum, I am going with a friend this evening. I forgot to tell you last night. You will be alone here. Of course, Sam can give you company..."

Ira waved him off. "Okay, I will go with him for dinner. He was asking for a suitable date for having dinner, not a *date* date."

"I understand. Bye, Mum. Have a nice evening together." Varun took his backpack and left the flat.

Divine thrill danced through Ira at the thought of a *date* as she returned Harry's call to make plans for the evening.

Ira put on a black western shirt with a short skirt. She wore a pair of high heels and a silver necklace. Her hair was tied into a knot at the back of her neck. The bottom of the skirt came to mid-thigh, exposing the luscious curves of her perfect figure.

She stood before Rahul's photo in Varun's room. "Rahul, didn't you always love to see me in sexy clothes? And you also wanted me to find a partner who would give me similar love, like you. I think I am close to the dream. But I will always love you with all my heart. Love you, Rahul."

A text pinged on her phone. *I am near the gate.*

It was four p.m.

Locking the apartment door, Ira slipped into the elevator, and within minutes she arrived at the building's gate. Harry was opening the passenger door of his black Ferrari. A smile pulled across his mouth, rendering Ira weak in the wrong places.

"Get in, please." He pointed at the passenger seat.

Ira tossed her cute curls and got inside. Harry rounded the front of the car and settled into the driver's seat.

"Where are we going?" Ira asked with a grin on her lips.

Harry tilted his head towards her and smiled. "Trust me. I am not the guy who would lure a beautiful girl for nefarious intentions."

A giggle slipped out of Ira's mouth. "I am also not a naïve young girl who would make love over the net. I am a mother of an eighteen-year-old."

Harry chuckled. "Yes, we both are sort of old, but still young in mind."

Bela Bhumi Sands. The Ferrari rolled into the wide gates of the resort. Ira had heard of this luxurious resort on the shore of the Bay of Bengal, hardly a forty-five minutes' drive from Varun's apartment and fifteen minutes from the border of Toshali City. A resort for extra wealthy tourists and affluent locals.

Has Harry booked a room for an overnight stay? But there was no such plan! We are coming for the evening only!

Harry drove the car on a paved road, leaving the reception area behind. A warm and pleasant breeze carried the scent of the ocean from about a hundred meters away when Ira lowered the tinted window. It smelled like salt and sand, mixed with the aroma of coconut trees. The sea was to the left; on the right were the cottages with tall pine and coconut trees in the background.

Finally, the car came to a still near a shed, facing the sea.

"These sheds on the private beach are rented out by Bela Bhumi Sands," Harry said as he got off the car and came to the passenger side as Ira exited. He looked really sweet. They were so close to each other, and Harry was smiling. It was a nice experience.

"Good afternoon, ma'am. Good afternoon, sir."

Ira swung around to face a young woman in a hotel uniform, with a tray holding a wine bottle and two wine glasses. She set the bottle and glasses on the table.

Harry pulled a chair and signalled Ira to take a seat as he sank in by her side.

"Would you like me to pour the wine into the glasses, ma'am?" the server asked.

"Yes, please," Ira said.

The woman poured the drink into the glasses and set out plates with nibbles. "Enjoy the evening, ma'am and sir." She pulled the thick curtain around the shed, leaving only the seafront open.

"Thanks." Ira cast a quick glance at Harry. He gave her a flirty smile. She felt the heat rise through her whole body, but managed to look away until she was sure the server had left.

Comfort brewed in her, knowing that a privacy hedge and distance separated the sheds from one another.

Harry reached for Ira's hand and secured it on his lap. The thrilling passion moved up in Ira's body as she enjoyed the masculine warmth of his skin and the strength of his fingers.

She met his eyes. "I am still not convinced a widow and mother of a teen should date a man."

"Times are changing, Ira. You have every right to lead a happy life, no matter what your past circumstances are," Harry whispered and brought his face closer, his hot breath massaging her cheeks.

Even when Ira was going out with Rahul before their wedding, they had never kissed. Public display of love was a western thing. But a private show of affection? Harry and Ira were in their private space and, as far as she could tell, the sheds nearby were unoccupied.

"Ira, I really want to kiss you. If you consent."

A giggle slipped from her lips. "Okay, dear." She took his face with both her hands and brought her lips to his. Harry kissed her, matching his mouth with hers. He threaded his fingers through her hair and then held her face in his hands.

Ira hadn't had so much warmth in a long time, and it was like getting a rebirth. For a new life, and a new love.

"Please drop me off at least a hundred meters from the building," Ira said as the car was about to reach the destination. Her first official date had come to an end, but she was happy about this.

"I forgot to say," Harry said, "tomorrow morning, I am going to Mumbai."

Ira slammed fists on her hips. "Why would you tell me? Who am I?"

Harry glanced at her with a guilt-ridden smile. "Nothing like that. The date for the Mumbai visit slipped my mind. Ticket was booked already. My secretary just texted now and reminded me about my flight, because in the past I have missed a few."

Ira chuckled at the reply. "You forget so many things. Don't feel like you have to get out of the car, Harry. Thank you for a wonderful evening. Good night." She exited and loped towards the building without looking back, afraid that someone would see her with a man on a secret romantic mission.

As soon as she approached the elevator, Reema called.

"Ira, good news. Guess what?"

A whisper of fear curled through Ira. What could have happened? Divya's uncle arrested again? So what? He would just get out on bail again.

"No idea, Reema. Please don't create suspense."

"Okay, my dear. I am the acting principal, as the principal is sick."

"Congratulations, Reema." Ira pressed the button of the lift.

"Did I call you only to say I am the officiating principal? No. I received a letter from the Board of Secondary Education, and they have approved your application. You are joining Kalyani Girls High School in Toshali. Not very far from Varun's apartment. So, start looking for an accommodation and move out as soon as possible. I haven't told anyone in the office."

Ira squealed and spun in a circle, her hand going to her head and her face splitting open in a wide grin. *I'm moving to Toshali permanently!* "Thanks, Reema, this is not good news, but great news! I will miss you in the school, but this is the best thing that could happen for me."

"You deserved it, dear."

The elevator arrived and doors slid open. "Thanks, Reema, good night!"

Harry stayed true to his word and reached out to his contacts. This transfer is happening so quickly because of him.

She entered the lift and quickly typed a message for Harry. *Thanks for the follow up, letter has come for my transfer to Toshali. Love you.* She inserted a heart symbol with an arrow in it.

CHAPTER 18

Ira handed a five-hundred rupee note as a tip to the building watchman as she entered her apartment in Raghupur, holding a bouquet and a few gift bags.

"Joining a school in Toshali. Transfer. Shifting tomorrow morning," Ira said to the watchman.

"Thank you, ma'am. And the bouquet is beautiful." The security guard grinned and saluted.

She typed a text to Varun as she entered the lift. *Farewell party at the school over. Got a bouquet and gifts. Colleagues are shocked.*

Her mobile chimed. Ira pulled it from her handbag. *Mum, the packer will arrive by seven in the morning. So, please empty the fridge and switch it off.*

All right, my child. She smiled at the mobile and tucked it inside the bag before unlocking the main door.

Oh my God, it was such a long and tiring day. She plunged into the sofa and stretched her legs onto the coffee table. To meet with each of her colleagues was not that difficult, but explaining to each of them why she was moving to Toshali was tough. The answer, *Varun and I would stay together* cut little ice. Only Reema and the principal knew the real reason behind it, but they had planned to keep quiet to save Ira from any retaliation from Divya's uncle.

"You must practise leaving your son alone, Ira," one teacher had advised. "He is a student there, and the day he finishes his studies, he will find a job. And what is the guarantee he will work in the same city?"

Ira had replied with only a nod and a smile.

"Boys at this age prefer to live independently," another colleague had said, as if she were a part-time psychiatrist besides teaching in a school. "He might find a girlfriend, and he will be looking forward to living separately from a mother who is constantly looking after him."

She would love if Varun came to her with a girl one day. But what type of girl would want to have a boyfriend who has no facial hair and loves to wear dresses? She knew most crossdressers were not gay, if she were to believe the Internet sites—she had gone through several times to confirm her belief.

"You are correct, Rita, but we both are aware of such matters." Ira attempted to convince her when there was no need. "And I would love if he came home with a girl. But he is so busy with his studies, he has no time for romance."

Only Reema, her closest friend among the colleagues in the school, was understanding.

"You must try to find single men in the city, Ira," Reema had whispered to her.

She loved that naughty smile on Reema's face when they both slipped away for a walk on the school lawn.

"Single men are not waiting for me when I visit Toshali," Ira replied with another mischievous chuckle.

She thought of telling Reema about her meetings with Harry, her dates with him. But something stopped her. How could Ira discuss the sexy texts Harry sent to her?

"This small town is so orthodox, there would be gossips if you even think of another marriage. But Ira, times have changed. In a multicultural city, you are an unknown person, even to your next-door neighbour. You are a beautiful woman. Don't miss this chance."

"All right, Reema. I will send you an invitation to my wedding. Only if I marry." She chuckled again. But a tickle had passed through her nerves, thinking of no longer being a widow. Another man would come into her life.

"And your son," Reema said, "he is smart. He should accept a stepfather in his life. Anyway, he is a major now."

"Varun has encouraged me to get remarried."

"You are such a lucky mother, Ira. I hope my son would be that understanding."

"But you have a husband already, Reema. Do you still wish to marry again?"

"No, Ira. But I don't understand why the thought of another wedding brings such a thrill to me. You know, I have an astrologer friend. She has said I have another marriage written on my hand."

"Is that true?"

Reema glanced around for eavesdroppers.

"Will you promise me you won't reveal this to anyone? You are the only one who I speak my mind to."

"I promise, Reema."

"My husband. He was so handsome when I married him. But now, he is fat—enormous belly and partly bald. You wouldn't believe it. Nowadays I avoid going with him to parties."

Ira had seen Reema's husband on her twenty-fifth wedding anniversary. But she also knew Reema stayed with her sister when she was in Toshali. Could she read between the lines?

"You never go with him?"

"He is always busy with his business, so I get the excuse to go alone. But sometimes I dream about having another man."

Ira pondered over Reema's startling confession while still seated on her sofa, but soon she drifted off.

She woke to a text on her phone. Varun had sent the name of the mover. She didn't have the luxury of sitting idly this evening and musing over Reema. She must pack her clothes and jewellery tonight. But Reema's last words were sticking to her mind.

I dream of having another man in my life.

Ira got up from the sofa and trudged to the bedroom, stopping in front of her dressing-table mirror. *Am I maintaining the same figure from when I was in college?*

She removed her saree and deposited it on the bed. Standing only in a petticoat and blouse, she glanced at her belly. It was no longer flat, but not prominently big. She must join a gym and take care of it. And boobs? They were proudly smiling at her from the mirror.

An urge snaked inside her groin. *Congrats, Ira. Your new romance is waiting for you in the city.*

Ira's stomach growled. *Oh my, why am I daydreaming? I have so much to do, pack the clothing and cook.*

The next morning, Ira's entire household sat in the mover's truck. She was ready to travel to Toshali. Ira went for a last time inside her apartment.

Rahul's photo smiled at her from her bedroom wall. She had planned to take the photo in the bag she would be carrying with her.

"You are still my love, dear." She kissed the photo. "Didn't you tell me I should start another life after you? I am sure that came from your heart. But Rahul, I will admit something to you from my heart. Will you listen to me?"

She felt Rahul was meeting her gaze and at any moment would jump out and kiss her. She removed the photo from the wall and held it tightly.

"You are a bold man. I'm sure you can take it. Rahul, I want a man by my side. Love you, Rahul."

"Whom are you talking to, Ira?"

The photo nearly dropped from her hand. Urvi's voice trespassed her living area. Did Ira leave the front door open?

Of course, the front door was open, and Urvi stood in her empty lounge room.

"I saw the mover truck leaving the premises. Watchman said you are moving to Toshali!" Urvi's voice hid lots of complaints.

Ira couldn't think how to face this cousin of hers. She was dressed like a college girl and feared this wouldn't go over well with Urvi's dirty gaze.

Did Urvi hear me talking about my forbidden desire?

Ira's brain felt trapped in quicksand, and she was sinking in it.

"Whose photo is that, Ira? Were you kissing the photo of another man? Who is he? Did you get a lover?" Urvi's eyes were digging into each of Ira's movements.

Thankfully, like a protective husband, Rahul came to her rescue. Ira held the photo in front of Urvi. "Yes, Urvi. A man's photo. The man I always loved."

A flash of embarrassment crossed Urvi's face. "Sorry, dear, I thought—you are such a beautiful woman. Any man would die for you."

Ira smothered a grin. For the first time, she heard Urvi praising her.

"Yes, Urvi. I'm still dying for this man, Rahul. This photo is my most precious possession. And sorry, I have nothing here to offer you to sit on. In fact, I was about to leave and take a bus to the city."

Ira wished Urvi would leave.

Urvi slumped to the tiled floor. Sweat beaded on her forehead, and tears pooled in her eyes.

"What happened, Urvi? Why are you crying?"

"You are a modern woman, Ira. You can convince my son."

"Your son?"

"I don't want to take that wretched boy's name. He has ruined my family and now will ruin my honour.

Ira had never imagined Urvi's high-flying, perfect family could crash to the ground with the slightest shock. But she was, in fact, in a hurry. She should arrive in Toshali before the mover's truck so that she could be present when they unloaded.

"Urvi, can we talk some other time? I promise, I will call you immediately when the mover unpacks my home in the city. I must arrive there before time. You know, Varun..."

"Your Varun is a likeable lad, Ira. So what if he has long hair. Nowadays, so many young men are sporting long hair and pierced ears. And look at this boy, Amit. He has now changed his name to *Amita* and propagating it on Facebook. He has no shame."

Varun's praise from Urvi's mouth?

"I feel I could have time to spend with you. To be on your side when you need me. But Urvi, control yourself. Times are changing, and we have no say how our children will live their lives."

"I don't care if he lives or dies. But I am worried about my husband's life. He already had one heart attack. And when he finds his son is becoming a man's *wife*, he will get a massive attack."

"I'm deeply sorry, Urvi. I didn't know this, otherwise I would have come to your home."

"What, you're sorry? You didn't even tell me you got a transfer and are leaving Raghupur forever." Urvi stood up.

Thank God, Urvi might leave. Ira looked at her watch. "I promise, Urvi. I will talk to Amit."

"You will? Please Ira, save my family."

"Promise. Please go home and be with your husband. Tell him to breathe and forget unnecessary worries. His life is more important than any Amit or *Amita*."

Ira ran to take the express bus. A sigh came out of her mouth. Urvi's weeping face glared before her mind's eyes.

A perfect family is breaking up! As sad as this made her, she knew God would help Urvi to cope.

As the bus crossed the boundaries of her soon to be ex-hometown and entered the freeway, Ira's mind speeded to the generation which was determined to have a different life. A life she couldn't understand. Ira looked through the window. Raghupur was slowly disappearing behind her.

She felt an overwhelming sense of loss. Ira took a deep breath and exhaled slowly. Getting out of Raghupur was not just an option for her. She couldn't stay in a place where she was not wanted. Where her humanly act was rewarded with offensive posters and threats.

"Ticket, ma'am." The conductor was standing near her seat.

"One ticket to Toshali City Centre, please." She took rupee notes from her handbag and gave them to him.

Would she call Amit and ask him to leave his gay life and become a straight person? The life society expects? Was this possible? Was Amit gay by choice or gay from his birth and his family knew only now? Ira was not an expert in sexual choices other than the love between a man and woman. She always thought men were straight by nature and some become gay. Was she wrong? But she must talk to Amit.

"But why? Why did I promise Urvi in a hurry?" she asked herself. "Was it because I meant it, or because I wanted to get rid of her as I was in a hurry to catch the bus?"

Her own life hung between two separate worlds. Could she just select one she liked and reject the other?

"Your ticket, ma'am. And here is the change."

Ira took the ticket and change.

"Your ticket, sir?" the conductor asked the passenger next to her.

"Ma'am, not sir," the passenger corrected and handed money to the conductor.

A strong masculine scent forced Ira to notice, and she cast a sideways glance at the person. He or she? She was also confused, like the conductor. Short, boy-cut hair, tall and flat chested. She was sure the woman must be gay.

No, how many men and women were coming out as gay? But at least this new world wouldn't frown if a widow married again even if she had an adult son.

Ira's head reeled when her thoughts oscillated between two radical situations. *What if Varun decides for a sex change operation? Could I show my face to my friends and relatives after my son became a woman? This is even more shameful than if a man becomes gay and lives with another man. At least he wouldn't be wearing a frock.*

Ira inhaled a deep breath and closed her eyes. She was fleeing to the city so that she could lead a life she loved. Get another love. What if some people found love with same sex?

"City Centre stop," the bus conductor announced.

"Your apartment is locked, ma'am," the truck driver said.

She didn't answer the driver as she hopped into the lift to her new third-floor apartment she had rented. Varun had always been a responsible boy, and he should have been there even before the mover's truck arrived. Didn't she text him the instant the movers left her building in Raghupur?

Locked door. Varun wasn't there. How could it be possible?

I forgot. Why did I forget to contact Varun when the bus left Raghupur? I was inside Urvi's collapsing world. But what happened to Varun? He also could have called me. Where do I get the key now?

She fished out her mobile from her handbag. This boy needed a little motherly warning. So what if he was eighteen and had become an adult?

Ira looked at her phone in disbelief when the screen stayed black. *Did I press the right button?* She flipped the mobile on its side and pressed the correct button, with full attention.

"You are so careless, Ira," she mumbled to herself. "You forgot to recharge your mobile."

Ira glanced around. Thank God there was no one to mock her for her self-talk. Impatience and guilt crushed through her chest. The movers would charge extra for having to stay longer. And where would she get a phone to call Varun?

She trudged to the lift and pressed the down button, trying to remember Varun's phone number.

"Hello, Ira. How are you?" A pleasant scent and familiar voice greeted her from inside the elevator as soon as the door opened and she was about to step in.

"I... I am fine." She stepped back, her gaze fixed on Harry's smiling face.

"Sorry, I am a bit late. Traffic jam." He pulled out a key bunch from his pocket. "The truck waiting below is carrying your household, I believe."

Ira's mouth went bone dry. Harry! With her house keys! When did she inform him she was moving today?

"Yes. And Varun couldn't come here in time. He is usually..."

"I know, Ira. Varun is a responsible boy. He gave me this key as he is in the hospital." Harry gave the keys to Ira.

"Hospital?" Ira staggered backward. "Where? What happened to him?"

Harry flashed an assuring smile. "Nothing. He is attending Sam. He had an appendectomy."

Ira spun to the door, holding the key bunch so that Harry wouldn't notice the frown on her face. She couldn't fathom Varun announcing on social media that he and Sam were a same-sex couple, or that Sam was his boyfriend.

"Varun said this flat is available only for six months." Harry's voice echoed as he stepped inside the empty apartment, following Ira.

"Sorry, can't offer you anywhere to sit until my sofa comes here."

"Don't worry. I will be here to supervise the movers bringing all your household goods and placing them correctly. Do you have a list of how many packages went into the truck?"

"Oh, yes." Ira took out a folded paper from her bag. "But Harry, don't you need to go to the office? I don't want to take advantage. I am s—"

"My CEO manages the company. And don't worry, this is my pleasure."

The movers brought the first item inside.

"This is the sofa." Harry ticked off one item from the list and bent down to remove the protective packaging from it.

Ira stopped him. "Sorry, Harry, I have a contract with the movers. They will remove the packaging and keep all the furniture the way it should be."

"Don't worry, Ira. Don't you want to unwind on a sofa while drinking tea?"

Ira tried to hold back her chuckle, but it came anyway. "Yes, I want to quit everything and just focus on the tea. But..."

"But what? Movers are doing their work, and you have a new manager called Harry to see the shifting finishes with no trouble."

This time Ira didn't even try to hide her smile.

The workers continued bringing piece after piece of her furniture, fridge, TV, and whatever they had packed into their vehicle that morning. All of Ira's worries seemed temporary as she drank tea, sitting with Harry and watching the workers.

"Love this tea." Harry had satisfaction written all over his face.

She loved his appreciation. "Yeah, I love to have some ginger infused tea in the morning."

Ira recollected how Rahul's assuring smile and convincing words almost kept her in a world where she never knew what stress was. Rahul's biceps and wide chest were her sanctuary from everything.

Did she have the same feeling sitting near Harry? Or was this just fleeting? Like a sweet dream? Only about two weeks ago she had gone on a date with him. Can Harry give her the same love she was getting from Rahul?

Without Harry's clout and active follow up, no matter of recommendation from the principal could have secured Ira such a quick transfer. A longing to hug Harry and feel his muscular chest brewed inside her. She had to control her urge. She was not a teen and must behave like a mother of a teen.

The movers had placed all the items and finished removing the packaging. Ira and Harry had finished three rounds of tea when she realised it was around noon. And Varun still hadn't called her.

"See this boy, he is so careless. Didn't get time to even call me."

"You are forgetting Ira. First, locate where you packed your charger and put it to charge. And Varun is a nice boy. He has been texting with me and knows exactly what is happening here. He knows we are having a pleasant time sipping tea in your new home."

Ira ransacked her belongings to find the mobile charger and connect it to a power point.

"Harry, I hope you don't mind if I cook something for lunch. I will try to be quick."

Ira opened a small box containing vegetables she had arranged last evening. But Harry reached for her and held her hand. A pleasant current–of warmth, of something else–flowed between them. Ira felt a rush of blood in her face. She pulled away from Harry and bent to put the box on the table. She turned to look at him. His face was bright with excitement. He moved closer and looked down at her. Ira smiled back at him.

"You must have been working hard all night packing, and this is not the time to cook. I'm sure you can manage one day with restaurant food," Harry said.

"But Harry, you have been helping me since this morning."

"Exactly. And Varun has texted me not to leave. He wants me to wait so he can have lunch with me. He is bringing takeaway food and will be here soon. Sam's operation is over, and he is free now."

"Varun? Coming here?" A sigh came from Ira's mouth, which she stopped just in time.

"He would have texted you, but he doesn't know if your mobile is alive now. But if you don't find it comfortable, then let me call him and ask to cancel the order."

"No Harry, all I said is that I would have cooked lunch for you. But if Varun is already on his way, then let's wait and have food together." How could Ira say like any Indian parent she was uncomfortable being with a man she adored in the presence of her own son?

"That's a nice girl." Harry chuckled and got up to arrange the vegetables inside the fridge. "At least when Varun arrives, he will see that I was helping his dearest mother."

Ira joined Harry and removed the vegetables from the cardboard box she had packed last evening, handing over one after another for Harry to place inside. Was Harry purposely trying to find some work so that he could be with Ira for longer? She smiled inside.

"Sorry Mum, I couldn't contact you this morning," Varun said as he lurched through the door with a bag containing food packets.

Ira spun back and let out a smile at him. "No, I'm sorry. Forgot to recharge the mobile last evening and thought it would last for a few hours today."

Varun engulfed her in a tight hug, and Ira kissed his forehead.

"How is Sam now?"

"He is all right. The operation is finished, and he is resting. You know, Mum, he's got no family support, and we are like his family here."

Ira forced a smile. She couldn't pressure her son away from Sam. He was a good-hearted young man. Ira would play host to him in her new home as long as Sam behaved like a man—the straight man he had shown himself to be so far.

Do straight men become gay? Ira thought and planned to Google it when she was alone.

"Harry helped me today in your absence." She flashed a seductive smile at Harry and removed plates from the buffet. She had drunk only three cups of tea since that morning, and her stomach growled at the aroma of veg pilau when she opened the takeaway food container and served everyone.

"This was just practice," Harry laughed as he fed himself the first spoon of pilau. "Within six months, you will move again, and I will be available to help you. Of course, if you hire me."

"Hire you?" Ira said. "I didn't hire you today."

"No, you're right. But your son did."

Varun focussed on eating, but Ira noticed a big smile on his face. How much had this boy revealed to Harry? Did Varun tell him that this apartment had low rent as the tenure was only for six months until the owner moved in with his family? Or did Harry know she was planning to sell her apartment in Raghupur and buy one here?

"I have friends who are builders. Whenever you are ready, I can talk to them and get one for a reasonable price."

She decided not to reply to Harry.

"Varun, we *both* should go to the hospital in the afternoon and visit Sam. You're right, he is like a family member."

Ira purposely stressed the word *both*, expecting Harry to notice. She didn't want Harry to come with them to the hospital and let the world know that they were lovebirds.

Ira had always advocated for friends to say *no*. But when it came to her, she couldn't use it successfully. Was she getting weak when Harry was nearby?

She feared that Harry would notice she was thinking about him too much. Who else did she have in this large city other than this man?

"I will also visit Sam in the hospital. Maybe tomorrow. This afternoon, I have a meeting."

Ira was glad Harry had other plans.

"Tomorrow the hospital will discharge Sam," Varun said as Harry was about to leave. "Mum, he will be alone in the flat. Can we bring him for a few days to live with us? You know his parents don't even know he is in the hospital and wouldn't have come to see him anyway."

Ira glanced around as if she could gather enough courage to say *no*, but Harry was also gazing at her with an answer she knew she would give.

"Of course, my boy."

"Ira, I like your support of Sam. I will pick him up from the hospital when he is discharged and bring him here. You are such a nice mother to both," Harry said.

Ira tried but could only flash a timid smile. Harry didn't know that one day she was about to sleep with Sam. How could she treat him as another son?

"Mum, you should forgive Sam."

Ira tried to control the sigh from escaping her mouth as the Uber cab left her new apartment complex that afternoon. Varun wanted to bring Sam home and nourish him for a week. That was okay. What called for a forgiveness? Who would forgive whom? She had already convinced her subconscious mind, whatever had happened with Sam, she was equally responsible. And she couldn't discuss this in graphic detail with her own son.

"Mum, you haven't said anything."

"What is there to say, Varun? I said it was okay to keep Sam in our new home for a while, and he can move back to his flat when he feels fit and healthy. What else do you expect from me?"

Varun gave her a pointed look. "You know what, Mum."

Ira tried to read Varun's mind as the cab stopped at a traffic signal. Did he plan to live with Sam even after she rented a flat in six months?

"You see, Varun, after your dad's death, there has been only one income in the family. The money we will save when you eventually move in with me would help in buying an apartment here. Don't you want that?"

Varun placed his arm on Ira's shoulder. She glanced at him. Ira was well acquainted with the flash of the *I love you, Mum* smile that had brightened his face. His touch had always felt like a soothing balm to her over the years.

"Why do you think I'm not moving in with you now? It is not like I'll be moving a house, just three suitcases filled with my clothes and books. Sam knows he can find another mate to share his rent."

A cool wave passed across Ira's nerves. Soon Varun would be living with her.

"But Mum, what about forgiveness?"

This was not the time, and that too when the cab driver was listening to each word of their conversation.

"Varun…" She tried to flash her motherly smile she always used to convey her decision whenever Varun didn't agree with her. "Can we talk at home about this?"

The cab entered the hospital compound. Ira knew for at least a week Varun wouldn't be able to talk to her about this forgiveness. Sam would be in her apartment for that week, and she was also on holiday for shifting, after which the school holidays would start.

Why didn't she think of this before? For an entire week, she would be alone with Sam while Varun would be at college.

"How many days' sick leave has Sam taken?" she asked.

"I think, one week. Until then, we both will nourish him back to health and send him back."

Ira smiled at Varun's joke-like sentence and got out from the cab.

A text chimed on her phone as she was about to walk with Varun. She took the mobile from her handbag. Harry's text: *Ira, is it ok to call you now?*

She stared at the message, stilling her fingers. Stilling her heart. Even the air around her stilled.

"Mum, are you okay?" Varun stopped and turned towards her. She was staring at the mobile with a blank expression on her face. "Are you all right?" he asked.

Ira had hit the pause button in her mind. Was it by mistake?

She flashed a smile to cover up her feelings. "Varun, we haven't come to visit Sam in the hospital, but to take him with us. Is it all right if I wait here and you bring him? Maybe I will buy a coffee in the meantime."

"Okay, Mum." Varun went inside the hospital, and Ira walked to the road looking for a coffee shop.

What did Harry want to talk about? She pondered over Harry's text message after placing the order for a coffee. Another date? She didn't want to race in a new romance world so quickly. At least not at a time when Varun was around—and Sam, as well.

She decided it was better for her to finish the conversation before Varun came back with Sam. She touched the *call* symbol over the text message.

"How are you, Ira? Are you in the hospital?"

"Yes." A thrill passed through her body. "Varun has gone to bring Sam, and we all will go home together. I'm waiting outside."

"You should have stayed at home. You have shifted homes today and are probably feeling tired. But when you insisted on the dining table that you would accompany Varun to the hospital, I didn't say anything."

Why didn't Ira think of this before? If she had planned not to go inside the hospital, she could have stayed back home and arranged her kitchen items.

"You are right, Harry. But Varun insisted I come with him."

"He is a child every parent would be proud of. I have a suggestion. Another meeting is about to start in the next five minutes. If you guys could wait for an hour, I can come and take you all home."

Ira never wanted enough help from Harry to make her obligated to him. But again, the word 'no' was far away from her tongue.

"Don't worry, Harry. I know you would have come and helped. But Varun and I are enough to take him home."

"I understand," he chuckled. "See you again soon, Ira."

Ira looked at her phone. How far will this thing she had with Harry go?

"Coffee, ma'am." The sweet voice of the female barista broke into Ira's muddy self-talk.

"Thanks." She smiled at the barista and took the coffee from her.

Ira needed to plan how Sam would stay with them. She had only two beds, and this apartment had three bedrooms. Sam was sick and should get a separate bed for a comfortable stay. Should she ask Varun to share her bed as they did in Sam's flat?

"Someone in the hospital?" the girl at the counter asked.

"Yes, a friend." Awkwardness filled her when she realised she was standing in the shop without drinking her coffee. Ira stepped out.

Varun was standing with Sam at the gate when Ira arrived.

"How are you, Sam?"

"Good, and thanks for allowing me at your home." Sam's face was pale; he looked weak but calm.

Varun was smiling. He took Sam's hand. Ira didn't like the closeness between them. *Varun is getting too close to Sam.*

She tried to make her voice friendly. "Varun, have you booked a cab yet?"

CHAPTER 19

The next morning, after Varun left for the college, Ira took a shower in her attached bathroom and came out wrapped in a towel. She would have loved to stay like that for a while and sip tea resting on the sofa in the drawing room. But Sam was in her home, and she didn't want to repeat the same mistake.

Standing in front of the tall mirror, Ira gazed at her own body. She was beautiful and looking much younger than many women her age. A tingle passed through her skin, and she moved her hand to remove the towel.

"Can you please take these inside your room, Ira?"

A stunned Ira spun around. Sam was peeking through the border of the door curtain, holding a bunch of clothes. A squeal of surprise flew from her lips as she checked if the towel covered her properly. As Ira glared at him, he stepped back.

At first, she didn't understand how to tackle this and stomped to the bedroom door. Sam was standing just outside the curtain.

"Sorry, Ira. Your clothes on the balcony were getting wet from the rain and wind. I thought I would bring them in while they are still dry."

A naughty confidence bloomed in her when she realised she was still wrapped with that towel. Sam was standing in front of her like a guilty boy.

"You should rest. Why did you go to the balcony?"

"No, I...just..."

"Okay, keep them on the sofa, and I'll come out in a minute."

She went back inside and stood in front of the mirror. Sam had seen more than this.

After putting on a dress, she came out. Sam was sitting on the sofa after depositing her clothes on another.

Ira's gaze fell on the balcony; rain was pattering on it. She took a deep breath and inhaled the aroma of fresh, wet air. It was like taking a stroll in a green forest with fresh, dewy grasses and the smell of rain-washed soil. It was the first time she had smelled such a scent in a long time. The cool breeze caressed her face and hair as she looked up at the clouds. The rain seemed to call out to her. It was an invitation to walk along the serene paths of a green forest. She felt her tension melting away.

"Everything all right, Ira?"

Ira swung around—Sam was looking at her like an innocent child. She flashed a smile as if he had not invaded her privacy.

"I will make breakfast for you, Sam. You must be hungry."

"I was famished, so I have already eaten two pieces of bread. Just now."

"Why didn't you call me? I could have..."

"I am not used to this, Ira. Even before I became eighteen, my parents were gone. I don't think anyone has ever taken care of me. Thanks for bringing me here."

"Okay, I will make some tea and we will drink together."

Ira walked into the kitchen. Her mind seemed to run down three separate paths. One moved slowly, into the romance world of Harry. The other raced to protect Varun from the modern trend of same-sex living. And the third, her own secret with Sam. The more she wished to bury that deep inside the ground, the more her guilt came back with unknown force.

She was responsible, to some extent.

And now that Sam was relaxing in her drawing room, could she make her and Varun's lives free from thorns?

Ira made two sandwiches by the time the tea was ready and brought them to Sam. He was sitting on the lounge, watching TV.

"Morning programs are usually boring." She slapped on a smile while placing the sandwich and tea on the centre table.

"What to do when one can't go to the office? Thank God you are here, I have someone whom I could talk to."

For the first time, Ira hated the school holidays, but still managed to slip into her facade.

"Varun will leave your apartment and live with me here. I am sure you don't want to lose a friend like him. What can we do, Sam? With the limited budget of a single income, I have to cut some expenditure."

Sam chuckled, as if Ira said something funny. "This is usual. I've been there for the last four years. Flatmates come and go. What is new about it? And as far as friendship is concerned, Varun is still my best friend, and we will remain friends forever."

Best friend! Didn't Sam just say so many flatmates have come and gone? So why is only Varun his best friend?

"Do you love it when Varun puts on female clothing and becomes *Varuna*? You are a naughty boy, Sam!" Ira threw a chuckle.

Sam also let out a mild laugh. "Yes, he looks beautiful when he dresses like a woman. But after all, there are lots of differences between a real and fake woman. But what I love—when Varun becomes *Varuna*, she looks so similar to you, as if she were your doppelgänger."

"Doppelgänger?" Ira had never thought of this. Yes, when Varun was a little boy, some of her friends had commented that had he been a girl, he would have been a younger version of Ira.

"Yes, Ira. I have taken her photo. See here on my mobile." He moved closer to Ira. "See this? Isn't she a beautiful and sexy woman, just like you?"

Is Sam attracted to Varun only because he looks like me when in a dress? Does it mean he is not gay? Ira was confused whether she should be a bit relieved to hear this.

Ira felt Sam's hot breath on her chest. A shiver passed through her body. She was trying to bury a secret, but soon, so many baby secrets would loiter in and around her home. Would they destroy all her dreams of beginning another love life?

She had not taken a photo of Varun when he had been dressed as a girl. She had always kept that picture hidden in her heart.

Ira felt as if she was being drawn into some sort of trap. Sam moved closer to her. He placed his hand on Ira's shoulder, then moved slowly towards Ira's chest.

It was then that Ira realised that the top of her dress was already a little open. His eyes were fixed on the gap in the neckline. He could see a lot more than she had expected.

"Ira, you're not saying anything."

Ira jerked into consciousness. Sam was at a respectable distance away. Did she experience a horrible dream sitting on the sofa?

"Yes, Sam. She is looking beautiful. But Sam, if you don't mind, can I ask you something?"

"Sure, Ira. Anything for you."

"See, society never likes boys to dress up like girls. They think the person is effeminate. Only you and I know this about Varun. Can you keep this a secret?"

Sam said nothing. An unease hung in the air for a few moments. Would Sam ask something in return which Ira couldn't give? Would he blackmail her?

Sam raised his head. "I understand, Ira. Didn't I say I'd do anything for you? Yes, this will remain a secret with me."

"Thanks, Sam. You are a nice boy."

Ira got up. "Already ten in the morning. I will go to the market and buy vegetables. Otherwise, this bread will be our lunch." She threw out a mild laugh.

The lift door opened as soon as Ira pressed the down button. She stepped inside the empty elevator, carrying a winning feeling. Sam agreed to keep Varun's crossdressing a secret.

But as soon as the lift door shut, claustrophobia engulfed her. She had only a week to find out if Sam indulged in an affair with Varun.

What would Ira do if her suspicion was correct? Her head reeled when the lift started moving down. Varun was an adult, and if he decided to do something, she had no option but to watch in silence. She couldn't imagine crying foul like her cousin Urvi. But how would she react?

She dragged her feet out of the lift when its doors opened on the ground floor and walked to the road.

"Hi Ira, so good to see you here."

The sweet and familiar voice greeted Ira as she was about to cross through the gate of the building. She spun around and found Reema walking towards her with a massive grin on her face.

Surprise tingled Ira. "What are you doing here, Reema?"

"As if you own the entire place? Since when?" Reema let out a giggle and hugged her. "Nice that you moved in here, to this building."

"Yes. And you live nearby?"

"I live here. I mean, whenever I come here during school holidays. My husband lives in that building." She pointed toward an elegant structure.

"Your husband lives there? Is that not your home too? Or you already got another love?" Ira winked at her.

"Of course, I mean. Yeah, my home." Reema gave a short, mirthless laugh.

Was Reema's marriage really falling apart?

A guilt washed through Ira. She could arrange a transfer because of Harry's excellent contact in government network. And her ex-colleague Reema was still commuting weekly for her job between Toshali and Raghupur. Harry had requested that Ira never divulge how he managed her transfer to the city. She must bring up the point without invoking suspicion. All Reema knew was the principal had recommended Ira's application because of the assault she had faced.

"Have you ever tried moving out of the school and getting a job here?"

Reema let out a loud cackle. "Never, my friend. I am happy there."

Ira weighed how much time she could spend with Reema. She wasn't in a hurry to buy vegetables and go back to her new home.

"Reema, if you have time, can we go to a coffee shop and sit there?"

"Time? I've got plenty of it. I know a favourite coffee shop here, and it's a nice place to pass the time. Only a five minutes' walk."

Ira looked above. The rain had stopped, and the sky was slowly clearing up. Sunrays started pinching her skin. "Let's go. I need something to get rid of the loneliness from the school holidays."

Reema was right. The shop was only minutes away. Ordering two cappuccinos, both friends settled in a corner table.

Before Ira could ask more about the school job, Reema winked at her. "How is it going with Harry?"

Surprise speared through Ira. "Harry? You know him?"

"Come on Ira, didn't you meet him for the first time at my party? And you are asking me if I know him?"

"Oh, yes. I forgot."

Ira pondered over Reema's question. How much she should divulge? Harry was, after all, a friend. Just a friend. What was wrong with it?

"He was here to assist you in shifting yesterday."

"So, you chatted with him?"

"Nope. How could he even see that I was here watching him when his focus was on you? Yesterday he was talking to the movers when I was here. He didn't notice me. But when he asked the lorry driver if this was for Ira, I understood you had become my neighbour. So sweet, Ira. I will come here more frequently now that I have someone to pass the time with."

"You don't come here every weekend?"

"No. That's for another day. Not now."

Ira noticed a dark cloud hovering over Reema's face. She couldn't stop thinking about her farewell day in the school, when Reema had mentioned she would love to have another life partner as her husband was now fat and bald. Was there something else besides this?

"Everything okay, Reema?"

"I am bringing up Harry's subject and you are trying to ignore it?" Ira noticed Reema suppressing a sigh and plastering a smile on her face.

"I am telling you the truth. I hadn't even told Harry when or where I was moving. But he knows Varun's flatmate, Sam. Varun was visiting Sam in the hospital yesterday morning when the movers brought my household goods. He should have been here, and I didn't have the keys to this flat. He asked Harry, who was also in the hospital visiting Sam, to bring me the keys. Believe me. I have no hand in his coming here."

Did Reema believe her? It was true. But something tingled in her heart when Harry's name came up. Should she reveal she and Harry had dinner together? Went out for a date? Kissed?

A teasing smile formed on Reema's face. "So, Harry came and gave you the keys and went back?"

The server girl came to serve their coffee.

As Ira took her first sip of hot coffee, she saw Reema's eyes staring at her from across the table. "I see the way you two are getting close to each other," Reema whispered.

Ira had a sudden attack of hiccups as she gulped some hot coffee by mistake. She gazed at Reema, not knowing how to answer. If Reema had seen him coming, she would have seen him leaving. And his posh Ferrari, anyone would notice.

A mild laugh appeared in her throat, which she tried to hide. But suddenly, both friends laughed loudly.

"No, he was here. Helping me arrange my things. And by noon Varun came home, and we all had lunch together. Varun was with me then."

"Yes, I understand. You are trying to say you were not alone with him."

Ira let out another laugh but didn't reply.

"Don't take his presence seriously. You are just making a mountain out of a molehill. Would you like some toast with your coffee? Sorry, I forgot to ask."

"No, Reema. Already had breakfast this morning. This cappuccino is enough."

"Ira, my gut feeling says you are about to start another married life soon. Believe me, my gut has never told me a lie."

Ira let out a third loud laugh, but soon she became conscious that she was sitting in a café. Thankfully, there were only two other customers sitting in the opposite corner.

"Okay, my friend. When that happens, you will be the first to know. But I have too many worries, and the wedding is the last."

"All right. When did I say you will marry next week? My advice is, build a new friend circle here, socialise, and soon the luckiest man on the earth will come to meet you."

Ira was expecting Reema to say Harry's name. She was disappointed.

CHAPTER 20

Brother Mehul's phone call that afternoon snatched away Ira's peace. He was still with his daughter in Delhi, but apparently the youngest brother, Rohan, had phoned him about the ancestral property. Now he wanted to divide the property with the older brother and deprive Ira of any share. She must fight the lawsuit in a court of law. What a novel idea to team up with the oldest brother and single out the dead brother's widow!

She knew the judgement would come in her favour, but it would take almost fifteen years the way millions of court cases were pending in India. She had dreamt of selling her share and buying a decent apartment in Toshali with the sale proceeds. The dream would now have to wait for fifteen or twenty years.

"Forget another romance, Ira. Rahul hasn't left any will, and your remarriage will affect Varun's future," she told herself while sitting on the balcony attached to her bedroom.

She didn't wish to take advantage of Harry's grace. She would never trade her love for her dignity.

The main door opened and then closed. Ira looked at the time on her cell phone. Five in the afternoon. Varun must have come from his college. She got up and went to the lounge room.

Varun's backpack was lying on the sofa. She could hear him talking to Sam in his bedroom. Since Sam arrived at her apartment, he was occupying Varun's bedroom. Varun had been sleeping in the lounge.

"Close your eyes, Sam. You shouldn't see a naked boy in your room."

What are they doing? Unease speared through her.

"But I can look at a naked girl!" Sam giggled.

Maybe Varun got the urge for a girly moment and was going to wear a dress. Ira had no intention to eavesdrop, but the apartment was small enough to pass on each word Varun said to Sam.

"Unfortunately, not with me. Not unless I decide to get a sex transformation surgery."

"Are you planning to?" Sam's voice sounded enthusiastic. Ira pictured him having gotten up from the bed and gazing at Varun, eyes widened.

"Never, my dear. Mum would either kill me or die. Never in this life. I'm a girl only for a short period. An '*occasional girl*.' And I told you to shut your eyes. Why are you staring at me like this? And please lower your voice. Mum will listen if she comes out of her room."

Ira suppressed a giggle.

She left Varun's bedroom door and walked to the open-plan kitchen. Time to cook dinner. Taking out vegetables from the fridge, she began chopping them for mixed vegetable curry. She must find a strategy to secure Rahul's share of the assets without disturbing Varun's studies. And prove that she was a strong-willed female.

A pale perfume filled her nose. "A mother can always know even if her child says nothing," Ira said and turned around to face Varuna, chuckling. "I bought a few more dresses for you, mostly for wearing at home. They are in my wardrobe. This one you are wearing is a party dress."

"Mum, you are saying I shouldn't go outside in a dress. Where would I put on a party dress if not at home?"

"All right." Ira chuckled. She came to Varuna and untangled her bun. The wavy, long hair tumbled on her shoulders. "And now, this is my beautiful daughter. Can I ask you why you changed into the dress in that room, in Sam's presence?" Ira said, bringing her voice to a whisper.

"Mum, that's my bedroom. He is with us only for a week, or even less."

"So what? No mother would like her daughter to change clothing in a male's presence. Varun can do anything there, but not Varuna. Do you understand?"

"Yes, my dear mother." Varuna took her in a tight hug.

"Now is the time to study." Ira continued chopping vegetables. "I will cook dinner in about an hour. And ask Sam not to sleep in the evening."

"He will come out, Mum. I have already told him. Let me help with cooking tonight." Varuna came and took another knife.

Ira sensed her face brightening with a smile. And the stress she was getting a few minutes ago vanished.

CHAPTER 21

The next afternoon Ira opened the door without even checking through the peephole. This was the time Varun usually came home from his college.

"How was your day, Varun?" A smile formed on her face.

Something fell on the tiled floor in the second bedroom.

Without answering, Varun ambled into his bedroom—temporarily Sam's room. Ira knew Sam was packing his bags. She stilled, expecting a storm might come out of the room.

"What happened, Sam? Why are you packing?"

Ira could hear the pain in Varun's voice, even though she didn't intend to eavesdrop. This happened in a small apartment.

"I have gotten enough rest. Planning to go to the office tomorrow. Why use all my sick leave?" Sam said.

Ira had planned to inform Varun that Sam was leaving. But look at this boy! Instead of talking to his mother, he headed directly to meet Sam?

"Right, Sam. But you can travel to your office from here, too. At least you wouldn't have to cook until you're totally healthy," Varun said, his voice full of emotion.

"I'm healthy. Much better."

Ira didn't wish to follow the conversation. She trudged into her room instead and continued reading a book, which she was halfway through.

She hardly finished a page before Varun rushed in, unannounced.

"Didn't you freshen up?" she asked without raising her head from the book.

Varun sat near her and wrapped his arms around her shoulder. "Mum."

Ira set the book on the bed and glanced at him, then planted a kiss on his cheeks.

"You are the best mum in the world."

"You are the best son," she said between chuckles.

"But Mum, Sam's mum is never around when he needs her. Is this because he is a grown-up man? Twenty-five plus? Will you treat me the same when I am that age?"

Ira brushed the book to the floor and took Varun in her arms. "No my child. You are the most important person in my life. I will drop everything to be with you when you need." She planted a kiss on his forehead and made him sit near her on the bed. "But think of Sam's mother. She is not here. And did Sam inform her he was going in for medical treatment? We shouldn't blame a woman for knowing nothing. And as far as your mother is concerned, I will be the same, whether you are eighteen or fifty." A cool wave touched Ira's heart.

Varun's voice nearly choked. "I know, Mum. I also understand you can't be a mother to Sam. But you both are at home, and you could have at least talked to him. He would have left after three more days, anyway."

"Talk to him?" Ira straightened and gazed at Varun. A silence hung between the two. "I talk to him. But do you think we are chatting the entire day? Eight to ten hours? He watches TV whenever he doesn't feel like sleeping. And when I finish household chores, I spend my time reading a book, sometimes on the balcony and sometimes in the drawing room. Today, after lunch, he said he is feeling a lot better and would like to go back to his flat. I insisted he stay until at least the weekend, but it seems he made up his mind. What do I do?"

Varun didn't answer, but kept staring at the floor. The tension in the room was hot, and she only could cool it down.

"Believe me, Varun, it's a hundred percent his decision. He wants to go back to his office tomorrow and would be comfortable at his home."

"All right, Mum. I am thinking of dropping him off at his apartment."

Sam and Varun together, again? Ira knew she couldn't stop this forever. But the mother inside her was not ready to digest this.

"Why only you, Varun? I will also come."

Sam knocked on the door. "Ira, I am ready to go."

"We are coming with you. Give me a minute, I will just change my dress," Ira said.

Varun got up and went to the lounge room with Sam as Ira closed the door to change.

"Mum and I both would love if you stayed with us for the entire week, but ... maybe you got bored?" Ira heard Varun say.

"No, not at all, Varun. My apartment is even lonelier. But anyway, I must go back to work tomorrow."

Ira changed as quickly as possible and applied lipstick before coming out.

"Your bags ready? Give me another minute." She took out four takeaway containers from the fridge and put them in a polythene bag. "This is your dinner for the next four days. During the daytime, you can get something near your office, right? You don't have to cook in the evening. Just take this out of the fridge and reheat. I will bring more when these are finished."

"Thanks, Ira." A grateful look flitted through Sam's eyes.

Ira noticed a silent smile on Varun's face.

A familiarity burrowed into her as they entered the Alkapuri mall after dropping Sam off in his apartment. This was the shopping centre where they had dinner with Harry.

"What do you plan to buy, Mum?"

"Nothing. This entire week has been the school holiday, and I'm bored sitting at home. We can do some casual shopping, dine, and then go back home. How does that sound?"

Dining outside was always a favourite for Varun. And spending some quality time with Varun was Ira's preference.

"Fantastic, Mum. And a pub?"

"Pub? You want to drink? Oh yes, you are eighteen plus now. Why not?" An idea struck Ira. She had been to a place with Harry a few times now, but never with her son.

The signboard of 'Lone Pine Pub' slowed down their pace as they walked along the corridor. "How about this one, Varun? But promise me you will drink responsibly."

Wednesday evening. There was hardly any crowd inside. Ordering two wines at the counter, Ira chose a corner table where she could have some serious mother-son talk.

"You know, Mum, Sam is my best friend," Varun said as they climbed into the booth. "He understands me and appreciates my way of life. You understand what I mean."

Ira flashed a smile as she settled in the seat. "It's good to find new friends. But why only one? You should develop friendship with more *girls* and boys. And not everyone should know about your private life. Sometimes 'just friendship' is also enough."

She hoped Varun realised she gave stress to the word girls. Varun looked at her, smiled, and nodded.

The server arrived with two glasses and poured their drink within seconds.

"Cheers to my adult son." She clinked their glasses. "You know Varun, I had never drunk alcohol until I dated your dad," Ira said after taking a sip.

Varun also took a sip. "Why, Mum? Your parents didn't allow? But I know Grandfather drank regularly. And you always blame his death for heavy drinking."

"Right. He was a party drinker until your grandma's accidental death. He was alone after becoming a widower. It was too late when I knew his drinking habit." Ira took a long breath. The memory of dead parents suddenly became raw in her mind. But she didn't want to ruin the evening. "That's why I said to drink responsibly. Society looked down upon women who were drinking those days. Mumbai was different then. Just imagine what Raghupur is today, Mumbai was almost similar. Only difference, it was huge, and interfering in another person's life wasn't easy."

Varun was twirling his wineglass. "Your parents were so backward! I thought Mumbai was much more modern. Westernised."

Ira chuckled. "That was only for Bollywood stars and other elite people. Not middle-class families. But my parents were not backward. Do you know they had a love marriage in the days when arranged marriage was the norm?"

"They had? Wow!" Varun's eyes sparkled with joy. "My grandparents were so contemporary! That's why they allowed you to marry my dad, isn't it? Did they tell you how they fell in love?"

Ira responded with a smile and glanced around. Weekday evening. The nearest occupied table was at least two meters away in this large pub. She wished to start a conversation with her son regarding Harry.

"Talking about love with parents is also a western concept and new to us. No, they never told me it was a love marriage. I came to know from my uncle. You might have watched in English movies how aged fathers or mothers bring their new lover home and marry in the presence of their children."

Varun chuckled. "Yes, I've also watched lots of old Hindi movies where fathers scream at the daughter when she has chosen a boy. They thought it was the privilege of the parents—no, rather, their right—to choose whom the son or daughter will marry."

Ira responded with a smile. "It was not a hundred present wrong, just the norm—which is changing. But you know Varun, my parents always encouraged me to know the boy long enough before making any decision. Finally, the decision was mine. But they advised me not to rush. Your dad and I were in a relationship for almost two years before marrying."

The server approached the table. "Ma'am, would you like a refill?"

Ira thought about it, but realized she needed more time to discuss her relationship. "Yes, please."

"Okay, ma'am. Will be in a few minutes."

"Mum, this means if you get into a new relationship, will you wait for two years?"

Unease rushed through Ira. "Varun, you are a generation ahead of mine. Even though people in Raghupur think I am a modern woman, I still have some old beliefs I cannot come out of or am still questioning. As a parent having those beliefs, I wouldn't feel comfortable discussing my love life with my son in detail. Just gave you a briefing."

"And with the daughter?" Varun winked.

Ira giggled. "A bit more than the son. But that would be at home. But what I am going to tell you—" Ira paused and glanced around. "I mean, you should never discuss this with anybody, not even your cousin Mansi. I know she has convinced you about my second marriage. But..."

"Mum, I will keep my mouth shut."

"I have met Harry a few times. Both of us are mature humans. We are taking it slowly. But I am still conscious of the family at Raghupur. Remember how your uncle Rohan somehow knew I had dined with Harry? Let it be a secret between mother and son."

The server came back with the wine bottle.

"Sorry," Ira said, "Can we order food instead?"

A smile pulled across Varun's face. "Yes, Mum."

It was nine p.m. when Ira and Varun arrived at home. As soon as they came out of the elevator and walked towards their apartment, the door of another apartment opened and a lady spilled out.

"Are you Mrs. Ira Ray?"

Ira had never introduced herself to her new neighbours in Toshali. "Yes." A dark thought entered her.

"A courier had come with a letter. She requested me to keep and give it to you."

Letter? Who could have sent mail to this address? She remembered she had provided her new address to the school in Raghupur. Ira's chest tightened. "Thanks." She took the letter and went to her flat.

"What is this, Mum?" Varun stood near her.

"Your—" Ira was still reading the letter— "your uncle Rohan has gone to the court for the ancestral property."

Varun released a sigh and slumped on the sofa. "Let him go, Mum. As per law, we still own a share of that. How can he prove in the court we don't have a right?"

Ira folded the letter and sank into the adjacent couch. "Right. But he is playing games. Court cases in our country take fifteen to twenty years. That means my plan to sell our share and buy some decent flat in Toshali will never materialise. Selling the flat in Raghupur will not be enough to buy an apartment here."

Varun stared at her with his mouth agape.

CHAPTER 22

Ira could have enjoyed the remaining part of her school holidays on Thursday morning after Varun left for his college, but the letter she received last evening occupied everything in her mind. She had told Varun not to worry and, as a capable parent, she would take care of the disputed ancestral land in Raghupur. Varun was against selling the Raghupur apartment, as that had the emotions attached to his father. Ira might get a new husband, but her son would never find another father. With the rapid growth of Raghupur and appreciating property prices, it would have been unwise to sell it.

How could Ira then afford to buy an apartment in Toshali without selling Rahul's share in the ancestral land?

Ira was about to go to the kitchen for another morning tea when her cell phone buzzed. It was a call from Harry.

"Hi Ira, how are you?"

A chuckle came out of Ira's mouth. She settled on the sofa, holding the phone to her ear. "Getting bored in Mumbai?" Ira asked, feeling like someone switched a bulb on inside her heart.

Harry chuckled. "The meeting is at eleven, so there's nothing to do now. Lest I could have been in Toshali during your holidays."

"So that we could have gone on another date?"

Harry laughed loudly. "Not necessarily. We would've met again. Maybe along with Varun."

Ira loved being able to meet Harry more frequently. But she wasn't a teen girl, like she was when she was dating Rahul. Yes, she needed another romance, not a problem-solver, influential man. She must try to solve her own problem.

"Everything all right, Ira?"

"Yes, why?"

"Because you sound tense."

"Me?" Ira stilled and took a deep breath, keeping the phone at a distance. "No, I was alone after Varun went to the college. Sam also moved back to his place yesterday afternoon."

Ira realised the explanation was not enough.

"Ira, I want to show you something. Can I hang up and make a video call to you?"

"Sure."

A giggle came out of Ira. Gone were the days when she had fallen in love with Rahul and was calling from the landline when their parents were out. Cell phones were not very common in those days.

Harry made a video call immediately. Standing near the wardrobe of his hotel room, he pointed at a beautiful dress that hung on the wardrobe. "I bought this for you last evening. I was thinking of showing it to you from the shop, but realised you wouldn't be alone at home."

Ira let out a smile of happiness. "You are right. I wasn't at home. Varun and I went out for dinner after dropping Sam off at his place."

"How do you like it?"

The dress was sleeveless with a plunging neckline. There was no lace or anything like that, but there was a lot of blue and silver in the design.

"Looks beautiful. But remember, I'm the mother of a college-going son. Not a college girl myself. Can I wear this?"

Harry smiled. "I am also the father of a college-going daughter. I don't think you have to put this on when you go to work, but when you go to a mall or travel to Mumbai, Delhi, and even overseas, you don't have to wear the traditional dresses."

Going overseas? Did Harry mean she could travel overseas with him as his wife? Was this his hint?

"Thanks, Harry. But how do you know it will fit me? I mean, the size."

"Don't worry, you are the same height as my daughter. I often buy dresses for her. It will fit you perfectly."

The doorbell rang.

"Harry, it must be my maid. Can we talk another time? Thanks for the lovely dress."

"See you again." Harry hung up.

Ira headed to open the door.

As the maid cleaned and organised the house, Ira kept coming back to the same thought—*I must talk to Reema and ask if she knows any good lawyer here.* After asking Reema if she could join her for coffee once the maid left, she loped to the elevator. Last time they had met near the banyan tree just outside her building complex, so Ira arrived there and waited.

A middle-aged woman walked by holding a bag of vegetables. "Are you all right? Looking for someone?" the woman asked.

"I am all good." She pasted on a smile. *Can't a woman just stand near a tree and wait? What is unusual about this?* She checked her mobile clock. Only two minutes had passed.

An old man walked from the other side with a dog on a leash. Life seemed very normal for all the other people except just one soul, herself. What happened to Reema today?

Ira walked to the main road, which was almost two hundred meters from there. The best option to kill time.

When she came back, she noticed Reema waiting for her wearing a nightie.

Reema in a nightie outside her home?

"Hi, Ira." Reema's voice was icy, hair disorderly. The woman who would never come out of her home without makeup looked twenty years older than her age. Guilt pushed through Ira's heart.

"What is this, Reema? You're in a nightie? What happened to you?"

Reema sat on the brick platform near the banyan tree. "Sit down, Ira."

Ira regarded her friend. "You okay?"

"I was sick and was sleeping." Reema was looking elsewhere.

"I'm so sorry. I didn't know and woke you up."

"No, don't. I was already awake when your phone call came."

Ira stared at Reema for a few seconds. "Are you feeling better?"

"Yes."

"I was thinking of going to the coffee shop, but..."

"I know, my friend. For today, let's stay here and talk. I have spent hours reading books beneath this banyan tree. And now..." A desperation clouded Reema's face.

"Now what?"

"Nothing. You called me only for coffee, or is there something else?"

Ira took a deep breath. The air around her seemed stuffy.

"You know about the property dispute with my brother-in-law? That is now going to the court. Had Rahul been alive, he could have handled it better. But I will not let him go. I need an excellent lawyer to fight for me. Your husband must know someone..."

"My husband?" Reema let out a sigh. "The court is in Raghupur. Hiring a lawyer from Toshali who will have to travel to Raghupur on the hearing dates would be costly. I think you should hire someone in Raghupur."

Silence hung for a few beats. Had Ira not been lucky enough to secure a transfer to Toshali, she would have hired a local lawyer, anyway.

"All right. I will do that. Reema, I think you should go back and get some rest. Today is Thursday. Still three days left of the holiday. We can go together for coffee another time."

Reema got up. "Bye, Ira." She left. Ira stood there, watching her from behind.

Ira's phone chimed. An unknown number flashed on the screen. A shiver passed through her bones. Who could this be? Did Divya's uncle find her number? She tapped the red button to disconnect, but a few seconds later, it rang again.

"Hello?" Ira said slowly into the phone, keeping her finger ready to hang up.

"Good afternoon, ma'am, I am Leela, Divya's mum."

"Oh, Divya's mum!" Ira smiled into the phone. "Sorry, I didn't recognise your number."

"That's all right, ma'am. How are you? I heard you have shifted to Toshali."

"You are right, Leela. How is Divya?"

"She is all right. Will go to the school after the school holidays. Ma'am, I have some advice for you."

"What?" Her jaw went tight.

"Please don't go to Raghupur for a few months. My brother-in-law was asking for your phone number from one of Divya's friends. The girl called Divya and informed her. He is a demon, you know."

Ira inhaled a deep breath.

"You know, ma'am, that man has bribed the land registration authority and put on record that his older brother died intestate and made all the properties in his name."

"Intestate? But his daughter is very much here. You should file a case of forgery against him. You have all the documents, like Divya's birth certificate, to prove she is his legal heir."

"That's right. I remarried, but his daughter still has a right. But he is threatening us. He said if we file a case, we have to come to Raghupur for a hearing. He will assault us, and we can't even come inside the court. My husband is suggesting we should forget those properties. He is ready to adopt Divya and she can inherit his property instead."

"Your new husband is a gentleman. But you shouldn't let that monster walk away with a trophy like this. You must teach him…"

"But ma'am, I am scared. He has already spread rumours that my daughter was pregnant. I don't know how many ways he knows to harass."

"Okay then. Anything else?"

"No, ma'am, please avoid going to Raghupur, for your own safety."

After the call ended, Ira pondered Leela's words. Her situation did not differ from Leela's. Divya's stepdad would adopt her. He had properties in Toshali.

But what about Varun?

CHAPTER 23

I ra took a deep breath when the express bus left the Toshali bus station for Raghupur. Leela's advice yesterday afternoon still knocked inside her brain. "No, ma'am, please avoid going to Raghupur for your own safety."

"Ira, you are the only one to fight for your and your son's rights," she told herself last evening and called the lawyer to book an appointment for today.

Last night she could hardly sleep. She would steal a nap on the recliner seat of the luxury bus. Ira closed her eyes and tried to relax her limbs. She muttered a prayer. The prayer she usually chanted before going to bed every night.

The Uber cab rolled alongside the Raghupur subdivisional court and stopped in front of a small building. *Naik & Associates, Lawyers and Solicitors*, the signboard read. Ira climbed out of the taxi and entered.

"I'm Ira Ray," she told the receptionist, "I got an appointment with Mr. Ashish Naik, advocate."

The girl at the reception flashed a smile which appeared to be her routine. "Please go to the room number one, this way. Mr. Naik is waiting for you."

Ira forgot to even say a 'thanks' to the receptionist. *I don't know how many years I will have to come to this place, considering the way cases take decades to see that justice is done.* Ira dragged her feet into the chamber.

"Hello, Mrs. Ray." Advocate Mr. Naik stood up and extended his hand for a handshake.

Ira brought a smile to her face. "Morning, Mr. Naik."

"Please take a seat." Advocate Naik sat in his seat and adjusted his tie.

Ira glanced around. The table between her and the advocate was full of papers and files.

She thought Mr. Naik was seemingly a young person.

"I thought the law firm was fairly established." The unwanted comment came out of Ira's mouth.

"My grandfather started this firm almost fifty years ago." Mr. Naik let out a chuckle. "And I'm the third generation in this family business. We have an excellent track record, and you can rely on our expertise. You are lucky you approached us before your opponent came to us. We refused to take their case."

Surprise slammed Ira. "Did anyone come to you?"

"Yes, a man came this morning, just an hour ago. His name is Rohan Ray. I realised it is the same property you had spoken of yesterday over the phone. So, I turned him away. But not before taking a photocopy of the land deed. You had said the original documents are with your in-laws. I have read a little, and it clearly shows your father-in-law had inherited this property from his father. And Rohan said there was no will. It happens with many people of the older generation. 'Will' was a foreign concept to them. Without a will, you deserve one third of the property."

Confidence snaked into Ira's mind. She needed a shrewd lawyer to take care of her rogue brother-in-law.

"Thanks, advocate." This was a nice beginning. She had already discussed the fee structure yesterday. It was high, but looking at the market value of the property, she had no choice. "I have a question."

"Please ask."

"What do I do if my brother-in-law makes it difficult for me to appear before the court? Meaning he would abuse, threaten over phone for blackmailing, et cetera?"

Advocate Naik smiled. "You think he will? You need to keep proof of such abuse. Normally such men show their strength in the places closer to their home. Not elsewhere. If we can gather enough evidence, we can apply to the court to move the case to Toshali. We have an office there as well."

Relief washed over Ira. "This sounds good," she said. "And one more question. Can my son sign the deed of attorney instead of me? He is now eighteen."

"But why? You are the widow of the late Rahul Ray. You have more right to the property."

Within a year or two, Ira might be someone else's legally wedded wife. Was it the right time to ask Naik if she could fight the case in such an event? No, there must be a way to transfer the case to her son's name.

She collected the papers and tucked them in her bag. "I will go through this and send by courier, along with the signing fee, if that is okay with you."

"That would be lovely," Mr. Naik said.

"Now I will take your leave." Ira got up.

Mr. Naik came with her to see her off.

"By the way, Mr. Naik, how long might the case take to get possession?" she asked while walking.

She noticed an elderly woman who was also walking towards the entrance. The woman stilled and glanced at her before looking away and continuing.

Advocate Naik stopped at the main door. "Maybe a few years. But each case is unique, and I will try my best to give you possession as soon as possible. You don't worry, we will take care of it."

Ira forced a smile. "Thanks, Advocate. Bye."

Ira stepped onto the street. It was almost one p.m. and her stomach was rumbling. At least the first step of getting her due was done. She would fight for her son's rightful possession.

"Hello, lady." A faint voice forced Ira to stop. It was the same woman who was going inside.

"Hello, ma'am." Ira looked at the woman. She looked to be around eighty, looking pale.

"I heard your talk with the advocate and was able to gather a bit," the woman said.

This is so wrong, why did she eavesdrop on my private conversation? Then she realised she hadn't stopped discussing it with the advocate even after she left his chamber. She was also partly to blame. *I will keep this in mind for the future,* she assured herself and brought a smile to her face.

The woman continued. "I was fifty-five when my husband died. Since then, I've been fighting for my share of his property, and now I am seventy-five. I don't know if I can get my share before my death. The lawyer of my in-laws is hand in glove with the judges and intentionally pushing the case longer. They understand that the case will never go in their favour. They had offered me something less than my share in an out-of-court settlement. I refused and fought the case. Trusted these lawyers. Now, after so long, I realise these so-called professionals have their fees only in their mind. I also think these people have some underhand dealings with my in-laws, to push the timeline of the case. I should have agreed then. I lost valuable years of my life."

Ira froze. She tried to at least thank the woman, but her lips quivered.

"This is just a piece of advice to you before relying on the lawyers and courts." The woman left.

Ira stilled, then swung around and looked at the Solicitors' signboard and inhaled a deep breath. She didn't know how many surprises life had preserved for her. But this is life, and she must fight to survive.

She punched in the Uber app and booked a cab to go to the nearest bus stand. She could get some quick lunch and get the earliest bus to Toshali.

Her cell phone shrilled. Ira quickly pulled the phone from her handbag.

"Hello, Harry." She walked into the bus shed.

"How are you, Ira?"

She had spoken to Harry last evening, but never told him she was planning to come to Raghupur. The trip was not a secret, but she didn't want to take his help for everything—not give the impression that she was using him for her own benefit.

"I am good, Harry. My holiday will be over soon. I thought to meet a few people in Raghupur, so I suddenly decided this morning and came here."

"Oh, I see. So, you will be there today."

Ira thought for a moment. She didn't intend to lie to him, only didn't wish to drag him inside her own problem.

"I will, and will come back by evening."

"It's good Ira, to connect with your own people. I will not disturb you. Enjoy your time. See you when I am back in Toshali."

Harry killed the call.

The Uber had arrived. She climbed into the cab.

Waiting for over two hours in the Raghupur Bus Depot wouldn't have been easy for Ira. Fortunately, she had remembered to bring a fiction book with her.

She opened to the last page she had read, but her mind was cantered on the property.

She looked at the wall clock. It was past two. Rupa must have begun her duty. An urge to drink coffee in that stall arose. She got up and walked to the coffee shop, but found a young man at the counter.

"Will Rupa be late today?" she asked the young man.

"No, ma'am," the man replied, "She is sick and won't come."

The desire to drink coffee vanished. Ira went back to the waiting hall. A known gait of a woman from behind pulling a suitcase signalled her brain. She loped towards the woman.

"Hello, Reema. You are back from Toshali? How are you? Better?"

Reema stopped pulling her luggage and stared at Ira, her breath still catching.

"So, you can't forget Raghupur. How can you?" A painful smile curled her lips.

"You are right, Reema. Something or other is coming up in Raghupur. But I wonder why you came back earlier when you have two more days of holidays still to go? You should have come here on Sunday afternoon. And you still look unwell. Why didn't you ask your husband to drive you here?"

Reema looked elsewhere. "He is busy with his business."

Ira failed to understand. What sort of husband didn't help his wife when she was sick?

"Are you in a hurry, or do you have some time? My bus to Toshali will be in an hour. If you can, we can sit in a corner and have some girly chat."

Reema chuckled. "Okay, dear. You never change. Let's sit down. I will wait until your bus comes."

Ira found the same corner seat still unoccupied. "This is my favourite corner of the waiting area." She sat down.

Reema sat next to her and slipped a glance in Ira's direction. "So, what brought you to Raghupur today?"

Ira inhaled a breath. "Same property dispute with in-laws. What else? I took your advice and met a lawyer here."

"I understand the mindset of these men. They think the husband died and they can take advantage. Why don't you ask Harry for help? He has good contacts..."

"No, Reema. He helped when Divya was in trouble. But I don't want to use his generosity for my personal benefits."

"But Harry is a gentleman. I don't understand why his wife misunderstood him."

"His wife? But she is dead." Interest rustled through Ira.

Reema wore a grim look. Did she know something which Ira didn't? Anything about Harry was igniting her curiosity.

"She was in love with another man. They were about to divorce. But she got cancer when the divorce was almost final. Last stage."

Harry had just said his wife had died. Nothing about the divorce.

"But Ira, Harry knows me. If he hasn't said this to you, please keep this a secret."

Secret? Harry had a secret he never told Ira? Her nerves vibrated.

"Of course, I will. Forget it, Reema. We can shift to another topic."

Ira noticed Reema's features freshened when both friends talked about the funny side of life and exchanged jokes. She didn't realise how the time fled.

'Dear passengers, the express bus for Toshali will arrive soon at terminal twenty-one. Please make a queue at the terminal. The bus will leave for its destination on time.'

"Now I will let you go, Ira," Reema got up.

Ira got up too and hugged her. "Let me know when you are in Toshali, I will come and meet you. Bye for now."

Ira trudged towards the terminal. A bitterness clouded her mind after hearing Harry's secret. Her life was now full of problems only. Where would she go in search of solutions?

Emotion boiled in Ira's throat as she arrived at her Toshali apartment. The bus journey from Raghupur to Toshali was the worst she ever experienced. The aircon on the bus didn't work, making the air stuffy. Several times she had thought to complain to the driver, but she had little energy left. The entire world seemed to be sinking, but in slow motion. Rahul was the only lucky star in her life.

"Why did you leave me, Rahul?" she muttered, standing before his photo on the side table of her bedroom.

Her cell phone chimed. She retrieved it from her handbag. Varun's text read, *Mum, Sam has invited me for dinner, I will be home late.*

Okay, my child, She texted back.

She hurried to the bedroom, letting her clothes drop to the floor and putting on light, comfy ones.

She was tired and in no mood to cook. Deciding to order something through UberEATS, she poured a glass of wine and settled on the sofa in front of her TV. After surfing a few channels, she found a movie that was about to begin on Cine TV. *Be-imaan,* Untrustworthy. An old Hindi movie.

Ira had watched this film twenty-one years ago in a theatre in Mumbai. She was a student then. It was just the beginning of her romance with Rahul. She still remembered the story as this was the first movie both had enjoyed together, sitting in the back row corner seats, his arm around her shoulder.

A dark memory unsettled Ira. Rahul's loss became raw again, and the story too.

She continued watching, even though she knew the plot. The story of a wealthy business owner who was having a relationship with a young and beautiful woman. The whole time, the woman thought she was getting a wealthy husband and would enjoy her life. But slowly she came to find the real psychopath behind the smiling face. The man used her only as a sex partner, and when the girl asked about marriage, he began harassing her.

"I hope you are not like this man," she had chuckled and muttered to Rahul when they left the theatre.

"I am not a wealthy person like you saw in the movie, rather a middle-class man from a small town," Rahul had replied. That same evening, he proposed to her.

What about Harry? Ira wondered while twirling wine in the glass. He had dated her without even hinting about marriage like Rahul did long before formally proposing. Would Harry also use her as a sex companion? Was he making all the arrangements to get her confidence before taking her to his bed? If he was so honest, why didn't he say anything about his divorce? Or the plan of the divorce before his wife died?

Reema might have only seen his public face, as she was just a friend—not a close one. So, she had a high opinion about him.

The phone buzzed. Ira was not interested in taking the call from Harry. She didn't have the courage to reject the call either. The phone rang for a minute before stopping. A text message followed. *Please call me when possible, nothing urgent.*

She took her tablet and typed *Harry Thomas's wife* on Google Chrome. The screen flashed with millions of results. There must be a million plus Harry Thomases in the world, and most of them should have wives. *Why didn't I ask Reema what Harry's wife's name was?*

She grabbed the mobile phone from the coffee table and punched in a text. *Hi Reema, can you please let me know the name of Harry's wife?* But her fingertip hovered over the send button for an indefinite period.

Why am I asking this name? And why to Reema? Didn't I tell her a few days ago that Harry was just a friend, and nothing more than a friend?

Ira wiped away the message from the screen. "What do I do?"

The room felt too warm, so she got up to open the window. Seated on the couch, Ira closed her eyes, and a gust of fresh wind hit the window, making it rattle. She opened her eyes again. The breeze blew open her curtains and stirred her hair. She turned to look at it, and a thought sparkled in her head.

Harry was on her Facebook since they first met at Reema's party. She scrolled through his posts. He was not active on social media, and she found little in his past interactions. She scrolled down, and within minutes had dug back almost two years. There was a post, *Happy Birthday to my Dearest Wife Jenny.*

Ira got her first success. Jenny, Harry's wife's name. Jenny didn't even acknowledge the wish from her husband. Strange!

How could Jenny have fallen in love with someone other than Harry? Harry was an age-defying, smart looking man any woman would die for. What could have prompted his wife to make such a decision?

When she clicked on Jenny's profile, surprise punched her. She didn't notice recent posts, she was sure Jenny never shared her account details with Harry.

Hundreds of Jenny's FB posts sprung to life on the screen and winked at her. But nothing referred to her husband or any lover she had planned to marry after the divorce. Some were regarding her fight with cancer. But she had videos, texts, blogs, stories. All regarding *psychopath, impotence,* and *narcissist.*

Another round of surprise opened a pit in her stomach. Was Jenny referring to Harry with all these? She remembered a few movies showing the heroine tormented by a male psychopath. Most of the time, a dreaded criminal hid beneath a gentleman's face and soft-spoken words. Like the movie she just watched. Bitterness gushed through Ira's heart. Who else could Jenny have been referring to, if not Harry? Did she wish to run away from her husband? Afraid to accuse him directly?

The windows rattled.

Ira could hear the wind whistling through the trees. It felt as if a tornado was coming, and the ground was vibrating beneath her feet. She wanted to run, but her legs seemed frozen, rooted to the spot. The wind kept getting stronger and stronger, howling like a beast outside.

Wake up, Ira. Wake up, she told herself. *There's no storm outside. It is inside your mind. You only can stop it.*

She sat up straight on the couch, took the cell phone, and thought to block Harry's number. Maybe unfriend him on FB. Let him know she was no longer interested in him. Let him understand she found the truths and was not being fooled like the young woman in the movie. Her finger hovered over the 'unfriend' symbol for a few minutes. Was it all right to just press a switch and finish a relationship in a moment? Or even possible? Ira was never one to harm someone's feelings, even if she might have been the victim. No, it should be rather a slow and decent action. But a convincing one. She put the idea of blocking his number in cold storage for the time being—until she could figure things out.

CHAPTER 24

"Bye, Mum. It's too early. Please go back to bed and get some more sleep," Varun called to her before leaving for an early morning class.

How could Ira say she couldn't sleep last night? She didn't feel like going to the bedroom and instead tried to get some rest on the sofa.

Each time she tried to close her eyes, a sense of urgency woke her up. She didn't understand why her brain was so restless.

Ira got up from the sofa, stretched her limbs, and felt the sun's rays on her face sneaking through the window. She looked up, then down, then up, then around. She turned her back to the window and gazed into the kitchen.

She took out her phone and checked the time; it was six a.m.

She could smell the morning air as she inhaled deeply. Her lungs filled up with air. It was like breathing in life itself. She felt relaxed as she inhaled the cool, fresh air. She closed her eyes and smiled.

Ira wondered why Reema went back to Raghupur, leaving her family when school didn't even open until Monday. She could have spent some time with Reema.

Should she knock on the neighbour's door and introduce herself?

It didn't seem to be a marvellous idea.

Sometimes living as an anonymous person had its own advantage, especially when one was averse to invasion of privacy.

She ambled to the balcony and opened to a page from the novel she was halfway through. But, somehow, the chapter didn't sound interesting.

Ira surfed Facebook, and a notification grabbed her attention.

Reema had just changed her status from *married* to *single*.

Ira's eyebrows shot up.

Reema had mentioned she didn't love her husband anymore. But Ira had never taken it seriously. Indian women of her age stick with the same husband until death, even tolerating abuse. Leaving a husband—a wealthy one—requires more courage than fighting enemies on the border.

She swiped out of Facebook and tapped on Reema's number.

"Hi Reema, how are you?"

Reema greeted her with a loud laugh. "I thought the paparazzi would hound me after what I just posted on Facebook. But you called first."

"Imagine I am the paparazzi."

"Is that so? Where is your camera?"

"This is the age of the Internet. I will interview you and send it to the press with a stock photo."

Reema gave another chuckle. But soon a pause came into the air.

"Reema, I assumed you both were made for each other. Didn't you celebrate your twenty-fifth anniversary in a five-star hotel?"

"Five-star hotel! That was his business advertisement. Most people who came were his customers only. Another marketing investment. The anniversary was just another excuse. Soon he will have his wedding party, also in the same hotel, and mostly with the same guests."

"Wedding? With whom?"

"A younger, model looking woman."

Ira found it hard to digest. Only a week ago, Reema had complained to her how she was no longer in love, as her husband was a bulky and bald man.

And now a model looking woman found him attractive?

"Some young women find money more attractive than the man himself."

Ira required no more explanation. Reema's marriage was over. And now both Reema and she were in the marriage market, looking for suitable men.

She got the urge to ask Reema the story behind Harry's spouse and her divorce plan, but the timing didn't seem appropriate. Even if Reema was laughing, she must have been keeping her emotions hidden beneath a rock and was displaying a smiling face to the world.

"Reema, I always follow your Facebook posts, but you have given no hints before. You had told me you don't love your husband anymore, but I never thought it would end in divorce."

"I never wanted people to guess and spread rumours. Now that everything is over, I gave the news, so there should be no gossip."

Ira wondered if she failed in her friendship with Reema because she didn't talk about her divorce. But Reema needed mental support, and she must provide it to her. The timing was definitely wrong to talk about Harry's wife.

"Reema, life throws so many surprises, and we all become mature after dealing with them. I know you are a brave woman, and you will take this positively. Your ex might have chosen a young beauty, but believe me, you are beautiful. And God is creating a path for you to meet a beautiful man who would be genuine."

Reema chuckled. "You are my best friend, Ira. Don't mind me, I didn't tell you simply because I didn't feel like it. It could have taken longer, but I agreed for a mutual separation to finish it quickly."

"Will you come to Toshali on holidays?"

"Yes, Dhiraj is giving me an apartment as part of the settlement."

"That's good. Please let me know, I will come and meet you whenever you are here."

"Thanks, Ira. Talk to you another time."

She opened the novel again, but within two hours, she arrived at the last chapter. Now she felt the urge to buy another novel from the shop.

She wouldn't wait until the evening to take Varun with her to the market. He should spend his evenings studying.

She thought about visiting the same mall she had visited last evening. That was the nearest to her home.

What about Harry? Did he live nearby, or was his office near the mall? Last time Harry met her and Varun when both mother and son were in a pub. He was supposed to return from Mumbai, and it was highly unlikely that he would come to a mall on a weekday.

Ira navigated to the Uber app and typed the destination, *Alkapuri Mall.*

She knew psychos followed the women they like. But after declining his calls a few times last night and avoiding replying to his texts, Harry had not called her back. Not even this morning.

Did he understand Ira was not interested in him? If not, he will, in a day or two.

She was so immersed in her thoughts, she didn't realise that she had arrived at the mall.

She planned to order a coffee at the shop near the entrance and then look for a book shop.

"One medium cappuccino, please." Ira fished out the notes from her bag and gave them to the counter girl.

"What name you would like us to call you, ma'am?"

"Ira."

"Miss Ira. Thanks, ma'am." The girl smiled at her as she took the notes. "Approximately ten minutes' wait, ma'am, if you don't mind."

She had enough time and could have waited even more.

"No problem. I will hang around here."

Miss Ira sounded much better than Mrs. Ira.

Ira waited on the side and noticed how customers lined up one after another for their turn, either to order something or collect their orders.

I could've ordered snacks with that. The aroma from kachoris and samosas hung in the air, igniting her tastebuds. But she cast a glance at her own reflection in the mirror fixed to a pole. A beautiful young woman in a trendy frock with the figure of a twenty-five-year-old grinned at her and said, *No, Ira. You must control your tastebuds if you wish to remain tens of years younger than your age.*

She felt eyes digging at her, and a thrill washed over her skin. *Be careful Ira. You are the mother of an eighteen-year-old. Be practical.*

Standing next to Ira and waiting for her turn to be served, a young woman in her early thirties muttered to her friend, "That man is here, waiting for his coffee."

"Who?" the other girl asked.

"Shhhh. He is the owner. I was working in his company. Don't look back. He threw me out for no fault at all. I was told it was a restructuring. Bull sheet."

I am lucky to be in a government run school, not a private company, Ira thought. She had no interest to look back and see the businessman. Why would it matter to her?

"He probably expected some favour from you, being a young and beautiful girl. Nowadays, after several attacks from the 'Me Too' activists, bosses are not asking favours directly. You need to be smart enough to offer yourself. He looks handsome, must be a womaniser."

The first woman paused. "Maybe. But what can I do now? Job is already gone. He must have recruited another girl."

"Mr. Harry," the girl on the counter screamed. "Your coffee, sir."

Shock sliced through Ira as she controlled her emotions in a second. There might be many people with a similar name in such a large city.

But that self-assurance didn't last long when the same Harry she feared the most came out from the crowd and stepped towards the counter.

This time, the shock hit Ira's heart as she felt it jump inside her ribcage. Was Harry watching her standing nearby? Why did she think Harry would never follow her? Were those girls talking about him?

Psychos always followed the girls they like. The scent of the brewing coffee seemed like the foul smell of an uncleaned gutter.

A shriek came out of her mouth as she spun around and ran.

"Miss Ira." She heard the girl shouting her name. "Ma'am, your coffee please."

She didn't look back.

CHAPTER 25

Ira stretched on her bed. Saturday morning. Varun had left for a picnic earlier, and she had come out of her bedroom for a few minutes before going back for a bonus round of slumber towards the end of her school holidays. She got a good sleep last night, despite the looming knowledge that the property case might drag decades and she might become an old woman like the one she encountered two days ago at the lawyer's office. Not only that, even her first dream to get another love in her life wafted into smoke.

Really? It wasn't just a dream. She went on a date with Harry. She even kissed him and felt his presence inside her soul. And after coming back, she saw Rahul's smiling face inside her mind. Wasn't this a sign he approved of this relationship? An emotion gathered in her throat and tears burned behind her eyes. Was it right to throw a relationship into the garbage bin just because of some Facebook posts?

Yesterday at the coffee shop, those two women talked about a businessman. That must have been Harry. They even accused him being a womaniser. But what if it was someone else?

She felt Harry was so genuine when she was with him. But wasn't it a fact that all psychos successfully portray a genuine image? The more she would spend time with him, the more she would be dragged into his net. *You are a strong woman, Ira. Don't mess up your and Varun's life for the love of a man you have doubted once.*

A chuckle came out of Ira as she sat up on the bed. The ancestral property was now worth almost fifty million rupees. And with the current rate of growth in Raghupur, after decades, it would multiply by ten or more digits. That might have tempted her to sell it had Rohan agreed to part with her share. A wiser Ira should wait a decade or two and reap much more than that.

And what was wrong with removing a man from her life altogether? It was always better to get away from a psycho at the beginning of a relationship than repent later and ruin her life. That old Bollywood movie was a classic example.

She got up and stood in front of the mirror and combed her hair. It was her routine since before she could remember. A grey hair got her attention.

"Don't worry, Ira," she said to herself, "accept age gracefully. A perfect partner will accept who you are. This is rather good, it will keep the daydreamers away. Getting another romance is not your priority. Varun's future is."

Ira became wise in a day. Now she understood why widows who were mothers found it difficult to remarry. Because when the husband dies, so many responsibilities came that remarriage became the last option. But some were lucky. Like Leela, Divya's mother.

Divya's mother. Ira had almost forgotten. Last evening she had accepted her invitation for lunch. Today. She must go to the market to buy a gift for Divya. And she must choose the outfit to wear. Salwar kameez would be appropriate.

The Ola cab dropped Ira off in front of a worn-out building. Ira climbed out, holding her handbag in one hand and the gift with the other. She cast a leisurely glance, noticing the ground floor was for shops and restaurants, and the upper floors were apartments.

Milis Ready. Ira laughed inside her mind at the small signboard fixed to an electric pole in front of the restaurant. She wanted to go inside and tell the owner that the correct English spelling is 'Meals' and not 'Milis,' but then thought, what sort of English man would come to have food in this rundown place?

Five-star hotel and restaurant. The restaurant's signboard got another chuckle from her mouth.

"Here *hotel* means you get lunch and dinner, and *the restaurant* means you get breakfast and snacks," Rahul had explained when she was new to Raghupur. Some parts of Toshali were also similar, mostly the underdeveloped localities. People here were trying to follow English without knowing the basics of the language.

"Where are the stairs to the upper floors?" she asked at the restaurant counter after struggling for a few minutes.

The smiling face of the man fell, probably realising the gorgeous woman wouldn't be his customer. "Please go to the rear of the building, ma'am, you will notice a broken door and when you go inside, you will find the stairs."

Ira came out and, before going to the backside of the building, cast a glance at the other shops. She saw a shop selling vadas, samosas and other deep-fried snacks, piled up on large plates, uncovered, flies having free feasts on them. She hoped Leela didn't buy snacks from this shop.

A sudden awareness haunted her. What if Leela invited Harry too? He was the one who had brought the chopper and rescued Divya from the clutches of her rogue uncle. She should have asked her yesterday if she was the only guest.

Ira stilled. She still had time to back out—send a message to Leela that she was not well or that some urgent work came up. No, it would be cowardly. She must take the bull by the horn. If she faced Harry, she would tell him she had too many priorities. She could part ways politely.

Ira trudged to the rear. The broken door of the entrance didn't surprise her. At least Leela's new husband wasn't living in a slum. She stepped on the uneven stairs, where chunks of cement plaster had fallen off. Some even had broken bricks. Thank God she didn't wear heels.

A familiar scent came into the air. Footsteps sounded. Ira stood still on the stairway and closed her eyes. Would she meet Harry here? The footsteps came closer. Ira inched close to the wall and waited; her heart bounced inside her ribs. Was Harry still living inside her soul?

She opened her eyes and saw the unknown man surpassing her. The scent also disappeared, along with the man. Ira resumed climbing the steps.

Second floor, flat number 203. She checked the text message of Leela. Correct. The door displayed a Hindu Swastika sign made of turmeric paste, with dried flowers on it. Ira remembered her deceased mother-in-law always drew a Swastika on the front door.

Leela opened the door before Ira knocked. "Namaste, madam. We saw you were arriving. From the balcony. Please come in."

Divya stood near her mother to welcome her ex-teacher.

Ira cast a quick glance around. A small but tastefully decorated abode. A small sofa and four-seater dining table on one side of the hall—or she should call it a room, as it was small. There was a single bed with a study table near it.

"This is a one-room apartment," Leela said, "bedroom for us, and for Divya, that cot." She pointed at the single bed. "And this is Divya's study room, too."

Ira chuckled, looking at the table with books.

"Study table and no chair," Divya said with a grin, "I sit on the cot while studying."

"What do we do, ma'am?" Leela said with a soft smile on her face. "There's no space for a chair in such a small flat. The market price of this flat now would be around five million rupees. We can't afford a bigger apartment."

Ira remembered the gift. "I'm so sorry, I forgot to give this to you."

She handed over the packet to Divya. "Thanks, ma'am." She took the gift and set it on the side table. Ira understood it was customary in some places not to open the gift in the giver's presence.

"Please take a seat, ma'am," Leela offered. "My husband works on Saturdays. You are single. So, I thought only we women should be together."

"That's good." A sigh was coming out of Ira's mouth, which she stopped. Thank God Harry wouldn't be there.

"Ma'am, it's already one p.m. and you must be hungry. Will it be okay to serve lunch now?"

"Sure." The aroma of hot food from the kitchen aroused Ira's taste buds.

"Ma'am, I forgot to tell you," Leela said when Ira stepped out in the afternoon. "My school friend Tina is your sister-in-law. I found out only yesterday when she called me. She said her husband had cancer and he would come to the city for treatment in Toshali's cancer hospital. She actually asked if she and her husband could stay with us during the treatment. But ma'am, our flat is so tiny."

Ira stood still and closed her eyes. Rohan's hate-filled eyes entered her conscious. Was it good news? But how? Rohan had two beautiful daughters. They both needed their only bread-earning father for survival and studies. A sigh came out of her.

"Ma'am, are you all right?" Concern sounded in Leela's voice.

Ira tried to look confident. "I am." Ira didn't know what else to say. She eventually left the place and went downstairs, her mind in a flurry over this new information. The Ola cab was already there. After climbing into the car, she immediately dialled Tina, but the phone went unanswered. She pocketed the phone. So many thoughts crossed her mind.

The cab dropped her off near her building, and she called Tina again before entering. This time, Rohan answered.

"Why are you calling?" His voice was rough, and he was coughing.

"How are you, Rohan?" Ira tried to be as polite as possible.

"Does it matter how I am? You only want the property. Once you get it, you won't call yourself a daughter-in-law of the Ray family."

Ira pinched the bridge of her nose. She didn't want to argue. "Can I talk to Tina, please?"

"Tina is busy and doesn't have time for unnecessary calls." He killed the call.

Ira let out a sigh. *How much poison is there in this man's mind? Doesn't he understand this poison is making him sick?*

She entered the elevator. She was about to unlock her door when she got another call. This time from an unknown number.

"Aunt Ira," a girl's voice startled her, "I am Lisa."

Lisa, Rohan's oldest daughter. "How are you, Lisa?"

"Aunt, my, I am..." Lisa's voice choked. She was weeping.

"Lisa, you can talk to me. What happened?"

"Aunt, I didn't know. Only an hour ago I heard my parents' conversation and found out my dad has cancer. He was also telling my mum I won't go to the college next year, because he can't afford it. Lots of money is required for his treatment."

"Lisa, don't worry. Government colleges in Raghupur are not costly. They charge only nominal fees. Still, if required, I will make sure that you continue your studies. I will pay. All right, my child? You are like my daughter, too. Please don't cry. Your dad needs your support now. He needs treatment."

"Yes, Aunt. Thanks, Aunt."

Ira worried Rohan might be angry with Lisa for talking to her. "Lisa, I was trying to talk to your mum, but she is not taking my call. If you can, just let me know through WhatsApp message where your dad will stay during his treatment. I am very much part of the family, and I want to know everything."

"Yes, Aunt. I will. Bye."

Ira's energy had all drained out when she entered her apartment after attending lunch with Divya and her mum. Awareness punched her guts. The man who was terminally sick might be her enemy, but he was Rahul's brother. His daughters were Varun's first cousins. Culturally, first cousins are equivalent to sister and brother. Ira, even in her dream, would never imagine Rohan's daughters suffering for their education because the sole bread-earner of the home became incapacitated.

Her mobile chimed with a text from Varun. Her mother's intuition told her Varun had other plans for the evening. She slumped on the sofa and opened the text.

Sam has invited me, The text read.

She immediately dialled him.

"Varun? Will you be late?"

"No..." Varun inhaled deeply. "Sam asked me to his flat tonight."

She paused. "So, you will have dinner with him."

"No, Mum. Yeah... Yeah. Dinner and a sleepover, too. Tonight only."

"But your clothes! Shouldn't you come here and collect your night-wear?"

"Actually, Sam has bought some clothes for me. Gifts from when I was attending him in the..."

"Clothes? You mean girls' clothing?" Ira snapped, an unease rising in her belly. She got up from the lounge and stomped to the bedroom to change her clothes.

A silence hung in the air for a few moments.

"Yes, Mum."

"Sam can't find a girlfriend for himself, so he wants you to entertain him as a girl? And will you also share his bed?" She yanked open the wardrobe door and stared blindly at her clothes.

"Why his bed, Mum? There is another room."

Ira reached inside the wardrobe and snatched her nightwear. "Another room? What about his flatmate?"

"Flatmate? He doesn't have one. That man who had planned to share the rent didn't come. And Sam got a promotion and planned to keep the flat entirely for himself. Don't worry, Mum. He knows I become Varuna only in the evenings. I will come back in the morning."

Ira sighed loudly. "All right, my child. Enjoy your evening." She placed the phone on the bed with its speaker on and removed her salwar kameez over her shoulder.

"Mum, I know you will be alone in the evening, why don't you call Harry and spend time with him?"

Ira stilled, leaving the salwar kameez pooled at her feet. *Harry? How would she now tell him Harry was in the past? No, there would be another time for that. Let him enjoy his evening.*

"Varun, I will decide with whom I will spend my time."

"Sorry, Mum. Are you angry with me?"

Ira released all her anger in one deep exhale. "No, my child. You are now eighteen plus. I will not treat you like a baby anymore. But I expect whatever you do, you will do responsibly. Enjoy your freedom. Bye. Goodnight."

"Love you, Mum. Bye."

Ira went to make a tea. She needed something to douse the fire burning inside her. Varun should have been with her this evening. But he was now a grown-up boy. And she shouldn't expect him to be the same Varun when he was in school.

She made a cup of tea and settled on the sofa. Its steamy aroma relaxed her nerves. But she must talk to someone.

Reema? Who else?

Ira took her mobile and brought Reema's number to the screen. But just before she dialled, she stopped.

Reema should have told her Harry was harassing his wife. Or the reason Jenny was divorcing him. Bitterness flushed her brain. But only for a while. Many women suffer from bad and insensitive husbands. Reema was also one of them. Who knew how much sorrow she kept suppressed beneath the friendly and smiling face? Why should Ira judge her for something which she probably didn't know?

Reema was in need now and could use Ira's time and sympathy. Ira placed the teacup on the table and took the cell phone.

"Hi Reema, how are you?"

Reema chuckled on the phone. "I am good, dear. Bored to death at home? Don't worry, only one more day. School will reopen."

Surprise hunted Ira, hearing how Reema sounded jolly even after so much had happened to her. Was it because she always wanted to show a cheerful face to the world?

"No, Reema, I am not bored at all. I had gone for lunch with Divya's mum. And now I'm considering what I should do for the evening. I was hoping to be near you and talk to you."

"Don't worry, Ira. We are close, just a phone call away. You sound miserable. Is there something I can talk to you about?"

Ira thought for a second. Did she really sound depressing? Did her problems affect her voice?

"No, Reema. You are already going through so much. I don't wish to bog you down with more."

"Me? Through so much? Who told you that? Trust me, Ira. I am happy. I also wanted to get rid of that man. It was good he started the process, and I got a good share of his wealth. Now I can plan how to enjoy it and also find a man of my choice."

"You are such an optimist; I really envy your attitude."

"You will be like me, too. The more problems you face, the more mature you become. Tell me, what's bugging you? That rogue brother-in-law?"

Ira inhaled a breath. "That brother-in-law is suffering from cancer. You see, without medical insurance, you almost need a fortune to get the right treatment. I don't understand..."

"Are you happy or sad?"

"How can I be happy? True, I was fighting for the property. But he has two daughters. And their studies are now in the dark because money is short for his treatment. The girls are my nieces. I mean, Rahul's nieces. They are still family, even though I have a dispute with their father. I promised the elder girl that I would support their studies."

"You are a fine human, Ira. I like this mindset. You did the right thing. But remember, never forgo the property right."

"I won't."

Reema let out a giggle. Ira took the teacup. It was already cold.

"What else, Ira? Any plans for the evening?"

"Evening? No plans yet. Varun will be with his friend."

"Can I give you an idea?" Reema sounded jubilant. "Alkapuri Mall is so close to your home, and I always visited the pubs in it. It is really safe for women. Who knows, you might find the guy of your dreams there! So many eligible middle-aged men come there to get away from their lonely lives. Some are widowers and some divorcees. You know, Ira. My sister-in-law, who lives in New York, she found her new husband in a pub, and both married within a few months."

"This is not America, my dear. This is India. I need some place to kill time. I am not fishing for a husband. But I have visited that mall many times." Just days ago she had run away from the coffee shop after seeing Harry, who knows if he might be there again? "Suggest another place."

"Another place? Hmmm, try Keshari Mall, near to Alkapuri, and equally good."

"Done. Talk to you later."

She must keep herself happy to fight against all odds.

She dumped the teacup in the sink and loped to her bedroom. Find a life partner in the bar? No, not that attractive as Reema painted.

Her nightwear and undergarments dropped onto the floor as she smiled at her naked figure standing in front of her dresser's mirror. She took out a pair of fancy lingerie and a slightly deep neck frock from her wardrobe and put them on.

The selfie she took immediately after looked great. When she typed the destination, the Uber app showed the cab would arrive to pick her up in just five minutes.

So quickly? She ran out of her home and within minutes was waiting in front of the apartment building.

Olive & Nuts Pub. The neon signboard of the bar smiled at her when she turned to the left after entering the mall, as Reema had advised.

A group of men sang on stage. The only thing she heard clearly was the clinking of glasses and loud talking. Ira could also hear the thudding of her heart and took a deep breath to calm herself. She looked around for a place to sit and found one empty two-seater table in the middle.

"One martini, please," she ordered when the server asked.

She fished out her phone and sent a text. *Hi Reema, the pub looks great.*

The one I had suggested?

Yes, and found an empty table, too. Difficult on a Saturday evening, I suppose.

First step is over. Now look to see if any man is alone.

You won't change!

Don't be shy, my beautiful girl. Had I been a pretty woman like you, I would have thrown the net.

A deep voice broke Ira's attention. "Hello, ma'am, can I share the table with you?"

Will talk to you afterward, Reema. Someone is here. She locked her phone and tucked it in her handbag. "Sure," she said, looking at the young man.

"Thanks, Miss..."

"Ira. Just Ira."

Her mind was flying even before her first drink arrived.

"Thanks, Ira. None of the tables are available. If there's no one with you, I might..."

"Don't worry. There's nobody with me."

Ira threw a smile and cast a swift glance at him. He must have been around twenty-five.

Twenty-five? Only seven years older than my son? Almost Sam's age?

"Can I offer you a drink, Ira?"

"No, my drink will arrive soon. Thanks anyway."

"No problem, Ira. Saturday evening. Server might take ages to bring the drink to the table. Maybe I will fetch one from the counter for me." He headed towards the bar.

Ira glanced around. Most tables in the pub had four or more people. She also noticed a few more two-seaters, with mostly couples occupying them.

By the time her drink arrived, the man was coming back with his drink.

"Cheers." He raised his glass for her. "I am Vick."

She flashed a silent but flirting smile. A man in his mid-twenties was certainly not husband material. But what was wrong with passing some pleasant and innocent time together?

Would he feel the same after finding out her son was eighteen?

"New to the pub, Ira?"

He must be a regular here.

"New to the city. And yes, not a regular pub visitor."

Something tried to regulate her actions from within. Was she conscious of her age?

Ira took a sip of her drink. She glanced around the fairly packed pub, and a feeling of comfort washed through her. She loved this place. The sound of the piano in the background reminded her of days gone by. A smile spread across her lips.

A chime notifying a text alerted Ira, and she fished out the mobile from her handbag. It was Reema again.

Enjoying my favourite pub? Met anybody?

She stole a quick glance and realised Vick was ogling at her. A tingle washed over her chest.

Yeah. A young man. Charming but too young for me, she typed back. *Who cares? Just relish the company.*

She was about to tuck the mobile away when a Facebook photo opportunity carved into her.

"Vick, would you mind taking my photo?"

"Sure." Vick got up, holding his phone.

"No, with my phone, please."

Vick took a few snapshots of Ira until she found the best one to post.

"Ira, can I take a selfie with you, with my phone?"

She couldn't say no to his innocent request.

Vick came to her side and crouched enough to bring his face along-side Ira's. One arm wrapped around her shoulder and the other held his phone at a position which could snap the best selfie.

"Splendid. Thanks Ira, and can I now buy you a drink? Please don't say no to me."

Her drink was about to be finished. She replied with a smile, and Vick ran to the counter.

What a fine evening I am enjoying! She tapped on the photo to post on Facebook with the caption, *feeling happy and enjoying liberation from all worries.*

Will Vick be my friend once he knows I'm so much older than him?

Within a few minutes, Vick came back with two drinks.

"Cheers, to the new friendship." He clinked the glass with Ira's.

"You, I mean, I have an eighteen—"

"Can I be your Facebook friend, Ira?"

"Sure, why not? Please look for Ira Ray, Raghupur. I haven't updated my profile since I moved to Toshali." *Good. Let him see my profile, and soon he will know I have an adult son. I don't have to say anything here.*

She unlocked her phone and tapped the Facebook app to accept Vick's friend request.

Her photo smiled at her from the Facebook page. The dress she donned was a little bold. But the drink and Vick's humorous talks made her comfortable. Comments queued up on her Facebook photo.

Hottie, one friend remarked.

Bold and beautiful.

Wow!

Pretty n hot.

You are always above the worries. This's not a selfie. Who took the shot? This comment about her caption got her attention.

Am I really away from the worries? At least I can enjoy this moment.

Her gaze fell on a table only metres away. Harry was sitting alone at a table and sipping a drink while surfing through a tablet. *Worry* had not vanished, but was all around her.

Is this the only pub in the entire city? A dark thought crept into Ira's mind. She gave a cold reply when he called last night and even declined his invitation for dinner. Harry should have understood she was no longer interested in him. *Did Reema tell him I'm in this pub, and he is following me? Had I been to Alkapuri Mall, I wouldn't consider his presence a coincidence. But I came to another place! For the sole purpose of escaping this man!*

She moved her chair's position a little so that she wouldn't meet his gaze. A noise began in her brain.

"Thanks for adding me to your Facebook, Ira." Vick chuckled.

"You are always welcome." Ira said in a low voice so that Harry couldn't hear, but her legs urged her to jump from the chair and run away. If Harry didn't notice yet that Ira was just tables away, she should be all right. Should she ask something about Vick to turn her mind away from Harry?

She inhaled a deep breath.

Ira planned a safe and neutral topic for conversation so that Vick would do most of the talking, and she would only listen. Sweat collected in her armpits. She struggled to find a question. "Is your office nearby, Vick?"

"Next to the mall."

Ira blinked. Vick's brief reply disappointed her. How could she find a topic that would encourage him to indulge in a long chat?

"Tell me about your girlfriend, Vick." *Calm down, Ira. Take charge.*

Vick chuckled. "Girlfriend? You will laugh at me."

"Come on, Vick. Can't imagine a young man like you having no girlfriend." She tried to slap on a smile, but it was too tough for her now.

"I had one. But she broke up with me."

Ira swallowed. "You didn't try to win her back?"

"I did. I showed up at her place unannounced. But she had already married her ex-boyfriend. What a joke!" Vick let out a loud chortle. "Ira, I believe we both need a refill. Let me go to the counter again."

She couldn't ask Vick to leave her alone. A shiver crept into her bones.

Ira found herself between two odds—sitting with a man much younger might give her pleasure for an evening. But if Vick was trying to woo her, she would blame herself for his misunderstanding.

The other odd was Harry, sipping his drink at a table nearby. She didn't muster the guts to cast a sideways glance again and see if Harry was still alone.

What if Harry came to her? Reema had claimed the city was safe. No. She was wrong. Psychos were prying on beautiful women everywhere. Ira's underarms dampened and her heart slammed inside her ribs.

Vick was about to arrive with her drink, and it would be awkward to leave before finishing another glass.

Ira tapped on the Uber app and booked a cab. She sprang to her feet, so that neither Vick nor Harry would notice her. Holding her phone to her right cheek, so Harry wouldn't recognize her, she tiptoed out.

She didn't think Harry followed her. In fact, he didn't—because he had already left the bar and was walking down the corridor of the mall, ahead of Ira.

Ira saw him from behind. Her head reeled. Why—no! When did Harry leave the pub? Was his presence in the bar unintentional? Her feet stalled. Before she could think further, Harry vanished into another pub down the way.

Ira glanced around. Vick had also come out of the bar and was watching her, confusion blinking in his eyes.

"Sorry, Vick. I need to leave. Emergency." She rushed away without hearing Vick's reply.

The Uber would arrive in two minutes. Ira trudged out of the mall.

CHAPTER 26

D espite so many tensions in her life, last night Ira slept well. Property dispute, Rohan's illness, getting rid of psycho Harry, and Varun spending the night with Sam—possibly as his girlfriend. Ira was sure her brain became confused with so many odds and let her have a peaceful rest.

Last evening, after running away from Harry, she sat on the bedroom floor, burying her head between her knees, and wept. The 'lover Harry' fought against the 'psycho Harry' for a long time. But finally, it remained unresolved until she went to sleep.

She sat up on the bed, stretched, and yawned. Sunday, last day of her school holiday. Ira realised, after she rushed out of the pub last evening, she hadn't opened her Facebook. She tapped open her cell phone and swiped the screen into Facebook.

Vick had posted the selfie of her along with him and written on her timeline, *Spent a wonderful time with you. You are gorgeous.*

She also noticed a message in Messenger. From Vick. *Ira, what happened this evening? Why did you run away? Did I do something silly?*

She scrolled through the comments beneath Vick's post, and what she saw scared her to the bone.

Your new girlfriend? most of Vick's friends had commented.

She is hot, a dozen other comments screamed.

Vick had not replied to those comments, inciting suspicions from his friends and more comments.

Ira stared blindly at the screen. Bile rose in her throat.

She could explain this to Varun; he was understanding and supportive of his mother. But what about Urvi? Instead of supporting her cousin, Urvi would rather love to sling mud on Ira.

But there was a silver lining to all that happened. Harry, if really following her, must check her Facebook page. He would find Ira got another love and might refrain from getting back with her again. A chortle escaped her mouth.

Would she really be Vick's girlfriend? A man only about seven years older than her son? There are several instances of men getting involved with girls younger than their own children. Even Reema's husband fell in love with a woman who was not even twenty-five. But society never takes it easy on women who are in love with younger men. And why such overthinking? She never even dreamt of a romance with Vick.

Ira typed a message for Vick into Messenger.

Sorry for leaving the pub. It was not your fault, but I can't discuss this with you. I am concerned with the comments on the FB post. I want to let you know that I have an eighteen-year-old son. Your friends think there is something between us two. I would appreciate it if you clarify I'm just a friend, that would be great. Thanks a lot.

She got up and left the bedroom. Time for the morning tea.

Ira was about to pour water into the kettle when the doorbell chimed. *Who could be here at such an early hour?* Varun wouldn't get up so early on a Sunday morning. And he, too, had the keys. The maid would take the day off.

Ira put the kettle back in its place and walked to the entrance, cautious. She realised she was still wearing the same dress she wore to the bar last evening, having forgotten to change into nightwear. She pulled up the top edge of her depleting neckline and opened the door. Varun was standing there.

"Good morning, Mum." Varun came inside. His voice lacked the warmth it usually had when he spoke with his mother. Was he angry because of the discussions on Facebook?

"I was going to make tea, want some?"

"You are dazzling in this dress, Mum. Love your photo on Facebook. How was the evening?"

She adjusted her neckline again. Her jaw became tight, as if a young daughter was about to face an angry father for an unwelcome relationship. She must explain the situation to her son and become a mother again.

"I was reading a book until late last night, didn't realise when I fell asleep. Let me change."

As she trudged to the bedroom, Varun stopped her. "No, Mum. Wait a minute and I will take a selfie of both of us."

"A selfie, now? Varun, I just woke up, and what will I look like in the photo?" Ira failed to realise what was going on inside Varun's mind, but a storm appeared imminent.

"Don't worry, Mum, I wouldn't post it online." He stomped into his bedroom.

Ira's brain stopped working. She didn't understand what Varun was going to do. She quickly slipped into the kitchen, switched on the electric kettle, and came back.

Within minutes, Varuna appeared before her in a stunning outfit.

"Nice, Mum. Now I am no longer your son, but your daughter, Varuna. Are you okay with me now?"

Ira let out a chuckle. Perhaps Varun didn't notice the Facebook comments from Vick's friends, or perhaps he just ignored them. "Wasn't I okay with you before?"

"Mum, you look stunning in this attire. A sexy woman any man would die for."

"Varun, you are my child. I don't expect this comment from your mouth."

Varuna giggled. "Cool down, Mum. I'm Varuna. Not Varun. At least while I'm inside this dress. Didn't you once say a daughter can be a closer friend to the mother than a son?"

Ira giggled and hugged her. "Yes, you are my darling daughter. Did you wear this last evening with Sam?"

Varuna appeared to study Ira's mood. "Are you doubting me, Mum? No, that dress is in my bag for cleaning."

"Okay, but a mother would always like to know who her daughter is with."

A moment hung between them.

"Do you mean if I slept in the same bed with Sam?"

"You understand what I mean."

"Mum, I think we should change the topic. But for your satisfaction, I slept in the other bedroom."

Ira didn't reply. She got up and poured tea into two cups and came back. "Here is your tea."

The steaming teacups lightened Ira's mood. Now was the time for some motherly talk.

"You're getting too close with that man, Varuna."

Sam was not gay. After all, he had a girlfriend. And she had read somewhere in an article, some heterosexuals, when they don't find a sexual partner in the opposite sex, become bisexual for some time. But that is temporary. And didn't Ira change her views towards homosexuals? Supporting Urvi's gay son Amit for his lifestyle?

"Mum, who is 'that man'? He is Sam, and he is a nice guy. You know him well. He has his own problems. I was his flatmate for so long and you never looked at me like this. What happened to you?"

"Nothing."

"Can we change the subject?"

"To what? Last evening? Nothing happened there. I spent some time in a bar and this guy was across the same table. I asked him to take a picture of me, and he took a selfie standing on my side. He is a young guy, like Sam. All right?"

"I didn't ask about that man, or any man. It's about Harry. Why aren't you meeting with him nowadays?"

Ira had not yet told Varun about her changing relationship with Harry. She was waiting for an opportune moment. How did Varun find out?

Ira left the tea and got up.

"Mum, what?"

"Nothing, I will change into something comfortable."

Ira flounced to her bedroom, changed into casual clothing, and came back. Seated on the sofa again, she sipped tea. Varuna also came back as Varun, her darling boy.

Ira looked at Varun and asked. "How did you know I didn't meet Harry?"

"He called me. And said..."

"Okay, Varun. I must make it clear. I have decided not to continue any relationship with that fellow. You have no idea about his dead wife. His wife had planned to leave him as he was a psycho. Unfortunately, she got cancer and died. Otherwise, their marriage was going to end in divorce. Possibly a nasty one. Do you want your mother to fall prey to a psycho?"

Varun drank the lukewarm tea in one big gulp. "Harry is psycho? I don't believe it. He looks..."

"All psychos appear like gentlemen to the outside world. But again, I have so many other priorities. My wedding is the least one now."

A silence hung for a while. The air inside Ira's brain was thick already. She also wanted to talk about the two young women in the coffee shop who were complaining about an ex-boss being a woman-iser, and Ira believed that man might be Harry as they referred to a man standing behind. Another time, maybe.

Varun's face clouded with something unspoken.

"You know your uncle Rohan is going to court to challenge our share of the property," Ira said.

"Yes, you had said. And the case might continue for decades. What can we do?"

"No, it doesn't end there. Uncle Rohan has cancer."

Varun sat straight on the sofa. "Cancer? He has cancer? See, those who harass others get punishment from God."

Ira gazed into his eyes. "No, Varun. Do you think your dad would have been this happy knowing his brother might die?"

The smile from Varun's lips vanished in a second. "No, Mum. I am sorry."

"It's true we will fight for those ancestral lands. But we should help your uncle. He has no medical insurance, and treatment for cancer costs lots of money. He can't afford it. His daughters are also afraid their studies will discontinue. Rohan might not send them to college after they finish school. I promised your cousin to finance her college education."

Varun's eyes glinted. "You are the best, Mum." He moved closer and hugged Ira from the side.

"There's more to it, Varun. I tried to call your uncle and aunt. They didn't speak nicely to me. But they had called Divya's mum. You remember who Divya is?"

"Divya? The girl you helped in Raghupur?"

"Yes, she is now in Toshali with her stepfather and mum. Her mum is your Aunt Tina's childhood friend. I found out only yesterday. Tina approached her for temporary accommodation with them. For Rohan's treatment. But they live in a single bedroom flat."

Varun gazed into her eyes. "Why can't they stay with us? We are family, anyway."

Ira liked this straightforward and kind nature of her son, just like his father. "You'd think so. Unfortunately, they don't. But I will try."

"That would be nice, Mum." A smile grew on his face.

"Okay, another tea?" Ira responded with a chuckle.

"Yes, Mum."

Ira got up and ambled to the kitchen bench top. A few hours ago, she had been bugged up with problems. Now she was in control. Yes, her problems were many. But they would take time to get out of her way. One at a time.

CHAPTER 27

I ra booked an Uber autorickshaw as she locked the front door of her apartment. Monday morning, and she shouldn't be late on her first day at Kalyani Girls High School in Toshali. An autorickshaw would be much cheaper than a taxi as she would need one each working day—unlike Raghupur, where the school was at a walking distance.

She made her way to the elevator, whose door just opened to let a maid-looking woman out. She sprinted into the lift before its doors closed. Each second was important, especially when she didn't know how long it would take to arrive at her workplace in the morning traffic of Toshali.

She had just spilled out of the lift when her phone rang. *Oh, no. Not now when I am literally running.* She grabbed the phone from her handbag. It was Lisa, Rohan's daughter.

"Hi Lisa, can I call you after..." Ira hurriedly looked at her watch; the Uber autorickshaw would arrive at her gate in about a minute. "Five minutes?"

"Okay, Aunt." Lisa sounded like she'd been weeping.

She loped to the building gate. The Uber auto was already there. Ira climbed inside and settled on the seat, setting her handbag on the side. "Please take me to Kalyani Girls High School," she said to the driver.

"Yes, ma'am. It is already in my Uber app."

Ira took her phone and called Lisa back. "How are you, Lisa?"

"Aunt, Papa will come to Toshali to visit the cancer hospital. Tomorrow. Mama, my sister, and I all are coming with him. He tried with some of his friends to get accommodations. Aunt, you have seen my Papa. He is so hot headed. He fights with everyone. Who will help him?"

"Don't worry. Are you at home? Is your mama there?"

"Yes, Aunt."

"Okay, give the phone to her."

Only yesterday, Tina had declined her call. And Rohan, as usual, abused her. Uneasiness trickled through her.

"Hello?"

Ira recognised the weak voice on the phone as Tina.

"Tina, how are you?" The autorickshaw stopped at a traffic signal. Smoke from the vehicles wafted through the interior from all sides, choking her. *Why don't autorickshaws have doors and aircon, like cars?*

Silence. Was Rohan there, near Tina? Was she afraid to talk to her?

"You know, *didi,* they have diagnosed Rohan with cancer."

"That is unfortunate. And Lisa said you are all coming to Toshali for treatment and looking for temporary accommodations."

"Yes. Rohan has so few friends, who will support us in this moment? We are trying to find some cheap Airbnb rooms, but it's difficult within our budget."

The autorickshaw rolled in packed traffic as the signal turned green. She infused her natural softness into her voice. "I tried to call you yesterday after finding out about Rohan's illness. You all are coming and staying with me. One room in my rented flat is for you and Rohan. As long as you want. All right?"

Ira could hear Tina's sob. "*Didi,* Rohan is taking you to court, and you are offering us accommodations?"

"Don't cry, Tina. I am your family. So what if Rahul is no more? The Ray family blood is very much there in Varun. If I can't help when you are in trouble, when can I? I will text you the address, and you can come straight to my home."

"I will, thank you. This evening. We have an appointment tomorrow morning."

The autorickshaw stopped. Ira glanced out before getting off. Kalyani Girls High School.

"Your uncle Rohan, aunt Tina, and both cousins are coming this afternoon," Ira said to Varun during her break at school, while looking for the teachers' common room. "When do you think you can arrive at home?"

"Four p.m., Mum. Will you be late?" Varun asked, his voice sounding dull.

"Excuse me, where can I find the common room for the teachers?" Ira asked another teacher, clutching her phone between her shoulder and ear.

"The second left on this corridor." The lady flashed a smile and hurried away. Ira should have introduced herself before asking.

"Look, Varun, this is my first day at this job in a new place, should I ask the principal to allow me to leave early? Doesn't look good. I wasn't expecting both girls to come. But they are terrified knowing their father has cancer. They think it's a sort of death sentence. If you can move your stuff to my room and clear the room for them, that would be nice. Yes, no girly photos should be there."

"Understood, Mum."

Ira arrived in the common room and found it empty. She was probably the only one to have a vacant period. Settling on a chair, she looked at her watch; she had almost thirty minutes before her next class. A memory of her parents-in-law whispered around the periphery of her mind. They lived in an old two-bedroom house in Raghupur. Rohan was living with them even after his wedding. At least once a month, the other two brothers, along with their families, would come to stay with their parents. All the brothers worked in the same town, so commuting to their workplaces from the parents' house was not a problem.

There was not enough space for four couples and their children to live comfortably. All the women would squeeze into one bedroom at night, two on the cot and two on the mattress spread on the floor. Mum-in-law always loved to sleep in the same room with the three daughters-in-law. "I have no daughter. You three are my daughters," she would often say.

Their house was small, but their hearts had enough space to accommodate so many people. Ira had enjoyed those moments. The sisters-in-law cooked together for the entire family, and all of them ate together. The six-seater dining table was pushed to the side, and all the family members sat on the floor to eat lunch or dinner, cross-legged, with plates laid in front of them.

Would that time ever come back? Probably never. Varun was a small lad then. But he should know how cramping inside a tiny apartment has a positive side to it. You get closer to the family.

Ira had never heard so much noise inside her flat since moving to Toshali when the lift doors slid open to let her out in the evening. The main door of her flat was hung open. She heard Varun talking to his cousins—Tina and Rohan's two daughters.

"Namaste, *bhabiji.*" Rohan got up from the sofa to greet Ira. It didn't surprise her. Rohan had forgotten that seniors in the family were never addressed by their first name—an Indian custom—for thousands of years. She was sure Rohan was inside a façade as he had bad timing and needed Ira's help.

"Good to see you here with your family, Rohan." Ira didn't ask 'how are you' as that would be inappropriate to a cancer patient who was unsure if he would ever get rid of the deadly disease. "And I believe you found the place without any hassle."

"Varun had come to the bus station, and we came here in two separate autorickshaws." Tina was all smiles at Varun. "He is such a nice boy."

"I arrived at the bus stop directly after my classes ended," Varun said while seated between the two girls on the other sofa.

Ira struggled to hide her anger toward Varun. She had told him to clear his bedroom before Rohan and his family arrived. What would happen to her reputation if they noticed girl clothing in Varun's closet?

"This boy is so careless," she said, "I will now clean up his bedroom so that you guys could use the wardrobe." Ira stomped to Varun's room.

"Don't worry, *didi.*" Tina scuttled behind Ira. "I will help you. You have worked all day in the school."

Why didn't Varun clear his wardrobe instead of going to the bus station?

"You take care of Rohan." Ira opened the closet and grabbed the five dresses hanging nicely on the hangers—thank God Varun was almost her height and she could claim the dresses as her own. "See, I am such a lazy mother, I used this closet when Varun was sharing rent with his friend and forgot to take them to my room."

"That happens with me too, *didi.*" Tina was standing close to Ira, looking into the cabinet. "Give them to me, you remove the rest." She took the dresses from Ira.

Ira's attention shot to the lingerie, almost five or six pairs. How would she explain to Tina why a woman's lingerie was inside a boy's room? Why did she hand over the dresses to Tina? She could have held them all together, concealing the bras and panties inside the folds of the dresses.

Tina had left the room holding the outfits. Ira hoped she hadn't seen the female undergarments. She grabbed them together in one bundle, hid them inside Varun's shirts and trousers, and sprinted to her bedroom—casting an angry glance at Varun, who was still sitting on the lounge with his cousins.

The muscles in her face relaxed as she deposited all the lingerie inside her large cabinet. "I will arrange them afterwards," she said, nervously looking at Tina who was still standing there. But a curious glance from Tina didn't go unnoticed. Did Tina see something and was keeping mum? Hiding what she had already found? A current passed through her. How could she confirm Tina hadn't been in the room before and seen the female garments and lingerie inside Varun's closet? Anything was possible with this shrewd woman.

"Now you can use Varun's wardrobe for you and the girls." Ira made up a smile. "Let's go and I will make some refreshments. And tea too."

"No need, *didi*," Tina said as she ambled out of the room to the living area. "Varun had brought some hot samosas on the way, and I have kept aside two pieces for you. I will make tea for all now. You must be tired, please relax. Didn't you say we are still your family? Then why would you alone do all the chores?"

"Tina is right, *bhabiji*," Rohan said, sitting in the middle of the three-seater sofa, occupying the whole lounge. "Tina will do all the errands of home as long as we are here, you enjoy a holiday from cooking." His smile was feeble, but sly.

Ira pulled out two folding chairs leaning against the wall and sat on one of them, while Tina poured water into a saucepan and placed it on the gas stove.

After drinking tea together, Tina went inside Varun's bedroom (temporarily theirs) to arrange the clothes she had brought with her. Ira wondered for a while what she would cook for dinner, but something sliced through her brain. Sam had printed several of Varun's feminine pictures on A4 papers in his office and given them to him. The photos must be somewhere in Varun's room. What if Tina or her daughters found them?

Bile rose in her throat.

CHAPTER 28

Ira stood in the crowd of passengers at the bus stop after booking the Uber autorickshaw after a busy day in the school. It was a perfect place to relax her mind before arriving at home for another round of duties for the extended family. Friday afternoon. She smiled to herself at how her first two weeks in Kalyani Girls High School had passed so well. And Rohan would also finish two weeks of radiotherapy. Doctors were optimistic he had a better chance of survival.

The changes Ira noticed during the last two weeks were unimaginable: Rohan behaved so nicely, and Tina managed all household chores even before Ira came back from school. Was this a dream which might vanish when the family goes back after the treatment? She didn't want to think further and stress her mind.

But she was worried about the girls. Being away from the school, their studies had taken a halt. Even Varun's study at home was affected. But Ira convinced her mind that this was temporary.

Her cell phone rang, and Ira quickly swiped on the call from Varun.

"Hey Mum, are you on the way home?"

"Yes, Varun, waiting for the autorickshaw. Maybe it is struggling in the traffic jam. Where are you?"

"Hospital."

The hospital was near Varun's college. Walking distance. Everyday Tina would accompany Rohan for radiotherapy, leaving the girls at home. And if Varun's classes finished early, he would go to the hospital to be with his uncle and aunt. Ira was happy with that. She wanted her son to connect with his family despite the property dispute.

"Varun, the therapy for the day should have been over by now, what happened? Why so much delay?"

"One radiotherapy machine broke down, so the hospital rescheduled the patients, and Uncle's appointment was just now. But Mum..."

Ira felt Varun wanted to say something. Since Rohan and his family began living with them, she rarely got the chance to talk privately with him. Except the first day when she had texted him to sneak the girly pictures out of his room and hide them safely, even though Varun was sitting near her.

"You want to say something, Varun?"

A cold sensation reeled through her stomach. She paced to the other corner of the waiting area of the bus stop.

"Yes." He paused. Ira heard him panting. "Harry was here. He was here to meet some patient in the hospital."

Ira inhaled a deep breath and glanced around as if people were keen to eavesdropping on her secrets. "Okay, Varun. Don't worry. Don't meet him."

"But, Mum..."

An autorickshaw arrived. Before Ira could check the rego number from Uber app, another man got into it. Her cab was still on the way.

"Varun, am I not clear? I said, there is no need to meet and say hello to him."

"Mum, I didn't go to meet him, but he saw me and came."

Fear rose in Ira's belly. She had stopped communicating with Harry. And now he was after Varun to reach her?

"Mum, are you there?"

A sigh leaked out of Ira's mouth. She closed her eyes for a few moments and then said, "Yes, my child."

"He came and asked me if I can help him meet you."

"He said this? Why didn't you say I'm not interested in him? I changed my mind. Don't owe an explanation."

"Mum, you are being too rude. You are breaking someone's heart. This is the way Sam's girlfriend broke up with him, and see? It still pisses him off."

Still pissed off? That's why he became bisexual and is using a boy to satiate his desire!

"What did you say? Be careful, your aunt shouldn't find about this. Otherwise..."

"Mum, she was there when Harry said it."

"She was there?" A voiceless scream bulged in Ira's chest, and she glanced around helplessly. *Why is the Uber Autorickshaw so late today?* "And Harry..."

"Mum, Harry doesn't know her. So don't think he said it intentionally. Even I didn't realise when Aunt approached me when Harry was talking to me. I am sorry, I should have been more vigilant."

"What else did he say?"

"He said 'your mum broke off from me for no reason,' and he needs one chance to talk to you."

Ira pulled in a long breath. "And Tina was there when he said this?"

A silence hung like a wall.

"Varun!" Ira's voice rose.

A few commuters who stood around her eyed her. Ira lowered her voice and said, "Varun, how can you be so callous?"

"Sorry Mum, yes, she was there. But don't worry, Harry used '*broke off*' in English. Aunt Tina is not that educated and wouldn't understand English."

"Tina is a graduate, and she knows English well. Don't think that because she is not a working female, she wouldn't understand English."

The autorickshaw arrived. Ira climbed inside and took the seat. "Okay, Varun, enough. Come back home."

The autorickshaw rolled in the heavy afternoon traffic on the streets of Toshali. But Ira's mind raced in the opposite direction. As per Raghupur standards, a middle-aged widow is not supposed to fall in love. But Ira had not only pictured herself falling in love, that too with a man from another religion. She couldn't even clarify that she had broken it off. For breaking up, one needed to be in love in the first place.

Guilt cut through her. A tear splashed onto her cheek, and she wiped it away quickly.

I ra's brain reeled as the autorickshaw dropped her near the front gate of her apartment building. She had intended to help Rohan and his family when they needed her the most, not to create conditions for getting taunted by them afterwards.

Could she muster the courage Leela did?

Ira arrived at the lift and pressed the up button. Her heart began to race. Her skin prickled with heat. She fought an urge to reach home and throw herself in the shower.

Ira dragged her feet inside when the lift arrived and its doors opened. She wished to escape somewhere for a while, but couldn't. She must plan what to cook for dinner for seven people.

But I am no longer in love with that man. Ira tried to console herself by the time her floor arrived, and she pressed the calling bell on her door instead of taking out her keys. She felt she should announce her arrival instead of throwing the door open to her unsuspecting nieces.

"Come in, Aunt Ira." Lisa and Leena stood there to welcome her. "Aunt, are you tired?"

"No, why?" Ira managed a smile. She must practise living inside her façade before Rohan and Tina arrived.

"You look exhausted," Lisa said. "Could I make some tea for you?"

"No, I will wait until your dad and mum come back. We all can have tea together."

"And brother Varun too," Leena said, a smile curving her lips.

A flicker of a chortle escaped from Ira. She loved this innocent little daughter of Rohan and Tina.

Rahul's absence haunted her. Nobody would love her more than Rahul did. Harry was nothing in comparison. *Why am I thinking about Harry again? He is in the past tense now.*

When are you coming back? She typed the text for Varun and hit send. A moment later, a reply pinged back. *On the way, about fifteen minutes to get home.*

Fifteen minutes? Ira had hardly any time. She must spend some time with Rahul and get some solace before burying herself in kitchen duty.

She had packed many items in boxes and kept them inside the overhead cupboard of her bedroom, and she had yet to have time to open them.

She dragged the dining table chair inside her bedroom and climbed on it. One of the three boxes had her and Rahul's wedding album. She yanked one of them to the floor and rummaged through it, hoping that was the suitcase containing the valuable photos.

Rahul's photo smiled at her.

Ira looked at her watch—only about five minutes left before Rohan and Tina would arrive.

"Love you, Rahul," she muttered after planting a kiss on the photo. "I am missing you so much." Tears filled Ira's eyes. "You see Rahul, your brother is here. Sick. I am doing the same as what you would have done. Supporting in the sickness."

She took the photo and placed it on the lamp table in the lounge room, facing the three-seater sofa.

Varun's gaze shot at the image when he entered the home, along with Rohan and Tina.

"Mum, this photo?" he asked.

"Yes," she said, sneaking a glance at Tina, "I've been meaning to bring it out since the day I moved to Toshali, but haven't gotten time."

Why am I feeling guilty for the short period of friendship with a man? Am I brainwashed after living two decades in Raghupur? Doesn't it look artificial when Rohan and Tina arrive after spending long hours in the hospital, and I am busy with the picture? But I need Rahul for my soul.

"I am sorry, Tina. You had a long wait today in the cancer ward. Rohan must be exhausted. Let me prepare some tea."

Rohan was already on the sofa, stretching his legs above the coffee table. Ira didn't like anyone putting their feet on the table but stayed quiet.

"Don't worry, *didi,*" Tina said, coming close and casting a glance at the photo, "he is tired, but not me. You have worked all day in the school, so I will make the tea and also cook dinner. You are still in your work clothing, why don't you change and relax?" Tina stared at the picture for a moment, then signalled Ira to come into her bedroom.

For a split second, Ira felt faint as she followed Tina through the door. "What happened?" she muttered.

"Rohan will be nervous about seeing his dead brother's picture. This afternoon he said, 'one brother has left the world hardly a year ago.' He believes next might be his turn. He is getting depression."

"Don't worry, Tina. I will hide that inside as long as you guys are here. You go to your room and change. I am coming in about a minute."

Ira kept looking at Tina as she left her bedroom. Hopefully, she was occupied in her own world when Harry met Varun in the hospital. She wanted to text a message to Harry, asking him never to talk to Varun even.

But her fingers shivered when she tried to type. A tear choked her throat. She threw the phone on the bed and opened her wardrobe.

Changing into comfortable clothing, Ira came out of the room. Tina had begun chopping vegetables for dinner.

"What is the plan for dinner?" Ira asked.

"Chapati and mixed veg curry. While coming from the hospital, I stopped the autorickshaw outside a veg stall and bought vegetables, as the fridge was almost empty." Tina continued chopping an eggplant without looking at Ira.

Ira remembered she had planned to go shopping for the kitchen after school, but Varun's call about Harry changed everything.

"Didi..." Tina placed the chopped eggplant in a bowl and brought an onion for slicing. "Can I say something? Rohan is busy watching TV and can't hear our women talk."

Women talk? A separate kitchen would have been much better. But this was an open-plan one.

"I have a friend Leela, she was my schoolmate," Tina almost whispered.

What is confidential with Leela?

"She is your schoolmate?" Ira pretended she didn't know. Why should she say she had been to her flat for lunch last weekend and that she was the one who told her Rohan had cancer?

"You know her. You have helped her daughter, Divya."

"Poor girl, hope she will see better days here in Toshali." She put some wheat flour in a pot and came to the sink to get water.

"That's true, *didi,* but I am talking about Leela. She is not educated like you but is a bold woman who got out of the hell she was in back in Raghupur. A woman who doesn't earn will always be dominated by men folk, either by a husband or other family members."

Ira mixed water with the flour but then stilled. *What is Tina going to say? Why does she sound so different today?* "She is courageous? How?" Ira asked, even though she thought she knew the answer. She craved to read what was in Tina's mind.

"She had the guts to find a man and remarry. Most women like us never get a say in whom to marry. Often parents choose the candidates for us. You are an exception, *didi.* And we depend on that man who would earn money for the wife and the children. What would happen if that man disappears or dies? Such women, if there is not enough family support, will be on the street. In the old days, there were joint families, and widows were getting support from the family. But what about now?"

Ira caught a glimmer of tears in Tina's eyes. She didn't know if it was from the emotion or chopping the onion. She also couldn't tell if Tina was serious or drawing parallels after eavesdropping on Harry's talk with Varun.

A text pinged in her phone. She dug it out from her pocket and swiped the cell phone open, and a text from Mehul appeared. *Coming to see Rohan. Flight arriving tomorrow morning. Have rented an Airbnb in the same building as yours.*

CHAPTER 29

I ra didn't know which apartment in her building Mehul rented for his stay in Toshali. All she knew was that a family tragedy always brought family members together, and forced people to look at problems differently.

Saturday morning. Mehul would arrive before twelve. Ira went to the market for groceries—vegetables and fish for lunch. Only about ten minutes' walk from her building.

"Fresh vegetables," a hawker pedalling a trolley rickshaw bawled, "direct from the growers, fresh produce."

Ira continued walking.

"Madam, fresh vegetables, please." The hawker pedalled faster and made up the short distance.

"No, I don't need," she said without looking at him. The Green-grocer Super Market was on her mind.

She halted and bought a cup of tea from a street stall. A yummy aroma perked up her taste buds. Vadas deep frying in another roadside vendor's large pan didn't let her move ahead. "I will buy some on the way back home for snacks," she assured herself.

This was the perfect time to talk to Reema. She dug her phone from her handbag and called while sipping and walking, leaving the snacks vendor behind.

"How are you, my girl?" Reema asked.

"Girl is busy with taking care of in-laws." Ira chuckled. But her heart said something was wrong with Reema. Her voice sounded unfamiliar, as if she hid a mountain behind it.

"So, your brother-in-law came to stay with you? Despite the court case?"

"Yes, you advised me to help them in time of need. How can I ignore a best friend's advice?"

"And that's why you never called me during the week?"

Guilt washed through Ira. She should have talked to her more during the last few days. She made a promise to herself to visit Reema after Rohan and his family went back. She could even ask her about the ex-wife of Harry. But what was the need when she wrote him off from her life, anyway?

"Sorry dear, this is my fault. Are you all right, Reema? When are you coming here next?"

A sigh sounded in her ears. *Is Reema all right?*

"I suffered from a health problem a while ago, and got cured even. But it came back."

"Is everything okay, Reema? Do you need my help?"

Reema giggled. "Yes, chatting with you might help."

A beggar woman came towards her with a little baby girl in her arms. "Ma'am, please help me. Husband threw me out of his home to bring another woman. I am homeless. No money to buy food."

Ira looked around and noticed a concrete bench beneath a large mango tree. "Right, Reema. Let me sit down. We will talk. Just hold on."

She took out a ten rupee note from her purse and handed it to the woman. The baby girl on her shoulder cast a curious glance at the note. An unknown emotion bespelled Ira. Her small help would hardly solve any problem of the woman. What else could she do?

This happens to women whose parents didn't educate them to fend for themselves. She found reasons to wash away her own guilt. She had already committed to Rohan's daughters to finance their college studies. And they are family. Ira convinced herself. With her limited resources, help to this beggar would be a drop in the ocean. The woman had already gone and was begging other people.

"Hello, are you still there?"

"Yes, Reema. Sorry." She sat on the cement bench, setting her bag on the side. "Please go on." She took another sip from the cup.

"You are so nice, Ira. You are patient with me, just like Jenny."

"Jenny?" The name rang a bell inside her brain. *Which Jenny?*

"You have never seen her. Harry's deceased wife."

The tea, instead of entering her throat, ran into the windpipe and made her cough.

"What happened, Ira?"

"Nothing. Swallowed hot tea. Please continue." Harry's name was never a good omen for anything.

"I had some problems with depression."

"Depression? You never told me about this." Ira wondered why Reema had never told her anything about this depression—or Jenny, for that matter. Did she like to bury the secrets, or were they buried beneath the weight of her own unhappiness?

"Ira, I never want to bog down my friends with my problems. I always try to keep them to myself. But for some reason, I felt like talking to you. In fact, Jenny's treatment almost cured me. But lately, I've been getting similar feelings to those I was experiencing years ago."

Jenny was not Ira's enemy, but being Harry's deceased spouse, her name brought a dark face to her conscience. A pause hung for a while.

"You okay, Ira?"

Ira swallowed. "Me? Ye...Yeah. Please continue."

The beggar woman was pleading with an old man for alms.

"Jenny was a psychiatrist. And her clients were mostly women who encountered domestic violence or betrayal from their husbands," Reema said.

"Really? I didn't know."

"How would you? You hadn't even met Harry then. It is sad that she passed away so young."

Why aren't you saying her psycho husband forced her death?

"Ira, are you there?"

"Yes, Reema." She swallowed.

"Yes, Jenny even had made an NGO to help women dealing with psycho husbands. She was regularly posting on social media to educate women, including those who weren't her clients."

Social media? Facebook? Ira had seen Jenny's posts about psychos, assuming Harry was an abusive husband. Was her suspicion based on misinformation?

"Did Jenny face any such situation in her life?"

"I doubt it, Ira. She had a childhood sweetheart whom she couldn't marry because of family pressure. But that old love reignited. You wouldn't believe Harry even supported her. I've never met such a large-hearted man. But she was unlucky. Cancer stole all her sweet dreams away."

A shock passed through her nerves. She felt like she had burnt something in the kitchen—burnt the only hope she had in her soul. Irrecoverable. Irreparable. The hope, which should have cooked to perfection, was now a puddle of black and flaming lava.

Ira inhaled a deep breath. It was not the time to mourn her and Harry. Now was the time for her best friend Reema. She had lost her marriage to another woman and was alone. Loneliness was the worst enemy of depression patients. And she must do something for Reema.

"Ira, are you all right?"

Ira controlled her sob. "Yes, Reema. Trying to digest what I heard. Jenny was the best doctor for you, but we can find another psychiatrist to help. Please consider me your family. Once my in-laws go back, I will come to Raghupur on a few weekends and spend time with you. And be with you when you are in Toshali."

Reema chuckled. "I knew you would be the one to give me support. I won't hold you now. Please take care of your sick in-laws. Talk to you again."

So many memories glared at Ira. She had run away after ordering coffee when she had noticed Harry in the same place. Did Harry smell she disliked him? Why else would he have left the bar when he saw Ira at another table? Or did he assume she was in a relationship with that young man? She had so many things she needed to sort out, but didn't even know where to start.

By the evening, Ira was out of her blue. Rahul's older brother Mehul and his wife Nirmala arrived in the afternoon. It turned out their Airbnb flat was on the same floor Ira lived. She never knew one flat on her floor had occupants come and go. How could she when she was busy in her own world of problems?

It was Saturday, and Rohan was a bit relieved, as no radiotherapy was scheduled for the weekend.

"How many more days do you need to go to the hospital?" Mehul asked while sipping tea.

Ira glanced at him while chopping vegetables on the kitchen bench-top. Her small lounge room choked with members from three families. Varun and the girls slipped into her bedroom to play cards. Both the brothers and Nirmala chatted while sitting on the sofa. Tina helped her with cooking dinner.

"One more week. Doctors said there's no need for chemo." Rohan's voice was low; the confidence in his features had died several days ago. "I had never thought I would be hit by cancer. I should have gotten health insurance, but now it's too late."

"But it's good news that the doctor is not advising chemo," Mehul said. "This means the tumour cells are not in an aggressive stage. How experienced is he?"

"He? No. She. Dr. Jillian Thomas. Specialises in oncology."

"Dr. Jenny Thomas?" Ira's jaw went tight realising her mistake. Why did Jenny's name mess with her brain? Or was it Harry?

"Sorry. I mixed her up with one Dr. Jenny Thomas I knew." The tightness in her chest eased. *You are going to be okay, Ira.*

Tina stopped peeling the garlic and said, "I don't know why it was him to get the disease, when I never missed a single day praying in the temple for his wellbeing, the only bread-earner of the household."

One day, her cousin Urvi also amused Ira with a similar confession. Didn't she also pray for Rahul even though she earned money for the family?

Ira set the vegetables aside and took out the fresh fish she had brought from the market and marinated with salt and turmeric. Nirmala came from the sofa and asked, "What are you making with the fish?"

"I was planning to make fish curry, but Rohan can't eat spicy food. After radiotherapy of his throat, his tongue became oversensitive. So, fish shallow-fry only will be good for him. Or should I just fry two pieces for Rohan and make curry with the rest?"

"*Didi,*" Tina intervened, "let's make curry for the rest. Let Rohan avoid any protein until he is cured. Lisa found on the Internet that protein is the favourite food of the cancer cells and said her papa should avoid nonveg dishes altogether."

Ira flashed a smile. "Lisa is such an intelligent and understanding girl, Tina. Then I will make mixed veg curry for Rohan with none of the spices."

She remembered Rohan before the death of his parents. A fun loving, carefree man whom she adored and considered equal to a brother. His inability to earn a decent income might have propelled him to take the wrong path of fighting against family members for the property.

The good old days became fresh in Ira's mind, when all three brothers and daughters-in-law would gather in the house of Rahul's parents. The joint family. A place one is never alone to feel any depression.

Could she replace Rahul with Harry in this love story?

"Where're you lost, *didi?*"

"Harry?"

"Which Harry?" Tina narrowed her eyes.

"Harry? No, I said sorry." An electric current stung Ira at her own slip of tongue. *Why am I thinking of him? I've already lost him. Forever. And I'm the one to blame.*

CHAPTER 30

"Not a single man's profile on the Second-Chance Dating site appealed to me. Maybe I became too choosy and compared each with my late husband."

It was the next Friday, and the atmosphere in the school was in weekend mood. Ira's attention shot at Mrs. Singh, seated opposite her in the teachers' common room at Kalyani Girls High School of Toshali. The school sat on a large lot on the edge of the city, and the teachers' common room witnessed the hill in all its splendour. The trees were blooming flowers, spring painting a riot of red, yellow, and orange.

So much cultural difference between Raghupur and Toshali! No middle-aged woman in sane mind in Raghupur would discuss her dream of another love so openly, Ira thought.

"Sorry to say this, Mrs. Singh—" Mrs. Mishra, seated opposite her, sounded like a marriage counsellor— "Often women who are deeply in love with their husbands do not find any other man attractive after becoming a widow. But *compromise* is a strong trait which helps humans to become happier."

"Really? How many times have you married, Mrs. Mishra?" another teacher remarked, and the hall morphed into a full-blown laughter.

"I will let you know, but another day." Mrs. Mishra got up, still chuckling. "I have a class now."

The school bell rang, signalling another period to begin. All the teachers except Ira left the room.

Ira's gaze passed through the window, and she tried to immerse herself in the spring colours of the hill. She could spend her free period watching the scenery. But Mrs. Singh's confession messed up her thoughts. True, nobody would compare with Rahul. Not even Harry. But she lost both men. One to death and the other to her own foolishness.

Man proposes, but God disposes. She is just a human.

She tried to push the thoughts away and focus on her home instead.

For the last three weeks, Rohan, Tina and their two daughters had been in her flat for the medical treatment. Rohan's doctor advised him radiotherapy was complete and he would come for a monthly check up for the next six months. Since last Saturday, Mehul and Nirmala had been staying in the Airbnb on the same floor. They would also be leaving tomorrow.

She looked at the wall clock. One more period and she would start another weekend. Should she, like Mrs. Singh, list herself on a dating site and look for new partners?

A voice inside her said, "NO, Ira, NO. NEVER AGAIN."

She would rather focus on Varun's education. Even Leena and Lisa would depend on her for their higher studies. Ira would never take the risk of choosing a new partner who might snub her financially supporting the nieces of her first husband.

Resolution to remain single pacified Ira's mind. At last, she understood what was best for her and the family. She was no more afraid of society. But this was her own decision, born out of choice, not fear.

Ira also found a changed Rohan. He would regularly ask her about her day in the evenings. Even beg her to come to Raghupur on weekends and stay in his house. But the ancestral property never came into the discussions.

At the end of the day when she returned home, Ira stopped at the Agarwal Sweets Stall on the way. The Ray family always celebrated auspicious days with sweets.

"One kilo *Rasgulla* and half kilo *Sandesh,* please." She took out her credit card and placed the order at the counter while the autorickshaw was waiting for her.

"When any danger comes to the Ray family, we all fight together. This older brother can finance your medical bills. If required, I will move out of retirement and go to the law profession again," Mehul said, seated on the sofa with one leg on the other.

This sounded like a temple bell to Ira while arranging sweets on a serving tray. She cast a quick glance at Tina, who was standing nearby, her eyes pooling. Ira came close to her and gently squeezed her shoulder. "None of us is alone. We are a big, joint family, even if we live in separate houses and places."

"Ira is right," Nirmala said, standing next to her.

Ira took the sweets tray to the lounge room. Before she could say anything, Leena spoke up. "Aunt Ira has promised me I will never miss my college education. She will finance my studies."

For a moment, Ira's heart swelled with pride.

Mehul shook his head, eyes glowing. "We are a wonderful family, supporting each other in need."

Ira felt Rohan's gaze, soft and full of gratitude. Difficult to believe it was the same man who one day spied against her and fired offensive words.

She set the tray on the coffee table. "This is an auspicious day for us. The doctor said positive words for Rohan, that he might be completely cured. This is to celebrate. Let me bring some quarter plates."

"Ira," Mehul said before Ira left for the kitchen, "please sit down. This is our last night here together, and we need to talk."

A buzzing noise began in her head. She hated serious talks. *What now?* She glanced around. Rohan sat in the middle of the three-seater sofa, Mehul occupying the two-seater, with Leena by his side, Lisa and Varun standing behind the sofa. Nirmala came out from the kitchen and pulled another chair for herself. Tina also joined and stood near

Nirmala, her arms resting on the shoulder of the chair. Ira pulled a chair off the dining table and sat facing the kitchen, avoiding direct eye contact with Mehul.

Women in respectable families of Raghupur avoid eye contact with elders, especially men.

Mehul harrumphed and said, "We, both the brothers, had a long discussion today when you were at your school."

Ira was sure something serious was about to be told. She was the only one who wasn't at home throughout the day. Any more pauses would likely be heavy on her heart. She glanced around for another breath, wondering what would come next.

Mehul started again. "Rohan admits the property dispute was totally avoidable."

Ira lifted her face and stared at Mehul. Her fingers stopped before pinching her thigh to find out if she was dreaming.

"*Bhabiji,*" Rohan's voice trembled, "I am sorry for my nasty behaviour."

"Ira," Mehul said, "you have one third right on it as the widow of Rahul. The right will never be affected even if your personal situation changes in the future, like your marital status. Tomorrow we both are heading to Raghupur, and next week I will prepare papers for transfer of ownership to each brother's family. That means one-third will be yours. I will let you know so that you can come to Raghupur and we will execute the deed. You can withdraw the court case after that."

A pin could have dropped, and everybody would have heard it.

Ira struggled with how she would react. She tried to say thanks, but her lips quivered, and tears pooled in her eyes.

She felt a touch on her shoulders and swung her head around. Varun stood behind her.

"Thanks, brother Mehul and Rohan," she muttered.

"No. Thank you," Mehul said. "You brought the family together. You will always remain a Ray family member, no matter how your life moves on from now."

Nirmala got up and took the sweets tray in her hand. "We don't need plates for each. Tonight, we will feed sweets to one another." She took one piece of sandesh and fed Ira. "This is to acknowledge the second daughter-in-law of Ray's family who is keeping the home together."

Ira took the sweet in her mouth and then took the tray from Nirmala. One after one, she gave everybody a piece, beginning with the children. "I am doing the same as Rahul would have done. He loved his family more than himself. Thank you all."

"Mum—" Varun came forward— "no more cooking tonight. Please let me order dinner from a restaurant."

Ira chuckled. "All right, my child. Ask everyone their choice and order. Remember, vegetarian food only for Uncle Rohan."

Tears of joy burned at the back of Ira's eyes, but she refused to let them out.

With such a family, she might not need a man by her side. But why did Mehul say, 'even if your personal situation changes in the future.' What did he mean?

CHAPTER 31

"Suddenly the home looks empty," Ira said with a heavy heart after the Rohan and his family left for Raghupur on Saturday morning. "Varun, how about another round of tea?"

"Yes, Mum."

The smile had disappeared from Varun's face. His slumped shoulders told Ira how much he missed the company of his cousins.

As Ira moved to the kitchen benchtop, Varun followed. "Mum, yesterday they were talking about you."

Ira was about to fill the saucepan with water, but she swung around. She did so much for Rohan and still they were talking behind her back? "But you were at college."

"Right—" Varun's face twisted with a smile— "But Leena was in the other room, and she overheard them."

"You mean, she was eavesdropping?"

"No, Mum. Both sisters were resting in the bedroom after lunch. Lisa fell asleep, but Leena was reading a book, and the conversation just drifted into the room."

Ira opened the tap and held the saucepan to fill with water. "What did they say?"

"Uncle Mehul said you are the first woman in the family to earn a living. And times are changing. You deserve a second chance. The family should support you if you decide to marry again."

Ira didn't even flick her eyes towards Varun. Mehul had told her this in her Raghupur apartment, before heading to Delhi to meet his daughter.

For the first time since Rahul's death, her heart felt free. Free to love again, free to remarry—and with everyone's blessing. But her heart soon dropped. Ira had already spoiled her second chance. Why didn't she think things through before breaking it off with Harry? It would have been a dream served to her on a platter. And she dumped her own future in a garbage bin from where retrieval was impossible.

She took a piece of ginger from the fridge and crushed it into the pot. She was sure she would get a severe headache after this.

"Mum!"

"I'm listening."

"Aunt Tina said, they all have daughters. Who knows what fate has stored for them? Ira should be an example for them. No woman should suffer her entire life for becoming a widow. She was even praising Leela."

She placed the pot on the stove and faced Varun. "Leela's case is unique. She needed a man for financial support and to get away from her rogue brother-in-law. For me, this is another option. I am, but..." She grabbed the jar containing tea leaves and added two spoonsful to the pan.

"Mum, you are adding turmeric, not tea."

Ira stared blindly at the pan. Then she realised the water in it had become yellow already. "Oh, I'm so sorry." She snatched the pan from the cooktop and dumped it in the sink.

"Mum, you should have just emptied the pan, rinsed it, and filled it with fresh water."

Ira knew what to do and what not to do. She didn't need any advice from a teenage boy. "I will use a tea bag instead." She took the electric kettle and filled it with water. She loved to boil loose tea leaves in a pan the traditional way, but her patience had run out.

Varun watched her but remained silent.

"You don't have to stand here, watching me, Varun. Go to the lounge and I'll come when the tea is ready."

He didn't move. "Mum, I couldn't talk to you because our home was full of relatives. That day, in the hospital, when Harry came to me..."

"Tina has sharp ears. She listened to everything I didn't want her to know. And gave me hints also the same evening."

The water in the kettle began to boil, and Ira took out two cups from the cupboard and set them on the benchtop. She grabbed a packet and took out two tea bags.

"Mum, how did you find out Harry is a psycho?"

Tear burned in the back of her eyes, but she held it back.

"I was wrong. I should have checked before reacting. I was, I mean..." She filled up one cup with cold tap water.

"Mum, you were supposed to pour boiling water from the kettle. You poured cold water instead. What happened to you? Why are you worried Aunt Tina heard everything? She also thinks you have the right to get another husband."

A dart of anger speared through Ira. "Varun, you are not my dad. I'm your mother. Don't preach like a father whose daughter is not marrying." She dumped the teacup in the sink.

"Mum, cool down. Please come and sit on the sofa. I will make tea instead."

"Can't you leave me alone? Shouldn't you go for the maths coaching? Or are they closed on Saturday? When is your class?"

"In half an hour. But it's only a twenty minutes' walk, Mum."

"Then go and leave me alone. Please."

Varun padded to his room. Ira flounced to the lounge room and slumped on the sofa. Within five minutes, Varun came out of his room with his bag packed.

"Mum, you are tired of serving the relatives. Please take a rest. I will help with cooking lunch after the tutoring session. Okay? Bye."

She kept staring at the door after he left. She had no reason to talk rudely to her son.

Ira inhaled a deep breath and stretched her legs on the recliner. The last few days she was sort of happy, even though a family member was suffering from cancer and the property case had hung over her head with all its uncertainties. Because she had no time to ponder about Harry.

Why then was Harry's memory forced back into her head this morning? Didn't she resolve against being in another relationship? Harry might be a wonderful husband, but Ira was incapable of loving him the way she once loved Rahul. In short, she would never be a good wife to him. So, it was in his interest to forget Ira.

Breaking it off without an explanation was the worst she did with Harry. She must meet him and explain that she had other priorities. Priorities to her extended family members. There was no guarantee Rohan wouldn't see cancer coming back to him. Ira must prepare herself to provide for his two daughters. She didn't want another Rupa who would stop her studies and work in a coffee shop to help the family. The futures of these two girls depended upon her.

But how would their studies be affected if Ira married a man who had a large heart? Wouldn't he also support Ira in her wise decisions? A billionaire would never ask a schoolteacher wife where she would spend her income!

Her head reeled. She needed a coffee urgently.

By evening, Ira's headache was gone. Life must move on. There was no point in worrying about Harry when he was already out of her life. Varun didn't raise any further question after coming back from the tutoring session.

"When is your exam, Varun? I'm sorry, as a mother I should have kept track of your important dates."

"Still more than a month to go."

"All right, when it's over, we both will go to a pub."

"Pub? Which one?" He leaned forward with eyes wide.

"Maybe Lone Pine Pub in Alkapuri Mall. Why do you look so excited? I was planning to go there today. But another time."

Varun came closer. "Mum, one evening won't ruin my studies. I will spend an extra three hours studying this weekend to make up for it. Let's go. Now."

"Now? Are you so crazy that when I mentioned the pub, you are ready to stop everything and go?"

"Mum, please. I'm tired of studying. A minor break would help me focus better. And you have also worked so much during the last week and the week before. You deserve a relaxing break. Don't you?"

Relaxing break? A smile touched her lips. She needed a break and also some quality time with her son.

"But on one condition, Varun. I would love to take my boy with me. Not the daughter."

"You forgot, Mum. Didn't I tell you my cross-dressing will be only at home? And also, would my beautiful mum put on the same dress she had posted on Facebook?"

Feigned anger flashed through Ira's eyes. "I'm going with my son, not with a boyfriend."

"Come on, Mum. Who knows, you might find a new boyfriend there. Please. You looked gorgeous in it."

She couldn't stop her giggle and glanced at the wall clock. Already half-past five, and further delay meant availability of a table would be difficult.

She breezed into her bedroom like a hurricane and yanked open her wardrobe.

Within half an hour, mother and son were in the rear passenger seat of an Uber cab.

"Mum, are you sure we are going to the Lone Pine Pub?"

"Yes, why?"

"Nothing, just asking."

Ira stole a glance through the corner of her eyes. Varun was typing a text.

"Whom are you texting, Varun?"

Varun flinched and cast a nervous glance at her. "Sam asked if I would like to meet him this evening, and I said we are going out."

A silent chuckle tickled her nerve. Varun was old enough to move beyond the mother's close supervision. She decided to throw all her worries away and enjoy the evening with her son.

They were lucky to get a table at the bar. Ira loved the ambience of this place. Different from any other bar in Alkapuri Mall. The pub was situated near the main entrance of the mall. It had a huge glass wall with a garden behind. There was soft music playing, and the air was clean. From her table, she could see the garden and the fountain. The water splashed up and over the edges of the fountain. The full moon was shining, and she felt herself relaxing in the tranquil surroundings.

Varun went to the counter to bring beverages. Ira was not a regular drinking person. Tonight, she wanted to drink to her heart's content. But she wouldn't. As a mother, she must be an example to Varun on how to drink responsibly.

"Here are our drinks, Mum." Varun set the glasses on the table and sat facing her.

Smiles came out of her heart. She held the glass to clink. "Cheers to the future of the Ray family."

"Cheers!" Varun let out a chuckle. "But Mum, you became a Ray because of marrying Dad, that means..."

"That means I will remain Mrs. Ray forever. No matter what comes." She didn't wish to give any reason for him to push for a new partner. Ira already decided against that. One day, she had wanted a daughter from Rahul. If possible, she might ask Rohan's daughters to come to Toshali for their higher education. Her small home would always be full of family members. She would never be alone.

"Varun, I am considering buying a three or four-bedroom apartment in Toshali. What do you think?" She took another sip.

"That would be nice, Mum. But I'm against selling the Raghupur home."

"Why do you think I would sell that? That's your dad's memory. Raghupur is also growing at a rapid pace. Who knows if we might need that in the future?"

"Do we have enough savings?" Varun took a big gulp from the glass.

Ira glanced around and flashed a meaningful smile. "No. But your dad's ancestral property. Your uncle Mehul and uncle Rohan would transfer one third in our name, and we can then dispose it off at a good price. That is over six thousand square feet of land. I mean, only our portion. Enough to buy a luxury apartment in Toshali and still be able to save something from the proceeds. Can you believe, just a day ago, we all were determined for a prolonged legal battle? Thank God, I don't have to pay through my nose to the lawyers."

Varun replied with a chortle.

Ira decided she would make more frequent trips to Lone Pine. Possibly, one day, she would meet Harry. She would use that opportunity to say a proper goodbye. And to say sorry for her behaviour. He was a perfect gentleman and should get a loving life partner.

She noticed Varun's lips were moving, as if he were talking to someone behind her head.

"Who is that, Varun?"

He stilled. The smile on his face clouded with a grave one. "Nothing. There's nobody." He twirled his glass.

Maybe she imagined it. Nowadays, her mind was working on a wrong level. She might need psychiatric help, like Reema. Were these symptoms of a mental issue? Ira looked at her glass; her drink was about to be empty.

She would force Harry out of her thoughts as long as mother and son were here, drinking together. But was Varun really talking to someone?

Ira made a show of checking her phone but was watching Varun's reactions.

Her gaze fell on a known gait trudging out of the pub. Harry! Was he here? Why didn't she notice him before? Was it Harry with whom Varun was engaged in lip talk?

She jumped to her feet and flitted after him, leaving Varun behind.

Harry had sneaked into the crowd in the mall. Ira considered shouting to stop him, but her throat became dry, and she was just a breath away from crying.

Harry stopped at a common area and sat on a bench beneath a decorative palm tree. Ira stilled. Harry was sitting with his back to her. Ira remembered the day Vick was with her, and Harry had left the pub, realising she was also there.

If she ignored this moment, even God wouldn't forgive her. She owed him at least an apology for the way she had ignored him—nothing less than an offence to a man who had done no wrong to her.

Ira inhaled deeply. Should she approach Harry? What if he didn't forgive her and walked away?

Ira, this is your turn to stomach the insult. Each karma has its result, and today is yours. Go ahead and do what is right. Don't wait to see if Harry will pardon you or not.

She glanced around. *Did I think aloud? Probably not, otherwise Harry is so close he probably would have heard.*

She tiptoed and stood on his side.

"Harry!" Ira couldn't think any further. Her heart was thumping inside her ribcage, her breath loud.

Harry turned his head. A gentle smile adorned his handsome face. "How are you, Ira?"

"I am, I, me?" Her jaw went tight.

"Ira, are you all right?"

"Yes, I am. Why did you leave the pub? Is it because of me?"

Harry stood up. "I'm sorry, Ira. I had no intention of disturbing your evening."

"Disturb? Me? No. Rather, my presence ruined your evening in your favourite pub. I come here once in a while. Harry, I'm sorry. Please tell me. Did you want to avoid me?"

"No." His throat jammed, his voice coming out like a whisper. "I hoped you wouldn't mind. The first time you ran away from the coffee shop. I felt it was because of me, but I was unable to gather why."

Ira gazed at him like a guilty person awaiting the verdict.

Harry continued. "I tried to call you. Many times. Even sent you a text. Then I felt something had gone wrong from my side. I wanted to ask but didn't know how."

"I'm sorry, Harry." Tears streaked down her cheeks. She was the one who ignored his texts and didn't take his calls. "Deeply sorry. It was my fault."

Harry came close and took her into a hug. "No, Ira. I am a business owner with hectic work schedules. I might have done something inadvertently."

"No, Harry. You are always thoughtful of others. It was me. I'm sorry."

Confined in his embrace, Ira lifted her face and looked into his eyes. His warm breath washed over her face. "Ira, can we remain friends, as before? Please. Trust me, you have done nothing to offend me. I'm like a tube light, which takes time to light up. I might not have understood the social reality you are facing. There's no reason for me to be angry. Unnecessary."

Ira giggled and nodded.

His face broadened with a massive smile as he freed her from his grip. "It is all right. Although I'm going to do something now which might offend you. Will you forgive me if you don't like it?"

"What?" Ira's nerves tingled.

"Want to know?" A mischievous look brightened Harry's eyes, which she had never seen before.

Harry dropped to his knees with his head up, meeting Ira's gaze. "My dear Ira. I know this may look too hasty on my part. Or unusual. I had planned to do this the fateful evening I couldn't reach you. But it's been on my mind ever since. I love you and adore everything about you. I also love your only son and wish to make him mine. Will you please marry me? I will wait months and even years until you are mentally prepared."

She didn't expect this to take such a lightning turn and didn't know how to react. She needed more oxygen to think. But Harry held the keys to all the fresh air!

Even though her in-laws were in favour of another relationship for Ira, announcing a wedding was safer than continuing as love birds for more time.

"Yes. Harry. Yes, I will, but please not here. Varun is..."

"I love you, Mum."

Varun was chuckling, standing at her side.

"Varun, what are you doing here? And Harry, you knew he was here. My son..."

Harry let out a laugh. "Didn't I once say I love your son and want to take him as my child? He is eighteen plus now, and legally I can't adopt him. But I can legally make his mother my wife. And you have already said yes. Please don't change your mind. Don't break my heart."

The clapping of a dozen people brought Ira back to reality.

"Such incidents are favourites of the shoppers here, especially those who come out of the pubs after drinking."

The voice sounded a bell in Ira's brain. She swung around.

Vick was standing near Varun.

"Vick? You too?"

"Sorry, Ira. The other day you stomped out of the bar when I had just posted our selfie on Facebook. I thought you took offence. Believe me, I had no such intention. Then I realised you reacted that way because of Harry."

"You know Harry?"

"Yes, he is my boss. But we are more like friends."

A wave of discomfort passed through Ira with so many eyes staring at her. What next? Would Harry kiss her? Here? They had kissed in privacy before. But since when did kissing in public become the norm?

She looked at Harry. He was now standing, holding one of her hands with a smile on his face.

Ira let out a smile. "Please, no broadcasting on social media until this is legal. There are vultures who will pounce on me and spoil everything."

"I promise." Harry chuckled.

"And Harry, please do not kiss my mum here in public. This is not a western country."

The public had already dispersed. Vick and Harry laughed loudly. Ira, too, joined them.

"You young guys can import that culture here. Your mum and I are still the same old-fashioned people." He wrapped his arm around Ira's waist. "Let's go to another restaurant and celebrate. Varun, my child, can you please come with us?"

All three left the place holding hands with Ira in the middle. *I got love back in my life. But what about Varun? How do cross-dressers move ahead in life?*

Ira promised herself never to ask Google for an answer to this. Rather, she would watch her son over the next few years and see how he would grow up. A straight man, a gay man, or something totally different, she didn't know. But she would watch.

FROM THE AUTHOR

Thank you so much for reading Shackled Dream. I hope Ira and Varun's story appealed you.

If you enjoyed this book, Please leave a review now. They can be as long or as short as you'd like. Even a star rating is amazing and appreciated. Thanks in advance. I love getting the feedback, and your review will help other readers discover the book. You may also leave a review on **Goodreads**.

Please connect with me on Facebook (https://www.facebook.co m/profile.php?id=100067209253293), Twitter (https://mobile.twi tter.com/SASpencer39) and Goodreads https://www.goodreads.co m/author/show/21306969.A_E_Spencer)

ALSO BY

Also Available by S A Sencer (Writing as A E Spencer)
The Pink Mutiny http://mybook.to/The_Pink_Mutiny
The Black Waters https://mybook.to/The_Black_Waters